I Will Always Love You

Learning to Love - Book One

Kaitlyn Calicott

Emma has dreams. Big dreams! She hopes to compete as a swimmer in the Olympics, fall in love at least once, and live her best life each and every day.

Swimming comes naturally. Falling in love takes work for a girl who believes she's invisible.

Life will forever change when Emma accidentally spills coffee on the football quarterback, especially when his hot younger brother shows up in town and starts paying attention to her.

When her dreams start coming true, will the saying "All good things must come to an end" become her reality?

Contents

Prologue

2 years earlier

"I can't believe we survived the first day of freshman year." Ashley grins at me as we stand in line for coffee.

Lou's Coffee House is a flavor shell of fragrances as the culinary perfume of coffee beans freshly ground to perfection wafts through.

My go to order is a skinny latte with a shot of vanilla. Lou always writes my name on the cup, *Emma*, but for some reason makes the 'a' really big.

Ashley loves the cappuccino topped with a thick layer of micro-foam and also has the privilege of the 'A' in her name written big by Lou.

Under two minutes my latte is handed to me. I take a whiff of the steamy goodness, turn, ready to sip this perfection of a drink when I slam into a hard body.

One hundred and fifty degree brown liquid soaks through his shirt, sticking to tight muscles underneath. I look up into the piercing sky blue eyes of the most handsome guy I have ever seen.

"I am so sorry!"

I grab some napkins dabbing at the spot on his shirt, feeling his muscles contract underneath my touch.

He grabs my hand with the napkins to stop me. I feel a shock of electricity run through me and a blush creep onto my cheeks as I realize I was practically feeling him up.

"It's fine." He laughs. "I never liked this shirt anyway."

"I can buy you a new shirt or let me at least buy you a coffee." I am just rambling at this point and make the mistake of raising my eyes to his again.

"I have more shirts. I might take you up on that coffee one day though." He winks at me and I am blushing once again. Or maybe the blush never went away.

Look away! Why are you gawking at him?

He leans closer and whispers in my ear. "You're cute when you blush!"

He backs away to order but never breaks eye contact. I am entranced and can't seem to look away either.

Look away! Turn your dang head!

I finally peel my eyes away and see Ashley smirking by the door. I practically run towards her, grabbing her hand and pulling her out the door.

We get to the end of the street and Ashley turns to me. "What was that?"

"I don't know." We stop walking because I can't seem to focus. "I've never even seen him before."

"Are you serious, Emma? How do you not know who that is?"

I shrug, seeming to have lost the ability to speak. I steal her coffee since I spilled mine.

"He is only the hottest, most popular guy at school. He's the starting quarterback as a sophomore. He hangs with all the juniors and seniors.

"Oh". I seem to be a fountain of conversation. Am I in shock? Yeah. Shock. No. Wait. What's wrong with me!

Ashley rambles on. "He plays baseball in the Spring. I heard he's rich and his parents already bought him a Porsche for when he turns sixteen this year."

"Oh." Once again, I seem to have lost the function of speech.

Ashley smiles. "In case you were wondering, his name is Jeremy Anderson."

Jeremy Anderson. Why does that name sound so familiar? I have never seen him before. Believe me I would remember. I'm pretty sure any girl would remember.

I take another sip of her coffee, shaking those thoughts away. "You got all of that after one day?"

"Yep." She pulls my hand and we continue walking. "Hey, at least he noticed you."

I glare at her. "I spilled hot coffee all down his shirt."

"Well, it's a start." She grabs my arms and forces me to look at her. "What did he whisper to you? You were kind of blushing."

"It doesn't matter. That was our first and last conversation."

"Well, I saw the way he looked at you and he totally checked you out when you walked away. Is it so impossible for him to like you?"

Yeah, it is. Ashley is gorgeous with her long brown curls and big brown eyes. She has guys flock to her. I'm just the nerdy girl that no one pays any attention to.

I chuckle. "Okay, Miss Cupid. Let's go before you start planning our wedding. I spilled coffee on the guy. That's it. I doubt he's going to propose marriage let alone ask me on a date."

I link arms with her and we continue walking. Ashley stops me before we get to the corner. "I can't believe you didn't know that was Jeremy."

"Should I?" I hit the crosswalk button.

"Oh nothing, I just thought with your dad being the football coach, you'd know the starting quarterback."

"That's why he looked familiar. Let's get away from here before he comes outside."

As we cross the street, I think about how I have seen Jeremy at practice, but didn't make the connection until now. I love football and go to the games but I pay more attention to the actual game than the players. I know. I am one of those weird girls that actually enjoys the game more than the hot guys.

One more reason why I need to stay away from him. This guy spells trouble.

The next day at school, I open my locker to find a cup of coffee exactly to my liking, and it's still hot. "Until next time…" is written on its side.

Ashley walks up and sees the cup in my locker. "I don't remember stopping for coffee on the way to school." She glances over my shoulder to get a better idea of what I'm looking at. "No way! Is that from who I think it is?"

"Maybe." I blush thinking about our encounter the day before.

I could barely sleep thinking about those blue eyes and the chance that maybe Ashley was right.

Do I have a chance with a guy like him? I'm just a lonely freshman and he may only be a sophomore, but he's still one of the most popular guys at school. He would never look at me twice if I hadn't spilled my coffee on him. Plus, my dad would have a lot to say if I started dating the quarterback of the football team.

The warning bell rings, bringing me out of my thoughts. I grab the books I need and my coffee before shutting my locker. We pass by a group of football players led by none other than Mr. Popular beautiful eyes himself.

I hold up the coffee cup and mouth "thank you". He barely glances at me before turning back to his friends.

I look at Ashley, "See? I told you, he doesn't care about me."

"Then how do you explain the coffee?"

"I don't know. He was just being nice. Plus, my dad would never let me date him."

"Well that little message seems to say he wants to see you again."

I sigh, watching as he turns the corner of the hallway. "He's probably just making a joke about me spilling my coffee. He is just a typical jock, doing nice things in private and then his friends are around and he hides it. It's okay, I know he would never go for a girl like me anyway."

"Well if he can't see how great you are, then he doesn't deserve you."

We continue to walk to class. Ashley holds out her arm to stop me. "Wait, how do you think he got it in your locker?"

I shrug, not really caring since it will probably never happen again. "Let's get to class!"

We link arms and head to first period.

Chapter One
Present Day

I see him walk down the hallway, hoping this will be the day he finally notices me. It's been two years since the day I spilled my coffee on him and he barely gives me a second look. He walks past without even a glance and so it seems this year I will be invisible, once again.

I try not to be upset. I should be used to it by now.

I turn around and run into a broad, muscular chest, dropping my books. I really need to watch where I'm going.

As I go to pick them up, he reaches down to help me. I get a whiff of leather, and is that... evergreen?

After collecting my books, I stand, catching a first glimpse of the mystery guy and almost drop my books again.

It can't be.

"Can't be what?" The mystery guy asks.

Guess I didn't say that in my head after all. "Ummm...nothing."

He looks at me like he wants to ask more but thankfully he doesn't push it. "Okay. I'm Logan, it is great to meet you...?" He asks, looking at me curiously.

"Em... Emma." I blush because apparently anytime a cute guy talks to me that is what I do. Dumb fair skin.

"Well Emma, I hope to run into you again." Then just as quickly as I ran into him, he is gone.

This must be some twisted joke.

Later, I walk into AP English Literature and see him again. We are reading Pride and Prejudice and Mr. Stephens, our teacher, puts us in pairs for an oral presentation. "Emma, you will be paired with Logan."

Why? Why? Why? I swear the universe is playing some cruel trick on me. I spot Logan on the other side of the room and he grins widely. My hands start to sweat and my heart starts to race.

The project requires us to give an oral presentation on the book but set in a different era. Each group is given a certain section of the book. Logan and I are assigned the 1920s and the ball chapter.

We have a few minutes at the end of the class to discuss basic details and exchange information.

We decide to make Mr. Darcy a club owner. That is where he first meets Elizabeth and the ball takes place.

That night I receive a text:

Logan: *Would you want to meet up after school tomorrow at Carson's?*

Emma: *I have practice till 4:30 but can meet after that.*

Logan: *In that case, would you like to grab dinner instead?*

I reread the message a few times when my phone buzzes again.

Logan: *To discuss the project...*

Can he read my mind? That sounded like he was asking me out on a date, until his second message came through. I'm not sure what to think but agree to meet for dinner.

The next day, I can't concentrate in any of my classes. My mind is waging a war as to whether dinner is a date or not a date.

At swim practice, I dive under the water, trying to put all my energy into my strokes. I have a meet coming up that I need to get ready for. I'm already a junior and need to start getting serious if I hope to make it to the Olympics one day. Swimming is my outlet, from the smell of the chlorine to the sound of lapping water.

When practice is over, I race home to get ready for dinner.

I choose a pair of skinny jeans and a nice blue blouse that shows off my curves. To finish off the look, I slip on some sandals. Summer is still here and the heat is not letting up.

I never put on much makeup, other than a little mascara and eyeshadow. Tonight, I add eyeliner and lip gloss.

On the drive to the restaurant, I try to calm my nerves by telling myself it isn't a date. It is just dinner to discuss the project.

When I arrive at the restaurant, I see him waiting there for me and have to blink a few times to make sure I'm not seeing someone else.

He looks amazing. His dark brown hair is long on the top and falls just above his eyes. He has a perfect smile with the whitest teeth I have ever seen.

When those piercing blue eyes see me, I remind myself again that this is not a date.

He casually puts a hand on my lower back, steering me into the restaurant.

My back feels like it is on fire. I am pretty sure I'll have a burn mark of a hand print.

As we are waiting for our table, Logan tells me how beautiful I look. I feel a blush rise up in my cheeks and somehow manage to choke out a "thank you".

Once seated, we look at the menu and I quickly realize this is an expensive restaurant. I've heard of this place but have never been here. I wonder how Logan can afford to pay for such an expensive place.

The lighting is low to create an intimate appeal. There are wooden beams lining the ceiling and each table has a lantern with a candle burning. The whole place reminds me of a cozy farmhouse.

I scan for a cheaper menu item and decide to play it safe with the chicken cacciatore. Logan orders the rib eye with a baked potato and broccoli. I can already feel myself salivating over his food.

After we order, he asks, "So, how long have you lived in Marshall Creek?"

"My whole life. What about you?"

"My family moved here three years ago. I was in Europe attending a boarding school that specializes in film documentaries." I can see a hint of sadness in his eyes but it quickly disappears. "I came back to Marshall Creek to attend school like a normal teenager. My film obsession can wait until college."

It then dawns on me why he looks so familiar but it can't be. I gather up the courage to ask my next question. "Do you have any siblings?"

He smiles. "I have an older brother who's actually a senior at our school. He's the all-star football and baseball player."

I nervously take a sip of water wondering if it really is who I'm thinking of when Logan cuts off my thoughts, "You might actually know him, Jeremy? Jeremy Anderson?"

I gulp, wondering what to reply when the waiter shows up with our food. Thankful for the interruption, I immediately take a bite so I don't have to answer him right away.

"Do you know him?" He asks again as he cuts into his steak.

I wonder if he knows who I am. Maybe that's why he asked me to dinner. This must be some sick joke that his brother put him up to. But then again why would he even care, since he seems to ignore me at school. I play it safe by saying, "I met him once. We don't run in the same circles."

"Gotcha." It seems as if he might have more to say about the subject but doesn't. Instead, he asks about my family.

Talking with him is so easy and I find myself having a great time.

"So about the project. I mean that is the main reason for the meal."

Logan nods. "Yes, I have a few ideas in my car and thought we could stop at Lou's and grab a coffee to discuss the details."

Dinner and coffee? I thought the point of dinner was to discuss the project. Now he wants to spend even more time with me.

Breathe, Emma. It still doesn't mean this is a date.

I take out my wallet to pay for my food but Logan places his hand over mine to stop me.

"No, no I got this. After all, a gentleman always pays for a lady's meal and if he doesn't, his momma will give him a whooping."

A whooping. Who says that?

I know fighting him would be no use so instead I say, "Thank you. If you'll excuse me, I need to use the lady's room."

I splash some water on my face and I tell myself that this is nothing. The guy out there only happens to be the younger brother of the guy I have been crushing on since freshman year. If he's anything like his brother, I should probably stay far away from him but at the same time I feel this force pushing me towards him. I laugh because this is just my luck. Wait till Ashley hears about this!

I head to the front of the restaurant where Logan waits. As we walk to our cars, I can feel the electricity and he hasn't even touched me. If I moved a few inches to the right, our hands would be touching.

I'm not sure if it's because this is my crush's brother or some-thing more.

I unlock my car telling Logan that I would follow him to Lou's.

We order coffees; black with one sugar for him, and a vanilla latte light on the foam for me.

We throw around some ideas for the presentation and I find myself grinning. I feel so comfortable with him that I can't help blurting out, "Is this a date?"

Logan looks up from his notes and grins even bigger than me. "Do you want it to be a date, Emma?"

"Uhhh...ummm." I'm still shocked that I said that out loud.

What is with these Anderson boys and my mouth having no filter?

Logan looks directly into my eyes as he says, "I would love for this to be a date but don't worry, when I do ask you out, you won't have any questions about it being a date."

Later that night, as I climb into bed, I can't help but have this sense in my stomach that everything is about to change.

Chapter Two

Ashley demands I share all the details of the night before but just before I can say anything. She clears her throat. I instantly smell leather and evergreen.

"Hey Emma. Would you want to come over to my house tonight to work on the project?" I hear from behind me.

I nod, not knowing what else to say. "I'll text you my address."

I watch Logan walk away, not able to stop myself from checking him out.

Ashley clears her throat again. Right, she wants to know about last night.

"So we went to Carson's and talked about everything from family to school to future dreams. Guess who Logan's brother is?"

"Let me guess, Jeremy."

"How'd you know that?" I ask, shocked. Then again, I really shouldn't be surprised. She seems to know everything about everyone.

"One, everyone knows Jeremy's little brother just came back from Europe and two, they're practically twins."

"Your way of finding out gossip astounds me every time." It's one of the things I love about her even though I don't really care what people think.

She shrugs. "Tell me more about this date."

"It wasn't a date," which he did confirm at the end of the night. But then he said something about me knowing it when he does ask me out. "We were only there to talk about the project. Although Logan did pay for dinner and I did blurt out about if it was a date. I don't know, I really liked him and we clicked. Maybe I could see myself falling for him."

"What about Jeremy?"

"Ash, we have been over this. Jeremy doesn't give me the time of day. Why would I continue to like him when Logan is actually paying attention to me?"

Just as I finish talking, Jeremy saunters past with his football buddies and smiles at me. Woah, wait. Did he actually just smile at me? Usually, he completely ignores me.

Ashley laughs. "Well this year just got a whole lot more interesting."

I break out of my daze. "I didn't imagine that?"

Ashley shakes her head. She links her arm with me as we head to class. "So now what were you saying about you blurting something about a date?"

I knew I wasn't going to get away with sneaking in that little part. At least now I can get her advice.

I think back to what she said about this year getting interesting. I don't think so. I am just Emma. Nothing ever happens to me and no one knows who I am. Some might even say I am a wallflower. It is just the way I like it.

Later, I drive to the Andersons' home. I pull through large iron gates and up a long driveway. My first glimpse at the house has my jaw dropping.

This isn't a house. This is a mansion.

The front of the house is some sort of light grey rock. There are giant windows next to the door that reach all the way up to the roof. I drive around a koi pond complete with a waterfall. There are gorgeous white and yellow flowers planted around the pond.

I grab my backpack from the back seat, walk up to the front door, and ring the doorbell.

A woman answers the door, "You must be Emma." She pulls me into a hug and I can't help but hug her back. I feel like she is sizing me up but at the same time welcoming me into her home, if that even makes sense.

"I'm Victoria, Logan and Jeremy's mother. Logan is out back on the patio if you'll follow me." All I can think is how pretty and young she is.

At first glance inside the house, it is just as exquisite as the outside but very homey. There are personal touches everywhere from photos to little knick knacks.

There is a homey smell with a hint of cinnamon. I get a whiff of something delicious like a roast or something in the oven.

There are two cascading staircases leading up to a balcony with huge doors on the second floor. Victoria leads me underneath the balcony to a small living room. On the other side are French doors which lead out to the pool.

I would think all the dark paneling would make it feel small but it somehow does the opposite. It might be the sun streaming through the French doors and giant windows overlooking the back yard.

On the patio, Logan's mom excuses herself back inside.

I see Logan sprawled out on a lawn chair. I decide to be bold and scare him.

After last night, we had this instant connection and while I have no idea what will happen to us, I know we will at least be good friends. At least I hope we will.

I quietly tiptoe over to the chair and reach out to tickle him. He immediately bolts up.

"Ahhhh!" I scream and blush when I discover it isn't Logan. If I didn't know they weren't the same age, I would think they are twins.

This is even more embarrassing than when I spilled my coffee on him.

I run for my bag, ready to flee from the house.

I run into Logan, holding a platter of snacks, almost knocking him and the platter over.

He sets the platter down on the table and grabs my arms. He looks at me with this piercing, concerned look.

"Is everything okay?"

"Yes." I stumble out and mutter something about having to leave.

Jeremy walks up, pulls me over to him and hugs me.

I stand there completely in shock. I feel like a robot being passed between them.

He extends his arms and gives me the same piercing stare as his brother only with a hint of amusement.

"Hello Emma. I didn't mean to startle you. It's great to see you, again."

His eyes roam from my head to my toes. To say it makes me feel good is an understatement. This is probably the first time he has ever really noticed me, at least since that day over two years ago at Lou's. The day I spilled my coffee on his shirt and how nice he had been.

After he seemed to completely forget who I was when he passed me in the halls.

Logan looks back and forth between us, clearly confused.

Jeremy lets go of me and salutes us. "I must bid thee ado for I have a date."

Just as he reaches the doors, he glances back at us. "Oh, one thing I remember from last year, Mr. Stephens has a flair for dramatics, so put something creative in your project."

Once he is gone, Logan crosses his arms. "Care to explain?"

I bite my lip. He doesn't look mad but rather curious. "Well… I thought it was you on the chair, and I thought it would be funny to sneak up on you but it turns out it wasn't you." Logan laughs and I smack him on the arm.

Eventually, I join in. His laughter is like a drug that pulls you in. I've never done drugs and don't plan to but his laughter is so consuming. You can't help but laugh with him.

Finally, the laughing calms down. "I actually was curious about the 'seeing you again' part but that was even better."

"Oh, that." I shrug, hoping he will move on from it but when I look at him, he's giving me the same stare he gave me at dinner. It's a stare that I am pretty sure could get me to tell him anything he wants.

I think it's his deep blue eyes or maybe it is the smirk he is giving me.

"Uh well about two years ago, I may have accidentally spilled coffee all over his shirt."

I stare down at my shirt, not able to look him in the eyes. I will never be able to live that day down.

When I glance up, Logan looks shocked, which is surprising.

"I wondered if that was you."

Now I am the shocked one. "Jer called me that night at boarding school and said he had met this awesome hot girl. He told me the story about what happened and then I never heard anything about you after that. I figured you had moved away or something."

I am too shocked to say anything so I turn to our project notes hoping he will get the hint and move on. That was one of the most embarrassing days of my life and here Jeremy had been blabbing about it to everyone including his brother. No wonder he never looked at me in the halls again. He thought I was some laughing stalk.

Logan nudges my chin to look up at him. "Hey, don't be embarrassed. It serves my brother well to get a hot beverage dumped down his shirt every once in a while. Plus, I knew after hearing that story, I needed to meet you one day. Not many girls can really catch my brother's attention like you."

"Yeah well, he never seemed to give me the time of day after that."

"That's my brother for you. He's a total player. You know what? I am glad because now I can have you all to myself."

Had I heard him right? Catch his attention? So much for that. I thought he was a nice guy but then he ignored me for two years. That nice guy getting me coffee never seemed to come back but here is his brother, who has been nice to me since I dropped my books in the hallway. Maybe it is time to finally move on.

"So... I... umm... So for the project. I am not a huge fan of public speaking. Do you think I could create the visuals and then you do the presenting?"

"Hmmm..." He puts a finger to his chin like he is thinking hard and I can't help but laugh. "How about this? Since you don't like public speaking but Mr. Stephens is all for the dramatics, how about we make it into a video? That way we can perform it here so no one can see, and you won't have to say as much in front of the class."

"Yes, that would be amazing." I lean over and kiss him on the cheek. I pull back immediately. "Sorry."

"It's fine." Logan grins and I see a hint of a blush creep up his neck but I can't be sure.

We start planning out our video. We'd act out the ball scene and dress in 1920s attire. We also put together a poster of what the club looks like and what clothing was worn back then.

Logan starts writing the scene as I get a head start on the poster.

Before long, I glance at the time and realize it's almost seven. I quickly start to gather my stuff when Logan's mother walks outside. "Logan dear, is your friend staying for dinner?"

She smiles at me.

Logan looks over at me. "If she wants to."

I pick up my bag ready to go. "Oh, I don't want to intrude."

"Nonsense." She flicks her wrist as if pushing that idea away. She puts her hand on my back and steers me inside. "When you have two teenage boys in the house, you make sure to make enough food for an army."

I laugh. "Okay, let me just text my parents." She nods and goes through a door I assume leads to the kitchen.

After letting my parents know, Logan steers me toward the dining room. Or well the other dining room. The first one we walk by has a massive oak table that would probably fit twenty people or more. The ceiling is so high with a beautiful chandelier that I can only imagine sparkles with the lights on.

The second dining room is much smaller and more intimate even with it being right next to the giant open kitchen. With only six chairs around the table, I feel much more at home until we are served the first course of salad.

I've never been served in courses before which makes the meal exciting. For the main course, we have meatloaf, mashed potatoes, and some sort of carrot soufflé. I knew I had smelled some sort of meat when I walked in.

My mom is a delicious cook but this meatloaf is sweet and the mashed potatoes are so buttery, they practically melt in my mouth.

By the time dessert rolls around, I am not sure how much more I can eat. That is until I see the brownie a la mode and my mouth begins to water.

I enjoy not only the dinner, but also the conversation with his parents. His mother is a sweetheart and I can tell she loves her sons very much. His father on the other hand is a jokester. I can see where Logan got his smirk from which is becoming a normal occurrence.

After dinner, Logan walks me out to my car. I thank him for the lovely dinner.

I wonder if he is going to kiss me and try not to glance at his lips. I still feel drawn to Jeremy but something is happening here, I just can't put my finger on it. Is it friendship or something more?

All I know is that I want him to kiss me. I want to know what it would be like.

Logan starts to lean in. This is it! But at the last second tilts his head so he can give me a hug.

He pulls back and does just what I was trying so hard not to do earlier, glancing at my lips before giving me a quick peck on the cheek. "See you tomorrow at school, Emma".

I slowly make my way to my car and can't help touching my cheek where he kissed me. I glance in the rearview mirror to make sure there isn't a burn mark because it suddenly feels very warm.

I see Logan still standing on the driveway. I give him a wave.

As I drive home, I think about how I fit right in with his family, like I have known them forever. I know I need to be careful but my feelings are growing each day and I have no idea how Logan feels. We have a connection and I hope he feels it too. I guess, only time will tell.

Chapter Three

The next few weeks go by in a blur and it's time for my English presentation. My swim meet is also later in the week.

I don't know which one I'm more nervous for. My meet is a qualifier for if I have the times to begin my official Olympic training.

I walk into class with the poster for the presentation, hoping Logan remembers the video. We are up third and I am so nervous.

When it is our turn, I walk to the front of the room. I feel myself getting more and more nervous. My palms are starting to sweat. My eyesight is getting fuzzy. *Is this normal?*

I see Logan at the front getting the video ready. How can he be so calm and collected?

As I set the poster up, my breathing becomes fast. Logan must see I am a nervous wreck because he places his hands on my cheeks and looks into my eyes. Now I really can't breathe.

"Emma, you are going to kill this presentation. Remember what we practiced and just take a deep breath."

I close my eyes, take a deep breath and feel my nerves slowly going away. How does he make me feel so calm, yet my heart is beating a million beats a minute?

When I open my eyes, Logan has already moved to the center of the room to speak.

Our presentation goes off without a hitch. I only stumble once.

When the video comes up, Logan talks about how one day he wants to be a filmmaker so he thought this would be the perfect opportunity to create a fun video.

As the video plays, the class laughs at the right moments. I swear I see a tear in a few eyes when Elizabeth finally dances with Mr. Darcy.

Logan did a great job capturing the romance of Mr. Darcy and Elizabeth. I didn't see the final video and am so surprised to see the conflicted emotions in my eyes as we dance the waltz.

Watching the video makes me realize the emotions I have been trying to keep hidden. I have been crushing on Jeremy for as long as I can remember, but somehow Logan slipped in when I wasn't looking. I have known him for less than two months. I have to remind myself to be careful. Maybe he feels the same way, maybe he doesn't.

I didn't realize I was staring at him until he looks over and smiles. Almost like he could feel my stare. I don't know how long we stare at each other until the clapping breaks my thoughts.

The credits roll, followed by bloopers. I didn't know Logan put them in but I am laughing all the same.

After class Logan walks me to my locker. He softly touches my arm and I feel a shock run through my arm.

"It was super fun working with you. Hopefully we can do it again."

Just as I am about to reply, Jeremy walks by with a bunch of annoying cheerleaders and Logan joins them. One of the cheerleaders, Amber, grabs his arm and I watch as Logan laughs at whatever she says.

Like brother like brother, I guess. I close my locker heading to my next class. So much for anything happening between us. Maybe I imagined the whole thing.

Thursday comes way too fast and my first big swim meet of the year is here. This is the first year I'm the anchor in the relay, and I can feel the pressure.

My classes are going super slow. All I can think about is what if I get a cramp or what if I swallow water and start choking. Every possible thing that can go wrong goes through my head.

I have never gotten nervous swimming. Probably because it was always for fun. This is a qualifier to see if I have the times to take it to the next level.

When the last bell rings, I race to the locker rooms to change and stretch.

I enter the pool house. I can smell the chlorine in the air. I hear the laughter and conversations of those in the crowd. This is one of the places I feel at home.

Logan waves at me from the bleachers. I want to ignore him but my curiosity wins out. I walk over to him. He gives me a big hug and exclaims, "Good luck — or is it break a leg like in theatre?"

"Good luck is fine." I laugh. "What are you doing here?"

Logan takes my hand and traces a line on the back before clasping his fingers between mine. "Well, you see there's this girl that is the talk of the school. People are saying she is going to the Olympics one day, and I just had to see for myself."

I try not to let him see how much I am freaking out with both his words and his hand in mine. I am pretty sure my hand is permanently scarred just like my cheek and back. What is it about my body parts feeling like they are on fire when he touches me? "Oh, that helps me feel better!"

He grins at me. "You'll be great!" At that moment, Amber, the same girl I saw in the hallway with Logan earlier that week sits right next to him.

A few minutes later, Jeremy and some other girl show up. I recognize her as the captain of the cheerleading team and Amber's best friend, Mallory.

I quickly remove my hand from Logan's as Jeremy glances down at them and then goes back to talking to Mallory.

I quickly return to my team. I'm not sure why I let go of Logan's hand. It's not like I don't like him.

"Are you ready for this?" Coach Johnson asks me.

This is the moment I have been waiting for my whole life. Or well... the beginning of what could be my dream life. If I can hit my times, then I have a chance at making the Olympics in a few years and the training will officially begin.

"Yes," I say, shaking my head nervously.

He squeezes my shoulder. "You have always been one of our strongest swimmers. I always wanted to put you in a relay but you were always so good on your own. This year we need to make you a well-rounded swimmer so the Olympic scouts can see your talent. Now breathe, stretch and swim as fast as you can!"

I stretch my arms above my head, relieving some of the stress. "Right, no pressure!"

"You'll do great!"

When the first set of swimmers take their place, I glance into the audience and find Ashley sitting next to my parents. They always come to my swim meets. They know this is not only the first meet of the year but an important one if I plan on becoming a professional swimmer.

Just below them, I see Amber chatting Logan's ear off but he is watching me. He gives me a thumbs up. *I can do this,* I think to myself.

I put on my cap, take off my sweats, get my goggles ready and face the pool.

The first few rounds, I kill it in freestyle and butterfly. I only place second in backstroke, but I'm feeling good.

Next is the relay. I take my place as fourth in line, ready to go when the third swimmer touches the wall.

I see her headed my way and I take my position. I dive as soon as she hits her mark.

The water is chilly but not too cold that it takes my breath away. It feels good as I glide through the water. I can feel the water guiding me.

Stroke, stroke, breath.

Stroke, stroke, breath.

As I hit the other side of the pool, I gracefully flip and use everything in me to get to the end. I am so concentrated on getting to the wall, I don't see where the other swimmers are.

When I tap the wall, I know I've done it.

As I rise from the water, I can hear the audience applauding.

I check my time to see we placed first for relay which put us in first overall.

The next few minutes go by in a daze. Jeremy comes over to congratulate me. The butterflies are still there regardless of the feelings I now have for Logan. Now I just have butterflies for both of them. *How confusing.*

"You were amazing." He says.

He kisses me on the cheek and walks away.

What is with these boys all of a sudden kissing me on my cheek?

I am so stunned that I stand there for a solid two minutes before Ashley runs up and gives me a huge hug.

She whispers in my ear, "Did I just see Jeremy kissing you?"

I pull back from the hug. "You saw that? I thought I imagined it."

She grabs my hand and squeezes. "Nope, it was real." She pauses, studying me. "So is it over between you and Logan?"

I look at her, confused. "Over? We never had anything except a school project. Now he's flirting with Amber and doesn't have time for me."

Ash glances over my shoulder and whispers, "Well that might change since he's heading this way."

I come face to face with those piercing blue eyes. "My brother is throwing a party on Friday night. Do you and Ash want to come?"

I shake my head no at the same time Ashley practically screams yes. I try to telepathically send Ashely signals screaming no.

"Give us a second". She drags me away and says to me, "This is the perfect place to get to know Logan outside of a school project."

"Yeah I know but—-"

"Ha! There, you agreed so you have to go."

I shake my head yet again. "No, I was going to say he isn't interested in me as more than a friend. He was just being nice."

"Well then go and show him what you have to offer."

I don't really know what I have to offer but I know whether I agree or not, Ashley will drag me to the party.

"Fine. But you owe me."

I start walking back to Logan.

Ashley catches up with me. "We're in!"

"Great." Logan smiles at me. "See you tomorrow night — or well in class too."

He joins his brother's group as I look at Ash and she is smiling. I sigh and take off to the locker room to shower.

Chapter Four

"Ahhh... I have nothing to wear." I throw a shirt onto the already growing pile on my bed. Ash walks over to the bed. She grabs a pair of dark skinny jeans, a purple tank with lace on the sides and a pair of silver ballet flats. She picks out a long silver chain with a locket on the end and hoops to match from my jewelry.

"Now hurry up and change, Emma, so I can do your hair and makeup." As she walks into the bathroom I stare at her, amazed at how easily she picked my outfit.

Thirty minutes later, I see my reflection and my jaw drops. She somehow managed to give my straight blonde hair a slight curl. My makeup is so subtle you would barely know I have any on except for the fact that my eyes pop.

We walk through the door at Jeremy and Logan's house. Logan spots us and heads our way. "Thanks for coming. You look beautiful tonight, Emma. Do either of you want something to drink?"

He leads us to the kitchen. My hands are already starting to sweat. This is Ashley's territory, not mine.

There is everything from beer to wine to every kind of liquor possible. I choose rum and coke since that is the only drink I know. After we get our drinks, we head to the living room where everyone is milling about.

"Make yourselves at home," Logan says, excusing himself. "I'll find you in a little bit." Logan whispers in my ear before rejoining his brother and friends.

A shiver runs down my spine. What is he doing to me? I have never felt a connection so electric with any guy before. Maybe with Jeremy, but I never got close enough to him to see what it actually was.

Ashley and I sit on the couch, not sure what to do. I have never been much of the party type but Ash said this is one of the biggest high school parties and I have to go, especially if I am going to date Logan. I laughed at her because I highly doubt anything is going to happen with us. I may feel some connection but he doesn't seem to feel it back.

Ash leans into me, "Logan can't stop watching you."

I glance at Logan who quickly looks away. I get up from the couch. "Ashley, do you want another drink?" She nods and gets up to go use the bathroom.

The kitchen is even more crowded than before. I spot the rum on the opposite counter and maneuver my way through the crowd of people.

As I am about to get to the counter, some girl spills her drink all over the bottom of my shirt. Just my luck. I can already feel the sticky liquid soaking through and clinging to my stomach.

I search for the bathroom to clean it off. There are a few people waiting. Ash is leaving the bathroom and sees me. "What happened to you?"

"Some girl spilled her drink all over me."

"I'll get us drinks and meet you in the living room." I thank her and wait for my turn in the bathroom. I rinse the bottom of my tank top and am able to get most of it out. I wipe my stomach where the liquid soaked through and fold it under so the wet spot isn't as noticeable.

I return to the living room but can't find Ashley. I see a couple making out while a crowd around them cheers. When they pull away, I see it is Logan and Amber.

Logan looks at Amber and smiles. A smile I wish he would use on me. I run out of the room before anyone can see my tears.

I find the nearest door and nearly bump into someone on the porch. I instantly feel a warmth surround me as I'm surprised to see Jeremy. He sees the tears running down my cheeks.

He takes my face gently in his hands, wiping away the tears. "Hey, what's wrong?"

I sigh. "Just someone I thought I knew. Turns out I don't."

"Whoever this person is, isn't worth your tears." If he only knew it was his brother, he might not be saying that.

"Why do you suddenly care? You barely even know me."

Jeremy smirks, "I actually know more than you think." He wipes my cheek again. "You're beautiful. Now let me get you a drink and we can go beat some people in beer pong."

I gulp as he pulls me into the house. I should be freaking out because Jeremy is holding my hand but all I can think is, *did he really just call me beautiful?*

I have never played beer pong before but after a few rounds, I finally get the hang of it.

We have one cup left. Jeremy takes his shot and then it's my turn. I line up the ball, throw, and it goes in! Jeremy picks me up and spins me around.

As he sets me down, Ashley walks up and gives me a "what is going on here?" look. "Emma, there you are. I was looking everywhere for you."

She eyes Jeremy and looks back at me. I shrug and mouth, "I'll tell you later."

I glance back at Jeremy. "Are you ready for another game?"

Ash jumps in, "I want to play."

"You can take my place," Jeremy says. "I need to make the rounds."

Ash bounces next to me. "Okay, so how do I play?" I explain the rules but can't help looking where Jeremy disappeared to.

A few losing games later and we are both getting tipsy. We take a break out on the balcony.

Ash asks the question she has been dying to ask all night. "So what was with you and Jeremy?"

I stare out at the backyard. "Nothing, he was just being nice and trying to make me feel better."

I feel Ashley's gaze on me. "Why would he need to make you feel better?"

I sigh. "Long story short, I was going back to the living room to meet you and then I saw Logan making out with Amber. I was upset. I ran outside and bumped into Jeremy. He said a bunch of stuff that didn't make sense then got me to play beer pong. So nothing happened between me and Jeremy. I'm not even sure why he's talking to me all of a sudden."

Ash throws her hands up in the air like it is the most obvious thing as she says, "Because his brother likes you!"

I rest my elbows on the edge of the railing and set my chin in my hands. "Well he sure has a funny way of showing it. You know what, I am done with him. Now enough of this serious talk, let's get drunk." Boys are confusing. This is why I focus on other things. I don't have time for their games.

We make our way into the house, ready to dance the night away.

I wake up the next morning and squint, barely able to open my eyes. The sun is so bright.

I roll over and Ash is snoring next to me.

I sit up and blink trying to remember where I am. When my eyes finally adjust, I see we aren't the only ones who stayed over.

I grab my phone. It is dead. My parents must be freaking out.

I get up to get some water for my dry throat. The second I stand, I feel dizzy. My head is pounding.

As I enter the kitchen, I am instantly hit with the sweet aroma of coffee. Jeremy is pouring himself a cup. He sees me lusting after his.

"Well I have definitely seen you look better." I'm speechless. Every time he says something to me, I have to think twice because I can't believe the words that come out of his mouth.

He grabs a bottle of Advil from a cabinet, shakes out two pills and pours me a glass of water. "Take these while I get you some coffee. How about a piece of toast?"

"Umm, sure—" I say, not knowing what else to say and wondering why he is being so nice.

I take a seat at the island, swallow the pills and down the water. My throat already feels better.

Jeremy sets a plate with buttered toast and a steaming cup of coffee in front of me.

"So how did the rest of your night go?" He puts more toast in the toaster, I'm assuming for himself and sits in the seat next to me.

I take a sip of my coffee, staring at my hands clasping the mug. How did he know how I like my coffee?

"Well as you can see, I drank way too much, but Ash and I had fun."

He squeezes my shoulder. "I'm glad you decided to let loose for once."

Just as I am about to ask what he means, the side door opens. Logan enters, looks between us then takes his headphones out and grabs a bottle of water from the fridge. He's mentioned he takes morning bike rides.

He chugs half the bottle, not taking his eyes off of me and says, "So what happened to you last night? I was looking for you everywhere."

I stumble saying, "I was... ummm... I have to go."

I rush out of the kitchen and race over to Ash. I shake her, telling her we need to leave.

She looks confused and I ask where her keys are. She points to her purse by her head.

We walk out to the car. I get in the driver's seat as she gets into the passenger seat and rests her head against the cold window. "Is it just my head pounding or are you turning into a crazy person?"

I start the car, thinking about Logan. I have no idea what is running through his head. One second he is nice and I think he feels something for me, but maybe I'm overthinking it and it's just him being friendly. "I just had to get out of there."

"Got it." She buckles her seatbelt. "Well for waking me up, I demand you take me to Lou's for some waffles, greasy bacon, and coffee."

I pull onto the road. "Deal. I'll definitely need food before I get home." I'm sure my parents are angry and waiting.

Chapter Five

Over the next two weeks, time moves quickly. I am grounded for the next month after the party.

My parents were waiting for me when I got home. My mom said, "You know the rules, Emma. If you're staying out past curfew or at someone's house, you need to call us."

"My phone died, otherwise I would have called." I was hoping it would be a short lecture so I could change before they saw the beer. "I'm going to go take a shower and a nap."

Just as I was about to escape, my mom saw my shirt.

"Were you drinking?" I never lie to my parents and figured telling them the truth was better. Then began the lecture about underage drinking and how I needed to be careful, blah, blah, blah... Then the grounding happened and that was that.

My second swim meet is a disaster and I barely make third place. I am so distracted and most of that had to do with a certain someone being absent in the audience. He was probably with Amber.

After the meet, I'm mad at myself for letting myself get distracted. Even more so over a boy. We haven't kissed, we aren't dating, and we barely talk. I've never let anything affect me before when I was in the pool.

Why is Logan affecting me so much?

I can tell my coach is disappointed in me too. After my first meet, I met with him to go over my training schedule. We start pre-training this quarter and then come January, it is time to get serious for the Olympics.

It is my dream to get to the Olympics, but I need to get my head back in it and stop letting a certain boy distract me.

The Monday before Thanksgiving, I have another meet and see Logan in the audience sitting next to Amber. Jeremy and Mallory soon join them. Logan sees me looking at them and waves.

Why are they even here? They have never come to swim meets before.

I quickly tune them out. Another girl, Stacey, on the swim team comes over to me. "I see Mr. Hottie is waving at you?"

She is probably talking about Logan. I just shrug and shake my head, "Yeah whatever."

Stacey must get that I don't want to talk about it. She glances back and forth between Logan and I. "Well I think you should kill it at this meet, and then you'll have a line of guys waiting at your door."

I give her a small smile because I highly doubt that is true. I like being invisible.

I do end up killing it at the meet and win first in all my races but backstroke. It is by far my worst stroke, but second is still good.

As I gather my stuff, Logan comes to congratulate me, but I run by him saying something about having to change.

A few days later, I'm in the kitchen with my mom prepping our Thanksgiving meal. We always eat early around one so we can snack on leftovers the rest of the day. All we have left is the mashed potatoes and about thirty minutes left on the turkey when my mom turns to me, "Why don't you go get cleaned up and I can finish here."

I go to my room and lay on my bed. I glare at the ceiling, as if it's the ceiling's fault, and think about how much I used to love this holiday. Now everything seems messed up and I don't know what to be thankful about.

I hear a knock on my door and shout, "Mom I'll be right out." My door opens and in walks Ashley.

"Looks like I'm just in time for food. I never know why my parents insist on waiting until four to eat. Do they want us to fill up on hors d'oeuvres before the good food?"

When I don't say anything, she comes over to me, "What's wrong? You're usually super cheery on Thanksgiving."

I sit up on my bed. "I know. I just don't feel very cheerful today. This whole Logan thing is bugging me more than I realized. I never meant to fall for him and then he hurt me. I just don't get him. At least with Jeremy it was a crush from afar."

Ashley sits next to me. "I think it is time for you to explain the whole story from the party."

I sigh. "Well, after you left me at the bathroom to go get drinks, I was headed to meet you in the living room. I walked in and saw Logan making out with Amber."

"So what then, you thought you'd make him jealous with his brother? What exactly happened on that balcony?"

I glance over at her. "No, I wasn't trying to make him jealous. After I saw him with Amber, I went outside to get some air and Jeremy was on the balcony like I told you. What I didn't tell you was that he told me I was beautiful and no one was worth my tears. He said we should go inside and have fun. Hence you finding us playing beer pong. It reminded me of why I had a crush on him for so long."

I stand up and start pacing. "When I fell for Logan, I realized my crush on Jeremy was never anything in the first place. It was only meant to be a crush. I'm over him now, but we still had fun and it makes me think their roles are reversed. Jeremy was always the popular jock that never had time for me, and Logan was the sweet guy. Now it's the other way around."

Ash scoots to the end of the bed. "Babe, I don't think that's exactly how it is. Jeremy is still the popular jock and I am pretty sure Logan is still the sweet guy you fell for. Plus, I bet that kiss you saw was part of some game."

I fall down next to her. "Yeah okay. You're just trying to make me feel better."

She touches my shoulder. I turn my head to look at her. "No Emma, I see the way he looks at you when you aren't looking. That guy likes you whether you want to see it or not. That kiss was part of a game because that's what happens at parties."

It probably was just a game. I have never been one to over-react but there is something about Logan that makes me crazy. "You're probably right. It's just if you had seen that kiss. Ughh." I fall back on my bed.

"I still think it was nothing." She pokes me in the leg. "Now get your butt up and let's go get some food." She yanks me off my bed.

"Okay let's go." I follow her to the kitchen where my mom asks if we can help set the table.

After lunch, Ashley leaves but says she would be back later for our Thanksgiving sleepover tradition.

Since the girls cooked, the guys, meaning my dad and brother, get clean up duty and I decide to go for a walk.

I head to my favorite park with a gazebo overlooking the mountainside with a creek below. Hence the town name — Marshall Creek.

Whenever I need to think I go here because the world around me ceases to exist.

I sit on the bench in the gazebo and pull my jacket close. The air is chilly and smells like pine trees. Winter is approaching quickly and it looks like it might snow.

I think about everything Ashley said and how she was probably right. I don't know what I really saw and I at least owe Logan an explanation. The next time I see Logan, I would talk to him.

As I turn to leave, a figure walks up to me and I realize it is none other than Logan.

So much for next time I see him. I meant back at school — not now. I look up at the sky laughing at God's humor. Now isn't the time. Maybe next time. I can't face him now.

I try to sneak by but he reaches out to stop me. "Emma please wait."

"I can't talk to you right now." I start to walk again.

I can feel his eyes on my back. "Please Emma. I'm not sure what happened, but it seems like I haven't seen you since my brother's party."

"Oh yes, the party..." I still don't turn around.

"It looked like you were having a ton of fun with my brother."

That makes me mad because nothing happened and he should let me explain. I march up to him and look him directly in the eye, "Yeah... did it? Well, it seems I wasn't the only one."

"What's that supposed to mean?" He is clearly confused.

"Nothing." I say crossing my arms and backing up because I quickly realize I am a hypocrite. I am mad at him for not letting me explain when I am doing the same thing to him.

"Look Emma, I didn't come here to fight."

"Just to stalk me then?"

"No, well... I found this place on my bike ride and saw you here a few times. I never wanted to disrupt you. I came here today hoping to find you because I've missed you. I do have something to ask you though." He steps towards me, taking my hand.

"What do you want to ask?" I see the sun setting behind him. I didn't realize how long I had been out here.

A gust of wind blows through the trees and I shiver, but this time it isn't from the cold.

He traces a circle on my hand and I once again feel like my hand is on fire. Does he feel that too?

"Do you like my brother?"

I gasp and pull my hand away. "What would make you think that?"

"Well you seemed to hit it off with him at his party and I just wanted to know." He looks at me curiously.

I stare down at my feet, not able to look at him. "I will admit I used to like him a while ago, but then I started to fall for someone else and I thought he..."

The next thing I know, Logan lifts my chin and his lips are on mine. They are soft as they move against mine. *Can I stay here forever?*

I sink into the kiss but after a few seconds I pull away and run.

I glance back and am surprised to see Logan hasn't moved.

When I get back home, I run to my room and fall on my bed.

I'm torn about what happened. It was the best kiss of my life but it shouldn't have happened.

He just keeps playing this game with me and I don't know how to feel.

Ashley shows up a little later and immediately knows something is wrong. I tell her nothing and she doesn't push me.

The next morning, I'm in a much better mood and ready for our annual Black Friday shopping trip. Ashley and I have had this tradition with our moms since we were little.

Every Black Friday we get up super early to get in line at 3 a.m. at Target. We bring hot chocolate in a thermos to keep us warm. The store doesn't open till 5 a.m. but the line gets long fast.

When the store finally opens, we are third in line. "Okay, you all remember the rules — 1. We have three hours to get everything we need, 2. No looking in anyone else's carts, and 3. Have fun! Ready? Let's go!"

We grab our shopping carts and are off.

I head back to the electronics first because that is where all the big sales are. I grab the Bluetooth headset my brother wants and then head to check out the DVDs.

For my dad's stocking stuffer, I plan on getting him a DVD set. I am deciding between *Indiana Jones* or *Pirates of the*

Caribbean when I hear a voice behind me, "Definitely *Indiana Jones*!"

My heart does a little flutter. I work up the courage to turn around, hoping things won't be awkward. "What about Johnny Depp?"

He takes the Indiana Jones set from me and points at the back, "But see Indiana Jones has adventure, lassos, and snake pits."

"First off, no one likes snakes and two…" I point at the Pirates set. "Pirates has thrill, hot pirates sword fighting and cute but evil monkeys."

Logan puts both his hands up. "Okay fine, you got me on the monkeys."

I laugh thinking back to the first day I went over to his house.

I was trying to find the bathroom and went into Logan's room by mistake. In the center of his bed was a very old stuffed monkey. I picked it up when Logan came in wondering where I went. I held up the monkey and asked him to explain. He took the monkey from me, "don't make fun of Bert. He's been with me since I was baby and I just can't let him go." He cuddles the monkey to his face and grins wildly.

I took the monkey from him and talked to him. "Okay Mr. Bert, well I need your daddy for this project but he'll be back soon." I laid him back against the pillows and left the room, laughing at Logan as I passed.

As I come out of my daydream, I see Logan has moved closer. He reaches out to touch my cheek and says, "Emma, we need to talk about the kiss last night."

Just as I am about to answer, Ashley pulls her cart up next to me, "Am I interrupting something?"

I step away from Logan blushing. "No, nothing."

Logan is still staring at me and whispers, "Meet me tonight at our spot at five," and then disappears.

As soon as he leaves, Ashley turns to me and puts her hand on her hip, "You kissed?"

"Maybe…" I turn around, throwing both DVD sets into the cart and moving on to the next section.

She follows behind me with her cart and points at me as she passes, "you have some explaining to do missy."

I know I will have to tell her the story but I am still trying to figure it out myself.

I head to the kitchen section to shop for my mom. She recently broke her mixer attachment for her Kitchen aid. I know she will need another attachment for her famous Christmas cookies.

I grab a few more gifts and then head to the register. The store is even more packed than when we first arrived.

When I get up to the register, I see a display of ornaments and spot one at the very top. It is a monkey popping out of a top hat wearing a Santa hat.

Without thinking too much about it, I throw it in my cart.

After I check out, I meet with Ash and our moms to grab some brunch to round off our Black Friday tradition.

Chapter Six

I fall onto my bed next to Ashley. "I forgot how tiring Black Friday shopping is."

Ash flips over on her stomach resting her head on her hands, "Okay now spill".

I laugh. "I was hoping you would forget." I know she won't let it go this time. "I walked to the park yesterday after you left, and then Logan showed up. Apparently, he found it a few weeks ago and has been coming back ever since. We talked a little or well, more like we had a disagreement. That's when he kissed me and I ran."

"Okay first off, what do you mean disagreement?"

I sit up. "We just fought about the party."

She raises herself up on her hands so she can see my face. "So you asked about the kiss with Amber?"

"Not exactly. He saw me with Jeremy. He asked if something was going on and if I liked him. I told him I used to but started falling for someone else. I was planning on bringing it up but then he kissed me. So I freaked and took off."

She leans back against the pillows. "Well I think you still need to talk to him." She gives me a knowing smile. "Plus he obviously likes you if he kisses you."

"So? He kissed Amber — does that mean he likes her too?"

"Ughhhh, I'm telling you that was a game and you're reading too much into what you saw. Go tonight and ask him about it. See what he says and then decide if you want to be with him."

I lay back next to her. "What's the point? I don't want to just be one of the many girls on the list."

Ashley looks over at me. "Logan is not like his brother and I doubt you could ever be one of the many girls." She slides off my bed. "Plus it could be the start of something great." She extends her hand towards me. "Only one way to find out."

I walk to the park and can't help searching the sky for signs of snow. Snow always makes everything more magical and I need all the magic I can get for this talk.

Logan is sitting in the gazebo looking out over the mountainside. I take a deep breath and approach him.

As I get closer, he hears me and our eyes connect. I feel the pull from halfway across the park.

I make my way toward the bench and he stands. He steps to me. I step back, knowing I'm a goner if he touches me.

"Thanks for coming. I just wanted to clear a few things up."

"Yeah, sure." I stand there awkwardly, not sure what to do with my hands or if I should look at him.

"So what happened at the party with my brother?"

Wait, what? That is not what I expected him to ask me. I glance at him confused.

"Nothing happened with your brother. He was being a good friend and comforting me."

"Why would he need to comfort you?"

"Ummm." I walk to the railing and gaze out at the mountains. Some already have snow on the peaks. "I saw something that made me upset."

He comes up next to me and I feel his gaze. It's like daggers piercing me. "What did you see?"

I decide to come clean. "You, Logan." I point at him. "Kissing Amber. I thought you might like me after the project but then you were so hot and cold. Then I saw you at your brother's party kissing Amber and I realized you only thought of me as a friend."

Logan stands there saying nothing.

I move away from him. This was a mistake. I knew he didn't like me. Why I even came today, I have no idea.

"You know what it's fine. It's dumb anyway. It's not like we were dating so you can kiss anyone you want. We can be friends. We can still have fun together as friends."

Logan still doesn't say anything, but a smile forms slowly on his face. I realize this is pointless. I'm just making a fool of myself. Time to go.

Right as I go to leave, Logan laughs. I throw my hands up. "What's so funny?"

He grabs my hands in his. "You! Jealousy is a good look on you."

I try to yank my hands away but he has a firm grip. "Yeah... well even if I was jealous what would it matter anyway." I stare out to the mountains knowing that one look into his ice blue eyes will suck me in. My body is already pulling me towards him now that he has my hands. One look and I'm a goner.

"First off, you have nothing to be jealous of. Amber and I are friends. Jeremy is dating her best friend — well, if you call what he does dating." He shakes my hands urging me to look at him. "Second, the kiss you saw was part of a dare, and it meant nothing."

I pull my hands away, immediately regretting the warmth from his. "I saw that kiss and it didn't look like nothing"

"We'll get back to the kiss in a second."

I swing my head back to him, confused. "Wait, why?"

He brushes off my comment. "I need to finish what I was saying. What number was I on?"

"Three".

"Right number three — do you know why I left the film program in Europe?"

"No?" I cross my arms wondering where he is going with this.

"Because film became more of a constant project and lost all the fun. I like making films that would impact someone and make a difference. Over there they seemed to take all that out and made everything about what would get the biggest rating. When I came back here and did that project with you, you reminded me of why I want to be a filmmaker in the first place. Even though it was just a silly school project, I had a blast with you. Then I started to fall for you and it scared me. That's why I might have kinda stepped back after the project. Plus, I thought you liked my brother and I didn't want to interfere."

"Your brother." I take a seat on the bench, knowing this conversation is only just beginning. "I had the biggest crush on him last year but he never looked twice at me until you got here. We did only meet once when I spilled coffee down his shirt."

He sits down next to me. "I don't think that's true. Any guy would be crazy not to notice you, including my brother."

"Yeah, well…" I don't know what else to say because it's true. He never looked or said anything to me after that day at the coffee shop. Unless you count the coffee in my locker but I certainly don't.

"Now about that kiss you saw. I want you to know it meant nothing. Jeremy dragged me into a game of truth or dare, and he left after that one round. I hadn't been able to find you so I just stayed when someone dared me to kiss her. I planned on giving her a quick peck but she grabbed my head and basically forced her tongue into my mouth. The only person I could think of while doing it was you and how I wanted to find you and kiss you."

"Yeah right." He certainly looked like he was enjoying that kiss.

I get up to leave. I make it past the gazebo and halfway to the edge of the park when Logan catches up to me. He spins me around and forces me to stare into those piercing eyes.

"I'm serious. Right after the kiss I even went searching for you and found you out on the balcony with my brother. I couldn't see much other than he was giving you a hug and saying something serious."

I chuckle, thinking back to that night. "He was telling me that whatever guy I was upset about wasn't worth it. He didn't know it was you."

Logan grabs my hands again and places them on his shoulders. "Well now that we have that straightened out, I'll ask permission this time." He grabs me around the waist, pulling me into him. " Emma, can I kiss you now?"

I pull away, not wanting to hear more excuses and being sucked in even more than I already am. If he kisses me again, that will be it. "Logan I don't want to just be another girl. I can't go through this hot and cold thing again."

"Emma, have you been listening to anything I've been saying these past few minutes?" He takes my face in his hands. "I want you and no one else matters. I like you. Like really, really like you."

I look away for a second. I really want to believe him. I remember what Ashley once told me, "The best moments in life are from the biggest risks". By moving forward with him, I'm risking my heart. I've dated before but I've never felt like this and that scares me.

Whatever happens, it's worth it. I can't help the big grin that spreads across my face.

"You said during your kiss with Amber that all you could think about was me yet she was giving you a horrible kiss. How do I know that it isn't you that's the horrible kisser?

Logan laughs at me again. "Well I would hope that I showed you yesterday that I am not bad but I guess I'll have to prove it to you again. So I will ask you again. Emma, can I kiss you?"

I wait a moment pretending like I'm thinking and grin big again. "Okay, Logan you can kiss me."

Without thinking twice, he kisses me. Just a short sweet kiss. He pulls away, his expression growing serious.

"Is something wrong?" I think of everything from I'm a bad kisser to maybe I'm too short or he changed his mind.

"Will you be my girlfriend?"

Well, that was not what I was expecting, but I'm dazed from his kiss and all I do is nod.

He picks me up and spins me around. I giggle because who wouldn't.

He sets me back down and kisses me again. At that moment, it begins to snow. I break away and look up to the sky. "Magical things always happen in the snow".

"That they do". He closes the space between us. This kiss is different from the previous two. It's deeper and I feel the kiss everywhere. It was one of those kisses you see in the movies. The one you see at the end when they get their happily ever after.

Not something I ever thought I would experience in real life. I just hope it lasts past the credits.

After a few minutes we break away. The sun is setting and the view is breathtaking. I lay my head on his shoulder and take in the view, not letting anything ruin this perfect moment.

Chapter Seven

The next day my mom and I are putting the leftovers into tailgating snacks. She watches me dance around the kitchen. "You're in a good mood today."

"Yeah well it's football day, and the odds are in our favor to win."

She gives me one of those knowing mom looks. "Okay if you say so."

Thanksgiving leftovers turned into tailgating snacks has been a tradition for as long as I can remember.

We form the mashed potatoes into football shapes, stuff them with cheese and fry them.

Then we use the turkey to make buffalo turkey puffs which are basically turkey, cream cheese and buffalo sauce rolled up in a croissant roll. They are always a favorite.

Last, we turn the stuffing into a sort of pot sticker meets egg roll.

As I take the turkey puffs out of the oven, the doorbell rings. "That's probably Ashley. Perfect timing, as always, right as the food comes out."

Mom and I laugh as dad gets the door.

I start putting the puffs on a plate when I hear a voice that is definitely not Ashley.

I wipe my hands. "Mom, I will be right back."

I run to the front door and I see a nervous looking Logan standing on the doorstep shaking my dad's hand. "Hey Dad, this is my umm... friend Logan."

Dad eyes Logan suspiciously. "The one you did the project with and then just stopped talking to you?"

I am so embarrassed; I lightly push him out of the way. I told him part of the story but I am pretty sure my mom picked up on a lot of what I didn't say. Which means she talked to Dad.

"Dad, that's not really how it all went."

He glares at Logan. "If you break my daughter's heart, I will come after you."

"Dad!" I give him a "stop it" look. "Mom needs your help in the kitchen and the game is about to start."

Before he leaves, he glares at Logan again. "I'm watching you," he warns.

"I am so sorry about that." I point to the swing on our porch for us to sit down. "Logan, you have no idea how sorry I am. My dad just gets very protective."

Logan smiles at me, "It's okay Emma. I get it. I'm sure one day I will be the same way with our daughter. Plus, I don't plan on breaking your heart ever."

He quickly kisses me in case my parents are spying.

I can't help grinning because not only did he say he wouldn't break my heart but he also said "our" daughter.

"Well I just wish you could have met him when we were doing our project then maybe he wouldn't have been so hard on you now."

"At least I met one parent when we filmed part of the project here. Your mother is such a sweetheart and she cracked me up."

"Oh yes, my mother. I think she suspects something. She was asking me why I was so happy today."

He smirks. "And why are you so happy?"

I lean back on the bench and sigh. "Oh I don't know. Some guy kissed me in the snow last night and it was magical." I try to be as nonchalant as possible but it doesn't stop my heart from trying to burst out of my chest because of him being so close.

"Hmm and who might this guy be?"

"Some guy I met at the park. No big deal." I say, staring at my nails trying my hardest not to look at him.

"Oh really. Some guy hmmm..." he starts tickling my sides.

I giggle and just when I think I can't take it anymore, Ashley walks up the porch steps. "Hope I'm not interrupting any-thing." She winks at us. "Are you staying for the game?"

"The game?" Logan questions.

"Only the biggest game ever — Florida versus Florida State." I exclaim.

"Don't we live in Tennessee?" He looks back and forth be-tween Ash and me.

"Yes, but both my parents went to FSU and that is actually where they met so I grew up a Seminole." I jump up from the seat.

He stands. "Got it. Well, I had come to whisk you away for a first date but that can wait. Bring on the football."

I give him a quick kiss. "Now that's my kind of man."

Ashley clears her throat. "On that note, I am going to go inside for some stuffing rolls before they are gone".

As she enters the house, I yell after her, "Ty is still here by the way."

Ashley freezes before slowly going through the door.

"Who's Ty?" Logan asks.

"My brother. He's back from college. He's a freshman at FSU. Come I'll introduce you!" I am halfway to the door when I realize Logan hasn't moved. "What's wrong?"

"He isn't like your dad is he?"

I laugh. "Tyler is a sweetheart like my mother."

"Okay good." He still looks very unsure.

"Although he might join forces with my dad if you hurt me." I wink and head inside.

Logan's mouth drops, but he quickly recovers following me inside.

We enter the living room a few minutes before kickoff. My mom brings the last plate of food and sets it on the coffee table. It smells like a fried thanksgiving dinner.

She sees Logan and runs over to give him a hug.

"Logan! It is so good to see you again." She grins at me over his shoulder. Guess I am caught now. Nothing gets past my mom.

"You too, Mrs. Collins." He hugs her back, glad that she remembered him.

"Now sit. I hope you're hungry. We have all the Thanksgiving tailgate snacks. I am going to grab the sweet tea." She hurries back into the kitchen.

"Thanksgiving tailgate snacks?" Logan repeats confused.

I begin to explain the snacks when Tyler walks in. I jump up and drag him over to Logan to make the introductions. "So, this is *the* Logan, huh?"

"Tyler...!" I give him a 'you better not say any more' look.

"We'll catch up later." He says to Logan and sits down on the recliner.

Logan whispered to me, "*THE* Logan?"

Of course he would catch on to that part. I shrug, "My brother and I are close. Now shush. The game is starting."

The teams take the field. Florida State sets up for kickoff. They kick the ball and Florida catches it on the 4-yard line. They run up the field before getting tackled on the 12-yard line.

By halftime, the score is 21-14 with the Seminoles in the lead.

My brother comes to talk to Logan. I excuse myself and go into the kitchen to help my mom with dessert.

We whip up fried cinnamon apple pie bites.

Using the leftover pumpkin pie, we turn it into our version of a pumpkin pie roll.

As we were waiting for the last batch of apple pie bites to air fry, I feel my mom staring. "So, you and Logan?"

"Yes. We talked and he explained everything. Then he asked me out." I pop a piece of pumpkin pie roll in my mouth, trying not to make a big deal out of it.

"Okay, just be careful. I like him, but I don't like how he has treated you." She kisses me on the head and takes the apple bites out of the air fryer.

A few seconds later, I feel arms snake around me. I jump. Logan laughs and whispers in my ear. "Hi beautiful."

I put my hand on my heart. "Logan, you scared me".

"Sorry, I just wanted to come in here and see what that wonderful smell was." He eyes the apple pie bites. "I thought those Thanksgiving tailgating snacks were good, but these look like heaven."

"Well, why don't you help me take them out to the living room and we can dig in."

Mom hands him a tray and pushes him out. "I take back what I said about being careful. It's him that needs to be careful. That boy is so smitten with you."

I giggle. "Nobody says smitten anymore."

I grab a tray before heading to the living room. Right before I leave, I say to my mom, "I don't plan on breaking his heart either. There's something about this that feels right."

Mom gives me a nod and a smile that says she knows all about what that is like.

As I sit down on the couch, I smile knowing my mom and dad's love story is one for the books.

Growing up, my mom lost her parents when she was young and moved in with her aunt who was always working. She had to raise herself but still managed to get straight A's through high school, became Valedictorian, and beat swimming school records. She was destined for the Olympics as I hope to one day.

She met my dad at FSU while working on the newspaper. He was playing football, a wide receiver.

After one of their games, sophomore year, she walked down to the field to interview the quarterback who totally blew her off.

Instead, Nathan, my dad, came over apologizing for his teammate's behavior and asked if he could do the interview instead. "I wouldn't want a pretty thing like you not having anything to write about." My mom instantly fell for his charming smile and way with words.

After that day, my mom didn't see him for a while, or whenever she did, he never acknowledged her.

She decided to move on and focus back on school and her swimming. The Olympics were in two years and she was in the middle of training.

She was studying in the library one day with her nose in a book when a voice interrupted her asking if the seat next to her was taken. She mumbled a no and continued to read.

When she finally looked up and saw Nathan, she frowned. He saw her frowning at him and asked what was wrong.

"Oh nothing. I just thought you were a decent guy but turns out you're just like the rest of those football players." She started packing up her books, ready to leave.

As she was about to turn, Nathan grabbed her hand, "Did I do something to upset you?"

Without turning around, she replies, "Yes... No... not really. It isn't your fault. You don't owe me anything."

Nathan stands and pulls her to face him. "I'm a little confused."

"You really don't remember?" Nathan shakes his head no. "A few months ago, it was the second football game of the season and I was supposed to have an interview with the quarterback. He blew me off and you jumped in so I wouldn't go back to the newsroom empty handed."

It finally dawns on him. "Elizabeth, right?"

"Yes. Now please let go of my hand. I need to go."

"Fine, but only if you agree to dinner with me tonight?"

Elizabeth looked at him a bit skeptical but after a few seconds agreed. "Pick me up at seven. I'm in Landis Hall."

With that she turned to exit the library.

Nathan took Elizabeth on their first date to the football stadium. He said it was where they first met and thought it only made sense. He had laid out a picnic for them and once the sun set, they laid back on the blanket and looked up at the stars.

Nathan turned to Elizabeth, "There's something about you, Elizabeth. I don't know how I could have forgotten about you and I have no excuse, but I plan to never forget you again." He kissed her right there and from then on, they were inseparable.

Fast forward to their senior year. Nathan played his heart out as FSU won the Championship, and Elizabeth swam as fast as she could for the Olympic pre-qualifying team.

Nathan was being scouted for the NFL and Elizabeth made the team, well on their way to making their dreams come true. It was going to be a happily ever after for both of them.

The draft quickly approached for Nathan and he was a second-round draft pick for the Tennessee Titans. He was going to be a wide receiver in the NFL.

That night Nathan and Elizabeth celebrated and drank a little too much champagne. One thing led to another and a promise they had made to each other to wait was broken.

The next day they talked and they had no regrets but decided to wait before anything happened again.

Graduation day was there before they knew it and Nathan's parents took them out to dinner. He grew up not having much but was very close to his parents. He grew up right there in Tallahassee and his parents attended every home game.

After dinner his parents excused themselves and Nathan took Elizabeth by the hand leading her to his car.

When they pulled up to the football stadium, she asked why they were there. Nathan just shrugged and said he wanted to reminisce on the college years.

They walked out on the field and Nathan led her to the center of the field where they once had their first date. Nathan looked at Elizabeth as she sat in a daze remembering the great memories.

"Elizabeth Davis, I knew there was something special about you since the day I met you." Elizabeth looked over at him and laughed, making him laugh too. "Okay, since the second time I met you. Every time I look into your eyes you have this sparkle and people can't help but listen to what you have to say with the words you write and say. You've become part of my family, well not in that way, but my parents love you and I love you. We've been through a lot and this summer I'll start training for the NFL. You will go off to the Olympics and win a gold medal in swimming. I want to do that together because I know without you by my side, none of it matters. So Elizabeth Davis, Liz the love of my life, if you feel the same..." Nathan got down on one knee and Elizabeth gasped. "Will you marry me?"

Elizabeth looked down at Nathan and started crying. Nathan immediately got up and grabbed Elizabeth's cheeks between his hand. "Hey don't be sad. This is supposed to be a happy moment."

Elizabeth just nodded and motioned to the bench on the sidelines. They walked over and sat down. She turned to him, "Nathan, you have no idea how happy I am but I have something to tell you. I am scared that what I am about to tell you will scare you away and you won't want to marry me."

"Nothing you say will ever make me run away."

"I'm pregnant!"

Nathan stared at her for a minute before getting up and taking a few steps. He turned back around to see Elizabeth with her head down. He walked over, lifted her chin up and got back down on one knee.

"I am going to try this again. Elizabeth, I love you no matter what and I will love our child no matter what. Whatever the future throws at us, we'll do together."

Elizabeth went to say something but Nathan put a finger to her lips. "Now don't say I am only marrying you because we are having a baby because I proposed before I knew about that." Elizabeth went to say something else and he kept his finger at her lips. "I don't care about the NFL or the Olympics if it means raising this baby with you and spending every day with you. Like I said, none of that matters if I can't have you. So, Elizabeth Davis, will you make me the happiest husband, soon to be father and man on this Earth and become my wife?"

Elizabeth whispered yes as the tears continued to fall. Nathan jumped up pulling Elizabeth up with him in his arms and kissed her. The passion radiated through them and Elizabeth pulled away to whisper in his ear, "Don't worry these are happy tears." Nathan kissed her again before bending down to kiss her barely showing belly.

They had a small wedding with only his parents, her aunt and a few close friends at their local church. She didn't want to be pregnant in her wedding photos, but if you look ever so closely, you can see a tiny little bulge where my brother was growing inside her.

They found out it was a boy the day before the wedding and shared it with everyone on that special day. My mom never did make it to the Olympics since she was pregnant with my brother, and then three years later getting pregnant with me but she never regretted it. My dad went on to play in the NFL for two years before twisting his knee.

I am sure with the right therapy he could have gone on to play again but he loved being a dad more. They both loved being parents and never looked back. My dad became the local high school football coach and my mom put her English major to use as a local blogger.

As I think back to their love story, I can't help but smile about how their love grew. I have always wanted that kind of love, that epic love, the love that can get you through anything, the type of love that you can't live without, the love that doesn't die.

I rest my head on Logan's shoulder thinking I may have found it. It may be too early to tell, but there is this feeling in my heart that I can't ignore.

Logan looks down at me. "Hey you. What are you thinking about?"

"Oh just life and what the future holds." I turn my attention back to the TV as the players run back onto the field to start the second half. "And how we're going to destroy these Gators!"

Logan stares at me a little longer before kissing my cheek and links my fingers through his.

The second half isn't as exciting as the first half. The Seminoles end up killing the Gators 45-21. I am screaming so hard by the end of it that I almost lose my voice.

As Logan gets ready to leave, he gives Ashley a hug goodbye saying he would see her at school on Monday. Then he says goodbye to my brother and promises they would hang next time he is in town. He gives my mom a hug and she whispers, "take care of my angel." He nods once, whispering, "I plan to for as long as she will let me".

I probably wasn't supposed to hear but I did and now I have a huge grin on my face.

He then turns to my dad and shakes his hand. I can tell my dad is finally warming up to him as he says, "I look forward to more football games with you."

Logan is just as surprised as I am. "Me too sir".

Before letting go of his hand my dad replies, "call me Nathan."

"Yes sir...I mean Nathan."

As we walk out, Logan leans in, "did your dad almost give me a compliment?"

"I think so".

When we get to the front door, Logan takes one of my hands, "can I take you out next Saturday?"

I put my finger on my chin pretending to think about it for a few seconds. "I think my calendar is free."

"It better be! I look forward to our date and you should too." I grin at him. "On a side note, are you ready for school? I'm excited to show off my girlfriend."

I blushed. "I think so. You might have to pinch me a few times to remind me it's real."

"Like this?" He pinches me in the side.

"I wasn't being serious!" I punch him in the shoulder.

He gives me a pouty face, "oww, that hurt."

"Aww you poor baby. Now go home. I have to go help my mom clean up."

"Oh, yes. Well then, until school on Monday. I bid you adieu." He tips off his imaginary hat.

"You're a goofball. I will see you on Monday". I lean up to give him a quick peck and turn to go inside when he grabs my hand.

"I don't think that was a proper goodbye." He kisses me much deeper this time.

I am in a daze that I barely say goodbye before he jogs down the stairs and gets in his car.

As I enter the house, my mom and Ashley immediately run up and tell me I have some explaining to do. I laugh and walk off into the kitchen knowing they will follow like little puppy dogs.

Chapter Eight

The only thing that gets me through the week is my AP English class when I see Logan. He even attends all my swim practices. I told him he didn't need to but he said he had nothing better to do. Plus, the sound of water splashing is kind of soothing background noise to do homework to, is what I am told.

I think he is messing with me but I am glad to have him there.

Finally, it's Friday and I can't wait for school to end. Ash is coming over to help me pick out my outfit for my first official date with Logan.

After swim practice, I meet up with Ashley and we drive to my house. When we get to my room, she asks me what we are doing on our date.

"I have no idea. He wouldn't tell me anything."

Of course, she freaks out because she needs something to work with and demands I text him.

I shoot Logan a text.

Emma: *Hey! Is there anything you can tell me about our date tomorrow?*

He texts back right away.

Logan: *Nope :) it'll be fun though.*

I know Ashley won't be satisfied with that answer so I try again.

Emma: *Can you at least tell me what I need to wear?*

He comes back with a very generic text that again won't work.

Logan: *Anything you wear will be great.*

I show the phone to Ashley and she grabs it from me. I try to get it back but she holds it out of my reach.

Emma: *A girl needs more than "you look great in everything". I'm trying to plan an outfit.*

I manage to grab my phone back right after she hits send. I read what she wrote and immediately send another text.

Emma: *Sorry that was Ash and she is set on making me plan out my outfit. Any help you can give me would be great or I'm afraid you will have to show up to a fashion show before we can leave.*

Logan: *A fashion show wouldn't be so bad ;)*

I smile and reply.

Emma: *Hey!*

It takes him about a minute this time before he texts back.

Logan: *Okay okay! How's this — dress warm but semi-formal.*

It's better than nothing. I tell Ashley and she disappears into my closet.

Emma: *umm okay I will pass that along. I'm super excited for tomorrow.*

Logan: *You better be. It will be a day you will never forget.*

I wonder what he has planned. He has been super secretive about it and said we would be gone the entire day.

Emma: *Oh really?!?!*

He texts back with nothing to do with the plans but I don't expect him to.

Logan: *Oh yes. Now be ready at 9 a.m. sharp.*

Emma: *Yes sir!*

Apparently, he has to go because he replies,

Logan: *Sleep tight!*

Emma: *You too.*

I am not surprised when I get a text back since he always has to end the conversation.

Logan: *:)*

I stare at our conversation, smiling to myself. Ash peeks out from my closet and sees me smiling. "What are you smiling about?"

"Nothing!" I glance back at my phone.

"Whatever you say. Now what did he say about what to wear again?"

"Warm but semi-formal."

"Oh perfect!" She glances at the outfits she has laid out on my bed.

"You know what that means?" I ask, shocked.

"Yes! Now try this on so I can see." She hands me a bunch of clothes. After years of living in a bathing suit, I'm not shy changing in front of other girls, especially Ashley, who is basically a sister.

Ashley practically lives at my house. Her mom is a flight attendant and always travels for work while her dad is a truck driver and often does long runs on the road.

She is close with her parents but since they are always gone, my parents have pretty much adopted her. I always wanted a sister to talk to late at night or in this case help me decide what to wear on a first date.

I put on thermal black tights and a deep purple sweater dress. It is so warm and soft. Definitely, one of my favorites to wear this time of year.

Ash always says it brings out all my curves or as I like to say lack of curves from years of swimming. She hands me black leather boots that go up to almost my knees.

To finish it off, she hands me silver earrings and a long silver necklace with a bunch of hearts on the end.

I look in the mirror. Ashley appears behind me and shows me what to do with my hair. She does a half up, half down twist thing. She is crazy if she thinks I can pull that off myself. As if reading my mind, she takes it down and shows me how to do it more slowly this time.

Once I think I get it, I thank her because she is my lifesaver when it comes to fashion, hair, and makeup.

Being a swimmer, I never do my hair or wear much makeup but Ash has slowly brought that girly side out of me. Three years later of caring about what I look like and I am still learning.

After she explains what to do with makeup, she heads home.

I change into my pajamas and fall into bed, hoping the hours will pass quickly.

The next morning my alarm clock rings at eight. I groan wondering why it is buzzing when it's Saturday.

Then I remember… my date!

I jump out of bed excitedly and get in the shower. I do my makeup just like Ash showed me and then attempt my hair. I am pretty proud of the finished product.

I only have five minutes before Logan gets here. My stomach growls and I realize I won't have time to eat breakfast. Now that I think about it, Logan didn't say whether we are eating breakfast together or if I should have something before our date. I pull out my phone to text him.

Emma: *Hey this might be a silly question, but am I supposed to eat breakfast before you pick me up?*

Thankfully he is quick to reply.

Logan: *That's up to you.*

What is that supposed to mean. Does he think I don't eat breakfast?

Emma: *Okay…*

Just as I hit send another text pops up.

Logan: *By the way I'm here.*

I realize it's already 9:05.

Emma: *I'll be right out.*

Logan: *Okay :)*

I quickly get dressed and head downstairs. I can at least grab some coffee and a piece of toast.

When I get to the kitchen, I smell dough and coffee.

I see Logan sitting at the breakfast bar talking to my mom. Spread out on the counter are bagels, cream cheese and coffee. I glance at my mom. "What's this?"

"Don't ask me. Ask your young man right here."

Before I can say anything, my dad walks in. "Do I smell Lou's bagels?"

"You do! Apparently, Logan brought them." I gesture to the counter full of bagels.

"Well Emma, you have a good man right here." He grabs some coffee and a bagel before sitting down next to Logan.

Lou's is the local bakery and coffee shop. We love grabbing breakfast there whenever we can. It also happens to be the coffee shop where I spilled coffee all over Jeremy.

I help myself to an everything bagel with delicious home-made chive cream cheese. Everything there is homemade.

I take a bite and moan in delight.

Her everything bagels are full of flavor and toppings unlike the ones you buy in the grocery store, that always lose all the toppings when you take them out of the bag.

The cream cheese is so creamy, and paired with the everything bagel, I am in heaven.

Logan smirks before turning back to my mom and whatever conversation they were having.

Chapter Nine

Thirty minutes later and we are finally leaving. I grab my coat and wave to my parents. I get in Logan's truck. "You're something else."

"Did I do alright?" He glances at me before turning the car on.

"Alright? I'd say you nailed it. Anything from Lou's and you are golden with my parents. I have to say I was confused about your breakfast text though."

"That was the point." He pulls out of the driveway, heading the opposite way of town.

About ten minutes into the drive, he pulls over on the side of the road.

"What are we doing?" I ask. Before I can say anything else, he leans over to give me a sweet kiss and then places his forehead against mine.

"I've been dying to do that since you walked into the kitchen this morning." He puts the car back in park and starts driving again.

Can someone say "awwwww?" That was the cutest thing ever and I feel like I am on fire. Basically, anytime he touches me, my whole body heats up.

Once I catch my breath, I ask, "Are you going to give me any hints about today?"

He continues looking ahead. "Nope! But I will tell you this, we are headed out of town." He gestures to the direction we are going.

"Oh really? I've lived here long enough to know which way is town."

He laughs and reaches over to grab my hand, lacing our fingers together. "Be patient".

The rest of the car ride is spent jamming out to music and getting to know each other.

We finally pull up to a giant outdoor ice-skating rink.

"I know you're good at swimming in the water, but how good are you when it's frozen?"

"Why don't we go over there and you can see!" I unbuckle my seatbelt.

Just as I'm about to open the door, Logan runs around to open it. He reaches up to grab my hand.

The air outside is cold and I am glad I have on a coat.

The rink opens at eleven and we still have fifteen minutes. We sit on a bench to lace up our skates. Logan is having trouble with his so I reach over to help him.

When the rink opens, I step on and glide around. I see Logan skeptically standing by the side. I skate over to him. "Do you need some help?"

"I'll be honest, I've only ever been ice skating once when I was younger. Growing up in hot Mississippi will do that to you."

"It is all good. Take my hand and I'll teach you."

He carefully steps on the ice and we start skating.

He picks it up quickly and before I know it, he is skating circles around me. He decides he is good enough to hold my hands and skate backwards. I try to warn him but he is set on doing it.

We are halfway around the loop when his skate gets stuck and he falls backward bringing me with him. I land on top of him and we both start laughing.

He kisses me, not caring about the other people skating around us. I pull away before it gets too heated seeing as we are in the middle of a public skating rink.

I am still getting used to even having someone kiss me. I'd had a boyfriend before but it wasn't like this. This feels real, while that felt like going through the motions.

We give it a rest for the day, deciding to get some hot chocolate.

We hold hands and sip our drinks as we walk around the park. The chocolatey goodness heats up my insides. Or maybe it's Logan holding my hand, sending warmth through me.

We pass by a gyro stand and Logan points to it. "Are you hungry?"

My stomach rumbles right as he asks. "A little."

He laughs as we head toward the stand. "Well we have a reservation at five but this will tide us over till then."

"I love me some good Greek pitas." We walk over to a bench to eat. I take in the creamy tzatziki sauce with the seasoned chicken.

"It is almost one now and we need to get going before our next stop."

He glances up from his watch and stares at my mouth.

"You don't have to ask to kiss me." I tell him hoping that he will get the hint.

"I know, but you have something right here." He wipes my upper lip with his thumb and licks it off. Then he pulls my head toward him and gives me another sweet kiss. "Let's go."

I toss my wrapper in the trash can as we head towards a large building. I see it is a museum and wonder what we are doing here. Not that I don't like museums, but this seems like an interesting choice for a first date.

We enter the museum to get tickets. Logan tells them we are here for the special exhibit and hands them the money. They give him tickets and some sort of pass that we are to hang around our neck. He tucks the passes in his pocket. Before I can ask what they are for, we are ushered into a giant ballroom.

I read the poster on the wall:

Special exhibit: Olympics of the Ages
Featuring special guest speakers from each sport.

I give Logan a hug. "This is amazing! I had no idea this existed."

"Well I know one day you want to be in the Olympics, so when I was reading the newspaper a few weeks ago and saw this in there, I knew I had to take you."

"Logan, a few weeks ago we weren't together."

"I know but I was still hoping. Plus, I still wanted to take you even if we were just friends. Being together is better because now I can do this whenever I want." He leans over to kiss me.

I lean into the kiss, showing my agreement while feeling those flutters in my stomach. I pull away, not wanting to but I am curious about where we are. "Now let's go explore."

At 2:15 p.m., they announce that those who have tickets for the panel should head to their seats. I am about to ask Logan if we have tickets when he pulls out the lanyards.

He shows the usher our lanyards who then directs us to the first row. I swear this boy shocks me every day. "Do we need to wear the lanyards?"

He shakes his head and puts them back in his pocket. I hope I can keep one as a memento so I will always remember this amazing day. I make a note to ask him.

A few different athletes talk about competing in the Olympics, the training they go through, and of course, what it's like winning a medal.

The last athletes are Natalie Coughlin and Michael Phelps. My jaw drops. I notice Logan staring at me, probably waiting for my reaction. I grab his hand, squeezing it with joy.

I listen intently to every word they say, wishing I had a notebook and pen. Yes, I am that much of a nerd.

I am sad when it ends because this truly has been amazing and I don't know how it can get better.

Logan pulls me to the stage door. I see him pull out our lanyards again telling me to put it on. Before I can read it, he shows the stage hand his, and they open a side door for us. We are ushered to a green room with couches.

I finally read the lanyard and almost faint when I read the words "meet and greet". I have no idea who we were meeting but I am excited nonetheless.

I almost faint again when Michael and Natalie walk in the door. They shake our hands. We introduce ourselves and my questions begin.

I ask them about the Olympics. I then ask the one question I never thought I'd be asking an actual Olympic swimmer. "I am currently working towards the Olympics. Do you have any advice?"

Michael replies. "Keep training and never give up. Getting there is hard, and once you're there the training is even harder. The coaches are stricter and the pressure is more intense. Having a sturdy team behind you to keep encouraging you and pushing you is the key to making it through."

I aim my next question at Natalie. "Backstroke is my worst and since you're amazing at it, do you have any tips?"

She nods. "Don't focus so much on speed, but rather keep your breathing in control and work on staying flat. After that the speed will come naturally."

When our time is up, we take pictures and they sign autographs. I give them both a hug and Michael turns to me, "I hope to see you on the team at the next Olympics."

When they leave, I wrap my arms around Logan and stare into his eyes, "How did you manage to set this up?"

He seems to contemplate what to say. I wouldn't have noticed the hesitancy if I hadn't been looking directly at his face.

"My dad's friend works with museums to host special exhibits and this is one of them. When I heard they were having this exhibit, I asked him to ask his friend if we could get tickets."

I give him a kiss. "Well thank you! This has been an amazing day."

Chapter Ten

"It isn't over yet." He grabs my hand as we walk to the exit of the museum. It's starting to snow.

Once in the car, we crank up the heater. I love the snow but it definitely has its disadvantages like the cold.

We drive for fifteen minutes and park in front of a restaurant. I see it is a Brazilian Steakhouse. I've never been to one but always wanted to go.

We enter and the hostess asks for our reservation. Logan gives his name and she leads us towards the back of the restaurant. My senses are on overload from the meats to something chocolatey wafting from the corner of the restaurant.

The table we are led to has a bouquet of roses and candles.

The waiter comes back with water and a bread basket. He explains that waiters will be coming around with different meats. In the meantime, we are welcome to help ourselves to the salad bar.

We hit the salad bar first and pass by a dessert bar. My mouth starts salivating. "Can we just skip dinner and go right to this bar?" He laughs, pushing me towards the salad bar.

The salad bar has everything you could possibly want on your salad plus multiple salad dressings to choose from. They have an array of fruits to choose from, other salads like different styles of potato salad, macaroni salad, and even jello salads.

We load up our plates and make our way back to the table. By the end of the meal, I am stuffed and didn't think I have ever eaten that much meat in my life. We have everything from filet mignon to pork chops, to lamb with a cranberry glaze, deer, and so many more.

We sit there for a few minutes. "Did you save some room for dessert?"

"Is that even a question?"

At the dessert bar, I once again load up my plate. I just can't choose between the chocolate cake I smelled when I first walked in to the assortment of fancy cookies and mini cakes. They even have over a dozen flavors of ice creams to make your own sundae.

When we finish, I moan and lean back in my chair. "I don't think I can move."

"Well our next stop is right around the corner so we don't have far to go."

Logan pays the check and as we get up, he grabs the vase of flowers and hands them to me. "These are for you. I called ahead and had it arranged."

I inhale the scent. " Thank you." I give him a kiss that quickly deepens. I cannot get enough of his kisses.

After we put the flowers in the car, he grabs my hand and pulls me in the direction of the theatre.

I see a sign for the Nutcracker and I instantly get excited. He hands the usher our tickets and leads us to our seats or should I say box. A waiter comes over and hands us each a glass of champagne.

After he leaves, I whisper, "Does he know we aren't twenty-one?"

Logan shrugs. "Perks of being in the box. We get complimentary champagne."

"Wow, okay." I take a sip and love the taste. I've never had champagne before and the bubbles are the best part.

The lights in the house dim and the overture begins.

Throughout the show, I am amazed at the dancers and how gracefully they move. Their strong but lean bodies as they leap and prance across the stage.

I always thought the view would be terrible from a box seat, with it being on the side, but I can see everything perfectly. I can see every muscle move as the girls are lifted in the air. I can see every facial expression as the soldiers and mice fight.

Just when the Nutcracker turns into the handsome prince and leads Clara to his castle, the curtain goes down and the lights come on. I know the story of the Nutcracker but I was so into the dancing that I just want it to continue to see what happens as if I don't already know.

I look over at Logan and see him staring at me. I glance away, embarrassed at how into the ballet I got. Logan turns my face back to him. "Have I told you how beautiful you look tonight? Because you do. Absolutely stunning."

Then he kisses me slowly and I feel the butterflies in my stomach. This kiss is different from the others we have shared. It adds a layer of promises of what's to come.

This may be our first date, but I feel myself falling fast and it scares me. I pull back from the kiss and excuse myself to the bathroom.

I run some cool water on the back of my neck and glance in the mirror. I'm practically glowing! *Just breathe, Emma.*

Back at our seats, I wrap my arms around Logan and whisper in his ear, "thanks for bringing me here and for this whole day. This is by far the best date ever. Although I'm not sure how you will top this in the future."

He chuckles. "I'm sure I'll think of something."

The lights in the house flash, signaling that the second act will begin shortly. Logan takes my hand in his and kisses the top. "I'm glad you are having fun."

The second act is just as good as the first with the Sugar Plum Fairy and all the other sweets incorporated into the dancing. The costumes are full of color and sparkle. The props look good enough to eat!

The final waltz is beautiful and so graceful as Clara and the Prince head back to their reality.

As the lights dim, Logan and I stand up and cheer. The dancers come back on stage to take their bows.

The drive home is quiet, not uncomfortable but rather peaceful.

As we pull up to my house, Logan runs over, once again, to open my door. I grab my flowers and Logan walks me up to my porch.

He takes my face in his hands and kisses me. It's a kiss that makes my toes curl and those butterflies, from earlier, come back. I want it to last forever but sadly it ends.

He gazes into my eyes, "I had an amazing night. I'll text you tomorrow." He gives me another quick kiss and walks back to his car. I see him get in and then wait for me to get inside before leaving.

When I get inside, I can't help sighing thinking back to what Ashley said. I really hope what she said is true because this sure feels like the start of something amazing.

Chapter Eleven

The Tuesday before break, Ashley and I sit at lunch. "Where's Logan?"

I glance up from my notes. "He was still working on the AP English essay."

When he finally joins us, he turns to me, "do you want to go out tonight?"

"I wish but I have to study for my Spanish final tomorrow. Plus, it's my last meet before the break so I have to get a good night's sleep. Rain check?"

He nods and goes back to his lunch. We talk about the finals we've already had. Ashley and I agree, so far, AP Art History was the easiest and AP Stats was the hardest. Logan is only taking AP Art History and said it wasn't bad but his Pre-Calc this afternoon is going to be even easier. I shake my head. "I still don't know why you are taking Pre-Calc when you want to be a filmmaker."

"Math is easy, and why not take a class for an easy A." Ashley and I giggle because we hate math.

I have always been more into Science and Ashley more into English and History. She can't decide between becoming a history professor or a journalist. "What other finals do you have the rest of the week?"

"Other than Spanish tomorrow, I have AP Bio and Honors Algebra II on Thursday. Nothing on Friday, which will be a nice break. This afternoon is my PE final, also known as running a mile in under twelve minutes, thirty pushups in a minute, fifty sit ups in a minute and swimming five laps. I can do that in my sleep so I plan on taking most of the afternoon to study since I'll be done with all that in less than thirty minutes. I am most nervous about Spanish and Algebra."

Ashley shakes her head. "Speak for yourself, AP Bio is going to be killer. I don't understand anything."

"How about tomorrow night after my meet, you come over and I can help you. I have to study Algebra but I can give you some Biology tips."

"Yes! That would be amazing."

Logan makes a pouty face. "Oh so she gets help but not me."

I lean over and give him a kiss on the cheek. "You can come too and study for your Honors Biology test." I stick out my tongue.

He still makes his pouty face. "I don't need Science classes for film but unfortunately it is a requirement for high school."

"You don't need Pre-Calc either." Logan glares at me. "Anyway next year I'm just going to take easy classes, especially with swimming and trying to make the Olympic team. I won't have time for these crazy classes."

"I may not be trying out for any Olympic teams but I'm right there with you on easy classes next year. Senior year is supposed to be fun and getting ready for college." Ashley agrees as she puts her lunch away.

Logan chuckles. "Well ladies, I have to go meet my brother before my Pre Calc exam but I will see you all later." He kisses me and leaves.

"I should probably go too. I have to grab my Spanish notes to study after my PE exam. I'll see you after school." I nod to Ash.

I am attempting to conjugate verbs when the doorbell rings. I am the only one home so I get up to answer the door, secretly happy for the break. I open the door to Logan. As happy as I am to see him, I am also kind of mad because I told him I had to study. "I told you I can't go out. This Spanish final is going to kill me."

"That is why I am here. I am taking you out to Sombreros. The whole menu is in Spanish and I am going to make you order in Spanish. It will be putting your Spanish speaking to the test."

"I don't know."

"You have the written part down, correct?" I nod. "I know you need help with the oral part and this will help, believe me. Now grab your coat and let's go."

"Okay, fine." I grab my coat, my purse and some of my notes too, just in case.

Fifteen minutes later we pull into the parking lot. We get a table and I read the menu. He wasn't joking when he said the entire menu was in Spanish. The waiter comes up to our table and asks what we would like to drink. Logan turns to him, "Estamos practicando para su examen de español mañana. ¿Puedes hablar solo en español?" *(We are practicing for her Spanish exam tomorrow. Can you speak only in Spanish?)*

The waiter nods.

"Tendremos dos tés helados" *(We will have two iced teas)*

When the waiter leaves, Logan sees my jaw drop. "Where did you learn to speak Spanish like that?"

"I had a film project in Spain and picked up a few things." He studies the menu like it's no big deal.

"That is amazing. I had no idea, and here I thought you just wanted an excuse to take me out." I am still in shock with his perfect Spanish speaking skills.

He closes his menu and sets it down on the table. "Well I did want an excuse but I also want to help you. Now what are you going to order?"

I glance at the menu and read what I want. "I want the Burrito de bistec. That is a steak burrito, correct?"

"Si."

The waiter comes back with our iced teas, chips, and salsa. He asks if we are ready to order, in Spanish, of course.

Logan points at me to go first.

"Me gusto el burrito de buster con arroz y frijoles." *(I liked the steak burrito with rice and beans)* The waiter writes it down and turns to Logan.

"Me gustaría las fajitas de pollo con guac extra" *(I would like the chicken fajitas with extra guac)*

The waiter says, "Eso será un dólar extra" *(that will be an extra dollar).*

"Eso está bien." *(That's fine)*

The waiter collects our menus. "So how did I do?"

Logan crosses his hands on the table. "You did great, except "I want" is "Me gustaría". You said "Me gusto" which is "I liked" the burrito. Just need to make it in present tense and not in past tense."

"I thought I had it but at least I was close. Those annoying tenses. When I write it, I can see it but when speaking, I always mess it up."

"You did awesome." He points to my bag. "Now take out those notes I saw you sneak into your purse and let me quiz you while we eat these chips and salsa.

I know my face has a "I'm caught look" so I reach into my bag. "Okay".

He tests me on different phrases and for each correct one spoken out loud, he feeds me a chip. The salsa is mild but every once in a while, I get a kick from the jalapeños.

The rest of dinner goes great. I am already feeling more comfortable with speaking Spanish out loud and making sure I'm using the right tense.

Chapter Twelve

Before my meet, I see Logan and run to give him a huge hug. "Thank you so much for helping me last night."

He takes my hand. "How'd it go?"

"Well I don't think I got an A but I feel like I did well. Last night helped a lot and it makes more sense".

"I am glad I could help." He gives me a pat on the butt pushing me towards my teammates. "Now go win this meet."

Did he really just slap my butt? He never stops shocking me. "Umm hmm".

I swim my heart out and manage to get first in my individual swims. The team places second overall. My coach pulls us into a group hug and congratulates us. "We can't win every meet but second is a great way to go into the Christmas break. Now have fun this break, but keep up with your cardio. I don't want out of shape swimmers in the New Year because of those food bellies. We have a meet the Wednesday we get back from break. I hope you all have a great Christmas, and I will see you at practice the Monday we get back."

Everyone groans but I can't wait. I love swimming and practices always push me.

I meet Logan outside and we head to my house where we are meeting Ashley to study. I find her inside with her stuff already spread across the table and some snacks, thanks to my mom.

We join her and I help them both with Biology, answering their questions and giving them tricks to remember the vocabulary words.

When it finally starts to sink in, I switch to my Algebra notes to go over the formulas. I ask Logan for help on how to remember them. He tells me about the songs you can sing. Why don't they teach these songs in class? It makes it so much easier.

Logan has to leave early but Ashley stays for dinner. After dinner, we are chilling on my bed going over our Bio notes, when she turns to me, "So what are you getting Logan for Christmas?"

"We said we weren't getting each other anything."

"You know he's still going to get you something, right?"

"That's what I am afraid of. I got him a little something at Target but it was meant more as an impulse joke gift."

"What is it?"

Embarrassed, I say. "It's an ornament of a monkey."

"I don't get it." I tell her the story of when I went into his room by mistake and found his stuffed monkey. Ashley bursts out laughing. "I take it back, you don't need to get him anything else. That is thoughtful, shows you know him, and is an inside joke. It's perfect!"

"Really? I thought it would be lame."

She claps her hands. "Nope, perfect!"

The rest of the week, I spend my lunch studying so I don't get to see Logan or Ashley.

On Friday, I have no exams. I'm waiting for Logan to finish his last exam so I can ask when we are exchanging gifts. Even though I know we said no gifts, I have a feeling he is still going to give me something.

I hear Amber whisper, very loudly, to Mallory, "So what are you wearing to the Andersons' New Year's Masquerade Ball?"

Mallory shrugs. "I don't know. Thinking about going shopping this weekend to get a new dress."

Amber agrees. "Sounds perfect."

Amber and Mallory are the girls that you love to hate because they have everything. They are popular, have great fashion sense, gorgeous, and get whatever they want. They are cheerleaders so they are always hanging out with Jeremy and his friends. I don't care much about being popular. I prefer to be in the background where no one notices me — but a small part wonders what it would be like to be them. I am, after all, a girl.

They walk by me and give me a disgusted look. Mallory whispers to Amber, "I can't believe Logan is dating her."

I have no idea what I ever did to them. Just as they pass me Amber says, "What are you looking at?"

"Nothing." I try to hide the fact that I was listening and this is the first I have heard of the party. I wonder why Logan hasn't told me. I know the party happens every year because Ashley has reminded me on more than one occasion. It is the biggest party of the year but it's invite only. I am sure he has a reason for not telling me.

Before I can think more about it, I feel arms snake around my waist and a kiss on my neck. I turn to face him and glare.

"Uh ohh. What happened?" He looks concerned.

"Well I just heard Amber talking about a Masquerade Ball at your house on New Year's and I'm wondering why I haven't heard anything about it."

"Oh... I was going to ask you tonight and invite Ashley as well. We throw the party every year and I didn't think it was a big deal."

"Big deal? Your parties are legendary and I've always wanted to go."

"Well, you are officially invited. I assumed you knew you were invited."

I feel embarrassed that I made such a big deal about it. "Thank you, and next time pinch me when I'm becoming a clingy jealous girlfriend. After hearing them talk about a party at your house that I wasn't invited to, it just made me jealous." Logan pinches me. "Hey what was that for?"

"For being a jealous girlfriend." He gives me his famous smirk.

"I meant next time." I say hitting him in the arm.

"Let's go. My brother is waiting for us."

Before we head out, Logan stops me. "Did she say anything else?" He asks seriously.

I think about the comment about me dating him and shrug. "Nothing worth repeating."

"Okay. If she ever does say something, please come and talk to me. I don't want a repeat of the party. She means nothing to me."

I just nod because I know Amber and Mallory like to cause drama. They mainly ignore me but the little comments have started now that I'm dating Logan. I trust him, but it doesn't stop the doubt from creeping in.

He links his fingers in mine, kisses my fingers, and pulls me to the front where Jeremy is waiting.

Chapter Thirteen

Christmas Eve is here. All day my mom and I have been baking cookies to give out on Christmas day. I glance at the clock and realize Logan will be here in thirty minutes. I tell my mom she has to finish the last batch of cookies because I have to start getting ready.

Exactly thirty minutes later, I hear the doorbell. I finish getting ready, keeping it simple with skinny jeans and a long sleeve red lace top.

Downstairs, I find Logan and Tyler chowing down on cookies. "Hey, those are for gifts!"

"No, those are for gifts." Ty points at all the Christmas tins on the counter. "These are for us!" Pointing at the tray of cookies in front of him and Logan.

Logan chuckles and comes over for a kiss. "I only had one because yes we are having dinner. Speaking of which, we need to go." He grabs my coat and helps me put it on. He looks over at my brother. "Tyler hit me up before you leave for college."

On our way out, I grab his present I had put next to the door so I wouldn't forget it. We decided to exchange gifts tonight. I was right about Logan getting me something.

Fifteen minutes later, we pull up to his house. I gaze up at the house, still fascinated by the beauty and size.

When I enter, I smell a delicious honey-baked ham wafting through the air. In the kitchen, his mom is scurrying about. I whisper over to him, "Your mom is cooking?"

"Yep, she loves to cook on Christmas. About the only time she cooks for the maids versus the other way around. Although between you and me the maids are still there to fix her little mistakes. I love my mom and she tries but she is still learning the whole cooking thing."

"I think it is awesome." I take my jacket off, hand it to him and walk over to his mom asking if she needs help.

Before I know it, I am mashing potatoes and adding crispy onions to the green bean casserole.

As we wait for the ham to finish, we join the guys in the living room. I sit next to Logan and he whispers, "I'm sorry I left you alone in there with my mom."

"Don't worry, we had a blast. And I may have seen a few baby pictures."

Embarrassed, he turns to his mom, "You showed her my baby book?"

"I only showed her a picture, but now that you mention the book..." She goes over to the bookcase and grabs a scrapbook. Logan and Jeremy both groan. "This here is a great book of my two boys when they were little."

We go through the book laughing at the cute pictures of them as babies and another with Jeremy at three attempting to hold a two-year-old Logan. There are funny ones of them a little older having a mud fight in the backyard and dressed up as shepherds in the church manger scene.

When the ham is done, we make our way to the dinner table and everyone sits down, including the maids.

I take a sip of my drink thinking it's cranberry juice but I practically spit it out when I realize it's wine. I glance up to see if anyone noticed and Logan and Jeremy are both laughing. I point at the glass of wine and whisper to them, "I thought we were just being fancy drinking cranberry juice out of wine glasses."

Overhearing, Mr. Anderson chuckles and says, "On special occasions we let our sons have some wine or a glass of bourbon. We figure if we give them a little here and there, they won't get drunk all the time and abuse alcohol." I just nod.

After dinner, Logan and I head to the back porch. The outside deck is decorated with Christmas lights. We walk down to the dock and gaze at the lake. It's dark and eerie, but you can see the lights along the edges from the neighboring houses.

I have never been out here but it is gorgeous. It starts to lightly snow so we go under the overhang. We sit near the fire warming ourselves up and cuddling on the bench. Logan pulls out a pretty big box from under the bench and hands it to me.

"Open it."

I unwrap the box and open the lid. Inside is some sort of shimmery material. I pull it out to find a dress. More like the most gorgeous dress I have ever seen. "I got your size from Ashley but I picked the dress out myself. I saw it and immediately thought of you. I figured you could wear it for the Masquerade Ball. Only if you want to."

"Yes! It is the prettiest dress I have ever seen."

"I hoped you would say that." He hands me another smaller box.

"Logan what is this?"

"Just open it." I open the box and inside is a mask that matches the dress perfectly.

"This is beautiful, almost as beautiful as the dress. Thank you!" I kiss him and then look back at the dress. "I can't wait to try it on."

"Well, then go try it on."

I want him to be surprised when he sees me in the dress. It is a ball after all, and I want a Cinderella moment. "I don't think so. I think I'll wait."

"Wait, why?"

"You can't see me in the dress before the ball. It's bad luck."

"I think that's only for weddings." He smirks.

"Well, same thing. You won't see me in my wedding dress before I walk down the aisle either." I pause realizing what I just said. "I... I... mean if we get to that point in our relationship then you know, you will have to wait to see my..." Logan interrupts my rambling with a kiss.

"I hope one day I get to see you in a wedding dress walking towards me but we don't have to rush anything. Okay?" He looks deep into my eyes and I swear he can see right through me.

"Okay." I give him a quick nod and then grab my present for him. "Here is your gift. Now it isn't as extravagant as your gift, but I hope you'll like it."

"Anything from you is great." He unwraps the small box and smiles wildly. "Where did you find this?"

"It is a secret!"

"It is perfect!" He gets up and reaches for my hand. "Now come here."

I set my dress box to the side and grab his hand. "Where are we going?"

"Inside to get some hot cocoa and put this ornament on the tree."

"You don't have to put it on the tree."

"Why not? I love it!" We go inside and he puts the ornament on the tree. I sit down on the couch admiring the tree and all the decorations while Logan grabs our hot chocolate from the kitchen. He hands me my mug and then turns on some Christmas music.

He sits next to me and I cuddle into him as I sip my hot cocoa. We sit that way for a few minutes, enjoying the peace and quiet. A slow song comes on, and he grabs my mug and sets it on the coffee table. He stands and pulls me up with him. "Dance with me!"

"Okay." We sway slowly to the music. It is at that moment I know I have fallen in love with him. I know it's fast, but sometimes you can't help your emotions. I look at him.

"Logan. I love yo... your taste in dresses. I can't wait to put it on and dance at the Masquerade ball."

Logan gives me a knowing look like he knows what I almost said. It is almost like he agrees, especially when he says, "me too!" Maybe it was for putting on the dress or maybe it was for loving me too, but either way I am content with where we are at this moment.

We dance for a while longer before he says, "Now let's get you home before your parents worry."

Chapter Fourteen

The next morning, Ty and I get up early. We run to our parents' room and jump on the bed like we are five. They sit up laughing at their grown children and our yearly tradition.

We run out to the living room, waiting for our parents to join us.

The tradition is to always open our stockings before breakfast and then we open the presents under the tree after. We stopped believing in Santa Claus when we were little but every year, we wrap a little gift for each person to put in their stocking from Santa.

Our parents finally join and we go through our stockings.

Every year we make a breakfast casserole and homemade cinnamon rolls.

We pop the casserole in the oven and start making the cinnamon rolls. The girls make the dough while the guys put their muscles to work, rolling and kneading the dough. We then roll them up in cinnamon and sugar and put them on a cookie sheet to bake. When there is fifteen minutes left for the casserole, we put the cinnamon rolls in the oven.

When breakfast is ready, we fill our plates and make our way into the living room. We like to sit in front of the fireplace and Christmas tree. When we are finished with breakfast, my dad takes our plates back into the kitchen.

We open presents and I receive everything from a new one-of-a-kind swimsuit from my parents to Florida State football tickets from my brother.

I got my mom a mani/pedi spa day since she is always working. I figured she could use some time to relax. She opened her other gift early since I knew she would need her Kitchen Aid attachment to make all our Christmas cookies.

I got my brother a Florida State jersey and my dad two DVD sets. After buying both, I couldn't decide which to give him so I wrapped up both. I was happy they all liked their gifts.

After presents, my mom and I grab our cookie tins for our cookie walk. We bundle up for the cold weather and meet the guys by the front door.

Every year we bring cookies to all our neighbors and sing Christmas carols. It is one of my favorite traditions. My mom and brother are the only good singers in our house. My dad and I try but don't live up to them.

Later that day, Ashley comes over to exchange gifts. I bought her a pair of knee-high leather boots she has been eyeing since forever. She got me a new gym bag and water bottle, both customized with my name.

After, she demands I try on the dress Logan gave me.

As I put it on, the silk material slides down my body. I have to glance down to make sure I actually have something on because the material is so light.

I turn around and Ashley gasps, pushing me to the mirror. I look at myself in and am in awe of the dress. It is long sleeved, slightly off my shoulder with a scoop neckline. The dress is tight up top and bunches on the one side, swaying loosely around my legs. When I spin the dress moves like water. The silver shimmers with hints of purple and blue, and is more beautiful than when I first opened it. "He sure can pick out a dress."

Ashley nods in approval. "He sure can. I think he's a keeper."

I sit down on my bed and think back to the night before when we were dancing by the Christmas tree. "Ash, I almost told him I loved him. I stopped myself but I really want to say it."

Ash stands in front of me. "Then say it."

I glance down at my hands. "What if he doesn't say it back?"

She takes my hands and pulls me up. She brings me over to the mirror once again. "Sweetie, if you could see the way he looks at you, you would have no doubt that he feels the same way. Probably has since the day he met you."

I see my reflection and her standing next to me. She has her serious face on. I make a decision. I just need to figure out the perfect time to say the words.

Chapter Fifteen

The Andersons' Annual New Year's Ball is tonight. This year is a masquerade. Ashley is headed over so we can get ready together. She has a date with Jeremy and says they are just friends. I keep teasing her about it but I know she really wanted to go with my brother. She has always had a crush on him. He was planning on going until something came up at school and he had to head back early.

Logan and Jeremy are picking us up at seven so we have a few hours to get ready. My mom is making a big salad with lots of veggies and chicken. She thinks keeping dinner light will make us feel better in our dresses, plus they will probably have light appetizers at the party.

When Ashley gets here, we eat and then get ready. I showered earlier so my hair would be dry for whatever crazy updo Ashley is planning.

An hour later, we are almost ready and still have fifteen minutes before the guys will be here. I'm amazed at what she has done with my normally straight hair. She swept all my hair to one side with a small braid halfway down and then curled the ends. She amazes me every time she does my hair.

We start to make our way downstairs when I realize I forgot my overnight bag. The Andersons insisted we stay the night since it would be super late. We, of course, will be in the guest room and not in the boys' rooms.

I run upstairs to grab my bag before heading downstairs where I see Logan waiting at the bottom. Our eyes lock as I make my way down the stairs. I decide this is the night I am going to tell him how I feel. Logan takes my hand and gives me a little spin. "Well that sure felt like a Cinderella moment."

Logan smiles at me. "It won't be the only one. You still have Junior Prom, Senior Prom, future Anderson Balls, your wedding, and I think that's it. Maybe more."

"As long as I am with you for those, I am good."

As I look into Logan's bright blue eyes, I can see what Ashley is talking about. It's like he's staring into my soul.

Jeremy comes over, "My brother is one lucky guy. You look stunning." He kisses me on the cheek as my mom starts taking pictures.

I put my hands on my hips facing my mom. "Really? You have to bring out the camera?"

"Yes she does." My dad comes over with the video camera having filmed my entire entrance. "Just like I'm capturing every moment and always have."

We pose for tons of pictures — everything from serious to funny before we finally manage to escape.

When we get to the Anderson house, the Christmas lights are still up and people are everywhere.

We walk up the left side of the stairs to the doors on the balcony, which are now open. The few times I have been to this house, I have wondered what lies behind these doors. I guess I am about to find out.

The boys usher us through the doors, leading us into a ballroom. *Wait, ballroom. I was not expecting this behind the doors.*

I look around and see a stage on one side of the room. The entire backside is windows and doors, leading out to what I know is the outside balcony overlooking the pool and backyard.

There are huge crystal chandeliers and streamers of ribbon hanging from the ceiling making it seem like waterfalls. It doesn't take away from the best part of the ceiling which is what looks to be hundreds of tiny lights.

I can't help but be in awe of the entire room.

A waiter comes over and hands us all a glass of champagne. I take mine, glancing back at the ceiling above the chandeliers. There are so many lights. It looks like stars. I'm amazed. Ashley whispers to me, "So this is an Anderson party?" I just nod not knowing what else to say.

Jeremy pats Logan on the shoulder, "We need to go find mom and dad."

"Yes." Logan gives me a quick peck on the lips. "I'll find you in a little bit. You and Ashley have some fun." He follows Jeremy.

I turn to Ashley. "So what are we supposed to do?"

"I don't know. I was admiring the ceiling and how gorgeous it is."

"Me too. How do you think they got all those lights up there? It's almost like magic at the Hogwarts Great Hall."

Before we can say any more, Mr. Anderson taps his glass. He is standing on the upper platform of the stage. Below him are Mrs. Anderson, Jeremy and Logan. I lock eyes with Logan and he smiles.

Mr. Anderson begins, "Thank you everyone for joining us. We couldn't be more excited to enter the New Year with all our friends and family. So please raise your glasses and join me in a toast to the New Year being the best year yet." We all raise our glasses and cheer. Logan points his at me and then takes a sip. "Now the dance floor is officially open." Mr. Anderson announces.

"Let's dance!" Ashley drags me onto the dance floor. I glance back at the stage to motion for Logan to join us but he is gone. I shrug, assuming he will find me.

We jump to the music and have a blast. A few songs later, a slow song comes on and Logan appears next to me. "Can I have this dance?" He says in a very good British accent.

"Why yes you can, Mr. Darcy." Attempting my best British accent. I remembered our project from earlier that year and how we kept trying to do British accents. He was really good at it, probably from his time over there.

He takes my hand, puts his other around my waist, and pulls me close. I lean my head on his chest and sway to the music. The electricity is there between us and it is like a force keeping us together. I don't think I could pull away even if I wanted to.

The song ends too soon and another upbeat song comes on. Logan spins me and even dips me a few times. I am amazed at his dancing skills and wonder where he learned it all.

I look over at Ashley and Jeremy. They are both laughing and having a good time. We shimmy our way over to them and the boys nod to each other.

Before Ashley or I know what is happening, they spin us and we swap partners. I stare up at Jeremy and then glance over at Logan. "Where did you both learn to dance like this?"

"We're just naturally good." I give Jeremy a "yeah right" glance. "We can't just be this good at dancing?"

Logan dances by with Ashley and chimes in, "our mother made us take ballroom classes when we were younger."

"That is great."

I feel someone watching me and see in the corner, Mallory and Amber glaring at us. I am still dancing with Jeremy and say, "Are you still dating Mallory?"

"We're having fun but it's not serious. Why?"

"She's in the corner glaring at us."

"Oh, don't mind her. She kept trying to get me to ask her but I just don't want the drama. She wants more and I just don't want to be tied down right now."

I know all about her drama remembering when she was trying to make me think that I wasn't invited tonight. "Is that why you asked Ashley?"

"Ashley is fun and she's your best friend. I wanted all of us to hang for a stress free New Year's."

"Okay well if you do pursue her, please be careful or I might have to come after you."

He steps back still holding my hands. "I am so scared," he teases. Then he flips me around again so I am facing Ashley and Logan.

We dance together for the next few songs. The boys start doing their own made up moves from when they were kids. Ashley and I attempt to follow them but decide to make up our own instead.

Another slow song comes on and Logan pulls me toward him. This time I wrap both my hands around his neck and he does the same around my waist. I give him a slow kiss. It quickly turns into a deeper kiss and I feel myself blushing.

I hear an "awww" from behind me and turn to see Ashley smiling.

Jeremy points at the clock on the wall, "you know we still have about fifteen minutes till midnight, right?"

"Oh and I can't kiss my girlfriend before then?" Logan dips me and gives me another kiss. It is a good thing he is holding me up or I would have fallen down from all his kisses. When he pulls me back up, Ashley and Jeremy are cheering.

Logan glances at me, "want to go for a walk?"

I nod, knowing I could use some fresh air right about now. After that display, I feel on fire and know my face is showing it. He literally turns my skin to lava when he touches me let alone when he kisses me.

We head out the back door and pass the pool. Instead of going down to the docks, we turn to the side of the house. I have never seen this side of the house and with what I can see in the dark, it appears huge.

We walk hand in hand around the giant backyard. I can see an outdoor basketball court and a sand volleyball court. We eventually head down to the docks. I notice a few boats on the lake and fireworks off in the distance.

I know this is the moment to say how I feel but I freeze up. *What if he doesn't feel the same?*

Logan puts his arms around me, tilts my chin up and gives me another smoldering kiss. As he pulls back, he looks deep into my eyes, my soul, at least that is what it feels like and says the words I have been longing to hear, "I love you, Emma."

Relief washes through me. "I love you, too!"

"I have been wanting to say those words since you ran into me in the hallway. You practically took my breath away that day. I thought I was just crazy but when we got assigned the project together and I sat there watching the final product, I knew it was true. I could see it in the video."

I think back to the video and how I felt the same way watching our chemistry on the screen.

"I thought I was seeing things in the video. I've been wanting to say it for a while now but thought it was too soon. Ashley assured me it is never too soon if it is truly how you feel."

"Well now you're free to say it whenever." He kisses my forehead. "I love you." He kisses my left cheek. "I love you." He kisses my right cheek. "I love you." He kisses the tip of my nose. "I love you." Finally, he kisses my lips. "I love you so much."

We break apart when I hear fireworks go off not far from us and then hear the countdown.

10... 9 ... 8... 7... 6... 5... 4... 3... 2... 1...

"Happy New Year, Logan."

"Happy New Year, Emma." Then he pulls me into another toe-curling kiss.

"Let's get inside before we freeze."

He grabs my hand and leads me toward the house. As we get closer, I see everyone outside for the fireworks. When we get to the deck, Ashley runs over to us, "I need to borrow Emma real quick." I just shrug at Logan.

"What is it?" I ask Ashley.

"So spill. Did you say it? By the looks on both your faces when you walked up here and that serious makeup session down on the dock, I'm guessing yes."

"Maybe...." I blush. Ashley crosses her arms. "Okay yes. He said it first and then I did. He told me he thinks he's loved me since he first bumped into me at the beginning of the year."

She squeals. "See I told you!"

"I know, it's still scary. I have never felt like this. I mean I had a crush on Jeremy and then those four months of dating John, but nothing like this."

"Well I am happy for you. He is a great catch."

"He is! What about you and Jeremy?"

Ashley shrugs. "He gave me a very brief friendly peck on the lips. As amazing as it would be to date the quarterback, we just don't have chemistry. He is super cool though, and I am down for us all to hang out anytime."

"Well I guess my brother still has a chance." I tease as I run back to Logan and Jeremy before she can say anything back.

She joins us as Jeremy asks, "What was all of that about?"

"Ashley just told me how you all are going to run away and elope." Jeremy's jaw drops. "I am totally kidding. We were just having a girl talk."

Ashley laughs and then turns serious staring right at Logan. "Don't hurt her or you go through me." She then grabs Jeremy's arm. "Now let's leave these lovebirds to some privacy."

Jeremy winks at Logan and they are off. Logan grabs a blanket from the pile his parents laid out for everyone to keep warm. We head over to their swinging porch chair and cuddle up on the bench, watching the fireworks as we ring in the New Year in a better way than I ever thought possible.

Chapter Sixteen

School starts back up in January and flies by. Before I know it, Valentine's Day is upon us. It happens to be on a Friday and Logan won't tell me anything. I walk into school that morning and Ashley runs up to me. "Have you seen it?"

"Seen what? I just pulled up to school."

"Come on." She pulls me towards my locker.

When I get closer, I see a giant heart on the outside of my locker. It reads, "Open me." I open my locker and out pops a bunch of balloons that say everything from "I love you" to "Happy Valentine's Day".

Halfway through first period, a student walks in delivering chocolate roses. It is a tradition every year that you can buy a chocolate rose for someone. You pick which period and they have Cupids deliver them. Basically, nothing gets done all day.

The Cupid comes over to me and instead of handing me a rose, hands me a coffee. "Here you go Emma."

First, I'm confused that he knows who I am and then second, why he is handing me a coffee.

He must see my confusion because he spins the coffee around and it says "every valentine needs something to wake up to. Maybe one day it'll be me."

I melt into my seat at the adorable message. I want to keep the cup forever.

In fourth period, instead of a rose, I get a box of chocolates with a note that says, "Check your locker before lunch for a special surprise."

As soon as the bell rings, I run to my locker and find a paper bag. Inside is my favorite burger from our local grille, Jacks. There are even still hot fries! Behind the bag is a thermos full of sweet tea. I take the bag with my sweet tea and close my locker.

At our normal lunch spot, I find Ashley talking to Jeremy but no Logan. "Hey where's Logan? I haven't seen him all day".

"I'm right here." Before I can turn around, I feel arms wrap around my waist and warm kisses on my neck.

I lean back into him. "I missed you this morning."

He leans around and gives me a kiss on the cheek. "I was getting things ready for tonight."

"Oh were you now?" I turn in his arms and kiss him back but this time deeper.

"And that is my cue to leave." Jeremy gets up and pats Logan on the shoulder. "Have fun tonight little bro. Don't do anything I wouldn't do". He leaves with a wink.

"What is happening tonight?"

"You will have to wait and see! Now open up that bag because I want some fries." He grabs the paper bag.

I grab it back. "Those are my fries. Some gentleman caller left them in my locker." I take a fry out and eat it.

I hear Ashley giggling. She has her phone out, texting someone. "What are you so smiley over there for?"

"Nothing." She quickly sets it down. "So what are you all doing tonight?"

"That is a good question. Logan won't tell me." I cross my arms and see out of the corner of my eyes, Logan eating my fries. I grab the bag from him, once again.

"Don't worry it'll be a good surprise." He gives me a pouty face for stealing the fries. I stick my tongue out at him.

Just then Ashley's phone buzzes. I grab the phone before she can and see a text.

Ty Bear: *I wish I could be there to celebrate but I'm excited for our Skype date tonight!*

I hand her back the phone. "Who's Ty bear?"

"No one." She blushes, which is weird because she never blushes. I didn't even think she was capable of it.

It takes me a minute but I finally realize who it is because there is only one person that would make her blush like that. "No way! Not Ty as in, my brother?"

"Maybe..." She looks away hiding her growing blush.

"Well it's about time!"

"It's nothing really. We just started texting over Christmas break and we're just friends. Neither of us had a date tonight so we decided to do a friend date. Nothing more."

"Okay, you keep telling yourself that!" I smile at her because I really am happy for her. Most people freak out when their friends like their siblings but Ashley and Tyler are perfect for each other. I would totally back their relationship if they went for it. They're just too stubborn to admit anything.

I look back over at Logan who is once again eating my fries. "So what time do I need to be ready tonight?"

"I'll pick you up from swim practice and we'll go from there."

"But I need to change and get ready."

"You look beautiful just the way you are."

"Umm are you forgetting swim practice? My hair will be a mess and I'll have no makeup." Ashley has finally started rubbing off on me when it comes to fashion and hair. I am nowhere near her expertise but I've gotten better in my own way.

He takes a lock of my hair and twirls it in his fingers. "First off, you look beautiful without makeup, and your hair dries perfectly straight so you don't need to do anything".

We've only been dating a few months and he already seems to know more about me than expected. What guy pays that much attention to how a girl's hair dries? Wait, how does he know what I look like without makeup? Even in the pool, I wear waterproof mascara.

"You have never seen me with no makeup."

"Yeah but if I imagined you with no makeup, I see a beautiful girl."

"Have I told you what an amazing boyfriend you are?"

"Not today." He smirks as he stands up. "I need to go, but I'll see you in English." He leans down to grab a few fries, gives me a peck, and winks at me before leaving.

Once he leaves, I glance to Ash who was watching us with a dreamy look in her eyes. One I have recently come to know very well in my own eyes.

"So tell me about this date with my brother!"

"I told you we're just friends."

"Right now tell me the real story."

Ash sighs. "It really is nothing. I wish it was more. You know all this. I've had the biggest crush on him but he practically sees me as a little sister."

"One day he'll realize you are a great catch." I would love for them to be together but I also know my brother is a player. He doesn't want to be tied down right now. I will have to remember to talk to him about Ashley. As much as I would love for them to be together, I also don't want either of them hurt. With my brother being in college right now, it would end up being Ashley that gets hurt until they figure out that they are perfect for each other.

"I hope so." She leans back against the wall.

The bell rings and we head to class. This time when the Cupids come, I get a teddy bear holding a heart that says, "I love you berry much!"

In English, we are talking about Romeo and Juliet which is very fitting for Valentine's Day. We are at the balcony scene and she asks for two volunteers. Logan immediately raises his hand and walks up to the front of the class.

When no one else volunteers to be Juliet, my English teacher glances around the room. I avoid her gaze but out of the corner of my eye, I see Logan whisper something to her. He then glances back at me with a very suspicious smile. I have a feeling I know what he said and I am going to kill him.

Next thing I know, she is saying my name and I am making my way up to the front of the room to reenact the famous balcony scene. I whisper over to Logan. "I hate you". He just gives me a smug grin.

Our English teacher has me stand on a chair and Logan bends down on the ground and begins the famous words. "But soft! What light through yonder window breaks? It is the east, and Juliet is the sun."

When he finishes the monologue, he pulls a chocolate rose off a nearby desk and hands it to me. He then sweeps me off my feet, literally, and holds me close to his chest. He gives me a quick kiss before setting me down on the ground as everyone applauds.

Our English teacher laughs and tells us to take our seats. I am glad she didn't get mad. "That was definitely one version of that scene, and only because it's Valentine's Day will I allow that display to be overlooked. Now everyone turn to Act 2 Scene 2 and we will begin reading the real version."

At swim practice, coach has us working on speed trials. I have never been good at sprinting. Longer distances have always been my thing so I can build up and beat my competitors in the last few meters. Coach Johnson tells me I need to work on everything so I have the best chance at making the Olympic team.

After practice, I change into my clothes from the day, jeans and a pink sweater. My hair is almost dry and I fix my makeup before heading out front.

An old school black Camaro pulls up in front of me. I take out my phone and glance down looking for a message from Logan but there's nothing. The window rolls down in the car and someone whistles.

I keep looking at my phone hoping whoever this creep is will leave me alone. I am also hoping Logan will get here soon. "I don't know who you think you are, but my boyfriend will be here any second."

I realize whoever this is doesn't want to leave, and I turn to the car ready to give them a piece of my mind. "I'm sure he is prepared to kick your--" I instantly see Logan peering over the driver's side.

"I think that boyfriend would be okay with it, since this is a pretty cool car and I'm cute."

I walk to the car and Logan runs around to open it for me. He gives me a sweet kiss.

We head out of town towards his house. When we get there, we go out to the back of the house into a greenhouse I didn't know existed. "Why is it every time I come to your house I see a different room?"

"Because this house is a mystery." He pulls me into the greenhouse and I see lights strung up everywhere. At the center, I see a table set up with candles. The air smells of cinnamon and chocolate. In the middle is a fondue pot – hence the chocolate smell. The cinnamon must be coming from the candles.

It is so warm and cozy here and I am not just talking about the temperature. Between the candles and the look Logan is giving me, I need to take my jacket off.

"I thought about taking you out for fondue but then I thought it would be more romantic to do it here." He says.

As I get closer, I smell the cheese fondue in the first pot and my mouth waters. We have bread and apples to dip in the cheese.

The next course is a garlic broth to cook the meats, potatoes and veggies in. Normally I would be worried about garlic breath but since we are both eating it, it's okay. *Right?*

As we wait for our meats to cook, Logan pulls out a box and hands it to me. I open the box and inside is a gorgeous necklace with a diamond heart pendant. "It's gorgeous." It isn't big and gaudy, but rather small and perfect with so much sparkle. Something I can wear every day.

I reach down into my bag and pull out my gift for him. He unwraps it. Inside is a coupon book I made for him with coupons like "foot massage" and "night of old school movies" and "eating Thai food". He loves Thai food and I've learned to love it too even if it still isn't my first choice.

"I will definitely be cashing in on some of these coupons soon."

When we finish the broth course, we move on to the chocolate. It's a dark and milk chocolate mix. We have all sorts of fruits and cakes to dip. It tastes even better than it smells.

I see a projector is set up and I ask what movie we are watching.

"It's a surprise."

I cuddle in next to him as he hits play. I am shocked when I see the opening credits. "You're actually watching The Notebook?"

"Every man can secretly have their favorite romantic comedies."

"This just made me love you more." I kiss him and settle back with my head on his chest. I can't help but look up at him and wonder "Is he even real?"

What a perfect night!

Chapter Seventeen

Between my AP classes and swim practice in the morning and afternoon, the semester is flying by. I finally have some down time at the end of March. The Andersons invite us over for a cookout.

The weather is sunny and warm, now that the snow has melted.

Ashley and I are lying on chairs by the pool relaxing in the sun when we feel a huge splash. The boys decide to do huge cannon balls right in front of us.

"Hey we are trying to relax here!" I hear Ashley yell at them.

"Well it's time to get in the water." Jeremy flips her chair into the water. She surfaces and if looks could kill, it would be one of those.

Knowing I am next, I hop off my chair and run over to the grill where Mr. Anderson is cooking steaks. "Hey Emma. What are you doing?"

"Oh nothing, just seeing if you need any help."

"No you're not." I hear a voice behind me.

"You're just trying to avoid the water." Logan agrees with his brother.

"What do you think we should do little brother?" Jeremy inches closer with Logan right by his side. I try not to look at either of the shirtless boys and the water glistening off their abs. It should be illegal.

Jeremy is bigger than Logan since he plays both football and baseball. He has muscle everywhere while Logan is leaner, but that doesn't stop the muscles from being there.

"I think my girlfriend needs to go for a dip." Logan is about a foot from me now.

Mr. Anderson laughs at his boys and whispers to me. "I think you better surrender now."

"Never!" I take off running through the grass. I hate running but with all the cardio I do swimming, I know I am fast. I take off towards the docks and see Jeremy ahead of me.

I turn around and see Logan behind me. I am the monkey in the middle. I take off to the side but Jeremy is faster and grabs my arms. Logan grabs my feet. I squirm hoping to get free but no such luck. Jeremy is strong and has a tight grip on my upper body. Logan may be slightly smaller but still very strong, keeping a firm hold of my legs. They take me over to the edge of the pool, swinging me as they count down. "1...2...3."

I'm thrown in and expect to feel the ice-cold water rush over me but instead it is actually pretty warm. They must have a heater which would make sense because even if it is warm out, the water would still be cold.

Ashley swims over to me. "You should have just gotten in when you had the chance."

"Yeah, yeah." I brush my wet hair out of my face.

Jeremy cannon balls in and swims over to us. "We should have a race. Whoever does two laps first wins."

"I'm out. I already know you'll all beat me." Ashley hops up on the side of the pool. "I'll be the judge."

I am excited because this could be my chance to beat them and get back at them for throwing me in the pool. "I'm down. You both may be faster on land, but I can beat you any day in the water."

Logan shakes his head at Jeremy. "Good luck. I've already raced her and have never been able to beat her."

"I bet I can beat her." He stands next to me. "You're on. Let's see if your words can meet your actions."

We set up at the end of the pool. Ashley stands above us. "Okay, you'll swim from this side to the other side and back twice. First person to make it back here and touch Logan or my hand first wins."

Logan hands us each a pair of goggles. "You ready?" We nod. "On your mark, get set... Go!" We both take off like rockets. I use the wall to push myself further and get in my element. This is what I was born to do and I won't let Mr. Hot Shot win.

Stroke, stroke, breath.

Stroke, stroke, breath.

I get close to the wall and flip, pushing off the wall with my feet. I head back to the starting wall. I get to the wall and flip again, knowing I am halfway to victory. I see Jeremy just ahead of me but I am not worried. I've always been a long distance swimmer, 400-meter or 800-meter, where I can use the first few laps to swim fast but not make myself tired. It's that last lap I live for when I gain the speed I need to get ahead while they are all worn out.

I flip and head back to the ending point. Jeremy is barely ahead and I am gaining on him. He is fast but I won't let him win. I stroke faster and touch their hands a second before Jeremy. "Emma wins!"

I take off my goggles and give Logan a high five. I look over at Jeremy as he says, "I let you win."

"Okay Mr. Hot Shot. Now don't let this inflate your ego, but you did give me a run for my money. Where'd you learn to swim that fast?"

"Coach makes us swim twice a week for cardio. But you, missy, are definitely an amazing swimmer. You keep that up and you will be giving the guys a challenge at the Olympics."

"I don't know about that but thanks!" I know I'm fast but didn't think I was that fast.

Mrs. Anderson comes over and says lunch is ready. We get out of the pool and dry off. I excuse myself to the bathroom before getting food. I fix my raccoon eyes and attempt to fluff up my hair. With no such luck, I exit the bathroom and find Logan standing there. "Hey winner."

He presses me up against the door and gives me one of those toe curling kisses. "Hey yourself."

"You were amazing out there, and you definitely surprised my brother." He pushes a strand of hair behind my ear.

I shrug. "I'm always up for a race."

He bends down to give me another kiss before pulling away and grabbing my hand. "Let's go get some food before I push you through that bathroom door and have my way with you."

Once outside, Jeremy winks at us. I blush, even though nothing happened.

I grab a plate, starving after all that running and swimming. My coach put me on a strict nutrition plan to start gearing up for the Olympics. I can eat everything but the potato and fill my plates with steak, corn and salad.

I sit next to Logan and across from Ashley. We are about halfway through eating when Jeremy says he has an announcement. "I officially got my acceptance letters back from colleges and need help deciding."

"Let's hear the options." Ashley chimes in.

"I got a full football scholarship to Alabama and Georgia. Both say I won't be starting quarterback till at least my sophomore year. Their current quarterback will be a senior the year I start." He looks at his mom. "Tennessee accepted me but no scholarship. They said I could be starting quarterback as a freshman since they're losing theirs this year." He glances at me. "And last is Florida State."

"Ding, ding, ding, we have a winner." I shout. Everyone laughs.

"Yes, Florida State offered me a partial scholarship and said I would be starting quarterback my freshman year too. They're losing most of their team this year so it will be a complete rebuilding year if I choose there."

Mrs. Anderson jumps in. "Well my vote is Tennessee because then you'll be closer to home. We have the money to pay even if there is no scholarship. Just think of the home cooked meals you can have and doing your laundry at home."

"Plus if you want to play for the Titans wouldn't you want to go to a Tennessee school?" Ashley says.

Logan replies. "I don't think that's how the NFL draft works unfortunately. He can go anywhere and still be picked up by the Titans when he graduates."

Mr. Anderson pats Ashley on the arm. "It's the way the football world works."

Jeremy looks back to me. "What do you think of the rebuilding year?"

I assume he is only asking me because my dad is his coach. "I think the rebuilding year is an advantage. Instead of playing with guys for two years and then them leaving and you having to start over with others, you get that in the beginning. No, you probably won't win any championships your freshman year, but come junior or senior year, that team will be super strong after working together for three to four years."

Mr. Anderson nods in agreement. "That is a very good point. Teams starting together in the beginning have always done better than teams having to start over halfway through."

"Plus if you go to those other schools, especially Alabama, I don't think I will ever be able to talk to you again." I lean back in my chair and cross my arms. Jeremy chuckles.

Logan leans forward. "I think she is serious. I was at her house Thanksgiving weekend with her family for the Florida — Florida State game and I have never seen a family take football more seriously."

"It's true. I've known Emma since we were practically born and Seminole football is life." Ashley agrees.

"Okay, well maybe I'll cross Alabama and Georgia off the list, but what about Tennessee? I'll be close to home and they have an awesome team."

"Tennessee isn't as bad as Alabama. I might talk to you if you choose there." I grin at him.

I pat Logan on the shoulder. "I hear FSU has a great film program. If you go there, you'll possibly have your brother with you."

"I think you need to make a pro con list for each and decide what would make you most happy. We will support whatever you decide." Mrs. Anderson adds before she gets up and starts clearing the table. Mr. Anderson stands to help his wife and clean the grille.

I love how supportive they are of their kids. They give their opinion but don't force it. They allow them make their own choices.

"Thanks Mom." He says when she walks back over. She smiles at him. "Thanks everyone else. You've given me a lot to think about. Now I just need to make a decision by the end of the week. I have a meeting with your dad too."

"We all know you'll make the right decision." I wink before standing and grabbing my plate to follow Mrs. Anderson.

As I head inside I hear Logan and Jeremy.

"You heard her man." Logan slaps him on the shoulder.

"That is one amazing girl you got there. Athletic, beautiful, smart, fiery and loves football. Don't let her go."

"I don't plan to. Not ever." I can't help but smile big. It has been a strange year but I wouldn't have changed anything.

Chapter Eighteen

Logan's baseball team makes it to the playoffs. The second playoff game is tonight. If we win, we will make it into the championship. I can't wait to watch him play.

The stands are crowded and thankfully we found some seats three rows up from the field on our team's side.

The clear skies and warm sun make it the perfect day for a game. Add in the smell of hotdogs and pregame chanting from the crowd and we have a ballgame.

Ashley and I have gone to most games since she started dating the shortstop, Daniel. They have been going out for about three months. I can tell she really likes him but is still holding out for my brother. I keep telling her, if it is meant to be then it will happen, but for now he needs to grow up and have "the college experience". I love my brother but I know he is not ready to settle down yet.

We cheer when the team runs onto the field. Jeremy is on the team as the pitcher. After a few warm up pitches, the game begins.

Logan does an amazing job at first base and I love watching him. He is so at ease with the game and could easily go pro, if he wanted to. Instead, he wants to be a filmmaker and says he only does baseball to keep in shape.

Every once in a while, he catches my eye and smiles. Even all the way up in the stands I shiver every time he looks at me.

I am excited about our double date with Ashley and Daniel after the game. We are taking the Andersons' sailboat out for a moonlight dinner on the lake.

By the seventh inning, we are down two runs with the score at 8-6. It is the bottom of the inning and this is it if we want to win the game. We have one out and Logan is up to bat. The bases are loaded.

"Let's go little bro!" Jeremy yells from third base.

Logan walks to home plate and I can't help checking him out in his uniform. Don't get me wrong, football players have always had my attention before with their big muscles and six pack abs. I may actually like watching football for the game but that doesn't mean I don't still notice the players.

Now there is something about baseball players. Maybe it is just because it is Logan or it could be the tight grey pants and the way his jersey hugs his broad shoulders.

With one strike and two balls, I can tell he is getting nervous. He steps out of the box to take a few practice swings.

I shout, "Hey number five, you hit this one and you'll get something special later." I wink at him as he walks back into the batter's box.

The pitcher throws the ball and Logan swings, hitting the ball into the outfield. He takes off running toward first and then turns toward second and then stops at third. The ball is thrown into home but our player is tagged out. Jeremy and another guy made it home so we are tied.

Daniel is up to bat and we only need one run to win the game.

Daniel hits a pop up just outside the infield. With two outs, Logan takes off the second Daniel makes contact. The other team misses the ball but quickly recovers and throws it to the catcher. Logan slides into home plate right as the catcher catches the ball and tries to tag him. The umpire yells, "Safe!" and we all go wild. We won and are on our way to the Championship!

Once Daniel and Logan shower and change, we head to the Andersons' house for what I am calling our dinner cruise. We say hi to Logan's parents before heading to the dock.

All the food is already on the boat. We hop in as the sun sets in the distance.

Once we get to the middle of the lake, we drop the anchor to eat.

We enjoy the time together knowing next year will be super busy. We will be seniors and as much as we want to relax and enjoy our last year of high school, colleges would be deciding our futures. It isn't the time to slack off.

After dinner, Logan and I head to the bow of the sailboat. Once the sun sets, the weather drops a few degrees. I shiver as Logan sits down behind me with me in between his legs. He wraps the blanket around us as I lean back against him.

I stare at the stars. It is so peaceful and quiet out here. The sky is pitch black but between the stars and the moon reflecting off the water, it is almost bright out.

I feel Logan shift. He places a light kiss just below my ear, whispering. "Do you know how much I love you?"

I grin. "Only a little bit." I don't think I will ever get tired of hearing him tell me that.

"Oh really? Is that all you think? Would someone that loved you only a little bit, do this?" Before I can do anything, he flips his leg around me, pinning me to the deck and starts tickling me. I am stuck and can barely breathe with how ticklish I am.

"Okay a lot. You love me a lot."

Logan stops for a second. "You sure?"

He tickles my sides again as I nod hoping he'll take it as a surrender. "Good, because I do so much Emma. We may have only been dating for six and a half months but there is something about you, about us." He gazes down at me before leaning down and kissing me. The kiss deepens as his tongue pushes through my lips. He rolls us over so I am laying on top of him. I feel myself getting carried away but I don't care. I love him and he loves me. My hands move down his chest.

Logan stops kissing me and pushes my upper body away. "Emma, we need to stop. As much as I would love to go there, we can't. We made a promise we would wait."

I sit up trying to catch my breath. He's right. We decided to wait and were treading into dangerous territory. I quickly roll off so we are laying side by side. I rest my head on his chest. "Thanks for stopping us."

"Of course. Now cuddle with me for a few minutes before we have to sail home."

I lay my head back down. I have never felt like this before and I know I need to be careful. I allow myself to be back in the moment and enjoy the night. I look out at the moonlit water with the twinkling stars above us. It truly has been a great night with friends.

Chapter Nineteen

The baseball team wins the Championship. The team celebrates by throwing a huge rager at an old abandoned barn, just outside of town.

There are old tractors outside the barn giving it a very rustic feel.

I'm not sure why they are throwing a rager on a Thursday night. Don't get me wrong, I am super happy for the win but couldn't they have waited till Friday night when we had no school the next day? Better yet, wait two days and have it on Saturday when I can sleep in the next day and not have swim practice.

Ashley persuades Logan and I to go with her and Daniel. We enter the barn and the music is blasting. We get drinks. I tell myself this is the only drink since I have practice super early in the morning.

I don't plan on being here long anyway since I have a curfew of eleven on school nights. My parents have never had to enforce it before. I'm usually in bed by nine since I have practice early. I decided this is a special occasion and I can still be home before curfew.

Logan and Daniel leave us to make their rounds. Ashley and I watch a few rounds of beer pong before sitting down on the couch. Logan and Daniel find us on the couches with Jeremy in tow. Other people fill in and ask if we want to play Ring of Fire. I say I will watch but everyone else decides to play. After a few rounds, I join in. If I am lucky, I won't have to drink much.

Several rounds later and I'm feeling the effects of three drinks. I think it was only three. I may have lost count.

By the end of the game, we are all pretty wasted. I must have fallen asleep because when I wake up there is sunlight coming through the windows. My head is pounding. I am laying on Logan's shoulder. We are fully dressed so nothing too crazy happened last night. I see we weren't the only ones that stayed. I don't think many people will be going to school today.

School! I forgot about school. I feel around for my phone and see fifteen missed calls from my parents and coach. I also see it is 6:30 a.m. I am already thirty minutes late for swim practice. My coach is going to kill me. I shoot my parents a text to let them know I am alive and will be home after my afternoon swim practice. Then I shoot my coach a text letting her know I missed my alarm and am on my way.

I shake Logan awake letting him know I have to go. Still half asleep, he asks, "What time is it?"

"It's a little after 6:30 and I have swim practice." He sounds as bad as I feel. His hair is slightly disheveled on top and his shirt is wrinkled but he still looks hot.

"You wake up Ashley and I'll call the car." He must feel bad because he instantly pulls out his cellphone and goes outside.

I try to wake Ashley up. She stirs but doesn't wake up. Finally, she opens her eyes and moans about the bright light. I let her know we have to leave because I am already late for practice and asks if she wants a ride to school. She mumbles something about finding a ride.

Logan comes back into the room and hands me my jacket. "The car will be here in a few minutes. Let's go out front and wait."

When the car pulls up, we hop in the back and I see water bottles waiting for us on the seat.

Ralph, the driver, hands us a paper bag and two coffees, as well. Logan must have told him to stop and get something.

Ralph is the Andersons' personal driver when they need him and he is always aware of everything. I never knew anyone who had a driver before I started dating Logan.

Logan tells him to drop me off first at my house so I can grab my stuff. "Actually you can drop me off at the school. I left my backpack in my locker since I went right to the game after my practice and then we came straight here to the party."

"What about clothes and your suit?"

"I always leave an extra bathing suit and clothes in my locker."

"Look at you. Always prepared." Logan hands me a water bottle which I quickly chug before taking a sip of my coffee.

In the paper bag is an egg white breakfast sandwich. Ralph thinks of everything. I have a feeling Logan also had something to do with this. Always taking care of me.

When we get to the school, I give Logan a quick kiss and thank him.

I quickly change into my bathing suit and go out to the pool. I see my coach sitting on the bleachers waiting for me. I make my way to her prepared for a speech. "I don't want to know the real reason why you are an hour late. Just get in the pool and warm up."

I dive in. After several laps, I feel my stomach rumble and don't feel good. I get out of the pool and excuse myself to the locker room. I barely make it to the toilet before emptying the contents of my stomach. I decide from there on out that I am not drinking that much ever again. I am pretty sure I told myself that the last time.

When I get back to the pool, my coach has put all my gear back in my bag.

"We're done for the day. I want you to go take a shower and get to class. Drink lots of water and I'll see you tomorrow."

"What about practice after school?"

"This one time only I'm allowing you to miss but Emma, I will not tolerate this behavior. If you want to go to the Olympics someday, you need to train. You are an amazing swimmer and I see your potential. I am not saying you can't have fun, but I won't have hungover swimmers in my pool. You got it?"

I nod and pick up my bag.

"Oh and Emma, I will see you at six sharp tomorrow morning and not a minute late."

"Yes ma'am." She walks back to the coaches' office area and I make my way back to the locker room. I am not looking forward to 6 a.m. practice tomorrow. Normally practice doesn't start till 8 a.m. on Saturday but I guess this is what I get for being late and almost throwing up in the pool.

I turn on the shower and let the warm water run over my body. It feels good after the night I had.

I dry off and head to the cafeteria hoping they have water and coffee.

The rest of the day is slow. By lunchtime, my headache is back and I debate what to eat. I am putting my books away when Logan appears behind me. "Hey you! How was practice this morning?"

"Not good. Coach yelled some and then dismissed me. She even told me not to show up at practice this afternoon."

"That does not sound good."

"It gets worse. I have practice at six tomorrow morning."

"I am sorry babe. This is all my fault. I know you didn't want to stay long at the party last night."

"Hey I could have left at any point. I chose to stay and drink."

"I know, but I still feel bad so I brought you something to maybe make up for it a little." He pulls a bag out from behind his back. Inside is a turkey wrap and homemade kale chips from Jack's.

"I might be able to forgive you." I close my locker and take the bag from him excited for the kale chips. Jack's uses this Cajun lime seasoning on them and I can't get enough.

"So where were you this morning? I missed you in class."

"Well my parents were waiting for me when I got home, so there was that — and then by the time I took a shower and got ready, I had missed the first few periods. I figured I would stop by and grab some lunch for us."

He pulls out a burger and fries for himself. I lean over and steal a fry. "Well thank you! This is just what I needed. I am not looking forward to going home. I had about ten missed calls just from my parents this morning."

"I am sure your parents will understand. You're the perfect daughter. They can't be too mad that you stayed out late one night."

"You're forgetting the first party of the year." I think back to before Logan and I started dating when I saw him making out with Amber. It had all been a misunderstanding but I was so jealous.

"Oh yeah, well maybe they'll forget that time."

"Very doubtful." I'm hoping I am wrong. Maybe they'll see my hungover state and that will be punishment enough. "Where did your brother end up last night?"

"I have no idea, but he was already home when I got there."

"You know you better be careful. My parents are going to start thinking you're a bad influence on me."

"Yeah right. Your parents love me, especially your mom. She always makes me goodies when I come over." He winks at me as he steals the kale chip out of my hand.

He isn't wrong about that. My parents are always doting on him, especially my mom.

When I get home both my parents are waiting for me at the kitchen table. I texted them to let them know I would be home early since there was no practice.

My dad points to the chair across from them. "Sit down."

"I am sorry I stayed out and didn't let you know. One thing led to another and it was morning. We were just trying to celebrate the Championship win and I wasn't planning on drinking. You both know how high school parties get. I already got yelled at by my coach this morning and have an early practice tomorrow. If you don't mind, I would really like to eat some dinner and then head to bed early. Whatever you want to do as my punishment I will take, but can we please talk later?"

My mom takes my hand. "Honey, we were very worried about you. We get celebrating, but couldn't you all have gone to Logan's house or come back here? Why the need to go to the party?"

"We were only going to go for a little bit. I should have called."

"We aren't going to give you the drinking lecture again and we had hoped you learned your lesson after the beginning of the school year. We spoke to your coach this morning and every minute you are not in school or doing homework, you will be training. You are grounded for the next three weeks, until the end of school." My dad says in a stern voice. I haven't heard that voice since my brother was in high school. He was always missing curfew.

"What about Prom?"

My dad glances over at my mom and she nods. "We will allow you to go to Prom, but no after parties. It is right to Prom and right home. And only if you behave until then. School, swim practice, and home."

"Fine. I love you both and I am sorry again for not telling you sooner that I was okay."

"We love you too honey. Now go get washed up for dinner." My mom squeezes my hand. Most of the time my parents get it since they were young once but that doesn't mean they don't worry.

At least I still have Prom to look forward to.

Chapter Twenty

Exams are here and Prom is right around the corner.

"One AP exam down, three to go." I take a book out of my bag to go over some notes before my next exam.

Ashley sits down next to me. "Lucky! I still have all of mine. But can you believe Prom is next week?"

"I know! Then only a week of school after that and we are officially Seniors."

Ashley pulls out her lunch. "We're still going dress shopping after you get out of swim practice today, right? Or are you still grounded?"

"I am still grounded but my mom said I can go shopping but I have to go home right after. I need a break from studying. It's all I have been doing since I can't go anywhere."

Just then Logan walks over with a sad look on his face. "Hey what's wrong?" I stand to give him a kiss. He sits down next to me. "Well, remember that film program I applied for this summer in New York?" I remember him coming to me before Christmas break and he was so excited to mail in his application. It was due the first of the year and he spent all break putting together his video submission. He took parts from our English project and other bits and pieces from previous films he put together. The theme was "What Captivates You".

"Yeah, it was your dream to get in. Plus it would look awesome on college applications."

"I got in." He lacks the enthusiasm he should have. After all, it is his dream internship.

"That is awesome! I'm so proud of you." I give him a kiss on the cheek but notice he still isn't happy.

"Yeah I'm super excited. The only thing is it starts the third week of May. I have to leave next Thursday to get settled in."

"But what about exams, and our last week of being Juniors?"

"Most of my exams are AP Exams which are this week and early next week anyway. I already talked to my teachers and I can take my other non-AP exams early."

I cuddle into him. "Well that's good. I'll miss you all summer. At least I'll be busy with summer classes at the community college and Coach Johnson is putting me through an intense swim training session. It's like she has never had anyone else want to go to the Olympics."

"I don't think she has ever had anyone as good as you." Ashley chimes in.

"Maybe." I turn my attention back to Logan and tap his lips, trying to make them into a smile. "I still don't get what the long face is for. We'll still see each other this summer. It's called a plane."

He takes my hand in his and looks directly in my eyes. "You don't get it. If I accept this program, I won't be able to go to Prom. I have to leave Thursday for the film orientation on Friday. Prom is Friday."

"Oh." I try to think of a way we could make Prom work because we have been planning this forever. "Okay so the orientation is during the day, I assume. What about you flying back just for Prom after the orientation?"

He shakes his head. "Orientation doesn't end till 6:30 that night, and I would never make it back in time. You know me, if there was anything I could do to make it work, I would." He looks so torn.

I decide to be a supportive girlfriend. "You know what, it's okay. You need to go, and we still have Senior Prom next year."

"Emma, I know you wanted to go. Maybe I can talk to them and just arrive a few days late?"

"No, I want you to get the full experience. This is what you want to do in life and I don't want to stand in the way. You go and I'll just hang with my mom."

"Are you sure?"

"Yes, I'm sure." I kiss him but we are interrupted when I hear, "sure about what?"

"Logan accepting his film program this summer." I grin at Logan.

Jeremy slaps Logan on the shoulder. "You got in little bro? Congrats!"

"I know! You can go with me and Daniel." Ashley adds.

I brush it off. "I'm not going to be a third wheel. It's fine really. I'll just go next year."

"But we've been planning this since we were eight years old. Logan won't mind if you're my date, right?" Ash bats her eyes at Logan.

"Ashley, you can't have two dates." I laugh at her.

"Ehh... Daniel is okay but I'd rather go with you."

"What do you need a date for?" Jeremy asks, confused.

Ashley looks at him like he was crazy for not keeping up. "Prom!"

"But I thought you were going with him?" Jeremy points from me to Logan.

"My film program starts next week so I'll have to miss it. I already told her I would see if I could go late, but I think you should go with Ashley, Emma. Make it a girl's night." Says Logan.

"Or you could go with me?" We all look at Jeremy shocked.

I find my voice first. "I'm sorry what? Don't you have a line of girls wanting to go with you?"

"Yeah but they're all annoying and shallow. I was going to ask Mallory but she is always so clingy. I can at least have a conversation with you." He smiles at me.

"Oh gee thanks. Just what I want to hear from a Prom date."

"So you'll go with me?" He gives me a cute little puppy dog face.

"You should go! If you can't go with me then why not my brother. At least then I know I won't be taking you away from a night you and Ashley have planned forever." Logan pushes his shoulder against mine.

I stand up, reaching down to grab my bag. "Guys, I am really fine not going."

Ashley grabs my hand. "Pretty please with a cherry on top come. I don't want to be stuck with Daniel all night. I want my best girl by my side."

I am shocked. "I thought you liked him?"

"Of course I do, he's my boyfriend but let's be real, later in life, I can look back at pictures at my hot junior prom date and my best friend."

Logan stands up next to me. I think it would be weird to go with Jeremy but we are just friends. Plus, I'll be hanging with Ashley all night. What could go wrong? "Are you sure you don't mind?"

"Not at all! If I have to hear in detail about another one of his dates, I might explode." He kisses me on the cheek.

"Okay fine." I point to Jeremy. "No special treatment or limos or anything like that."

"What about a corsage?"

"Fine, a corsage." I glare at him.

"Oh, I can't wait to hear how this night goes." Logan laughs at us. "It's like watching fire and ice".

I glare at Logan too. I swear he thinks it is funny.

"Alright Mr. Smarty Pants. Let's go find our spot before the bell rings. I want some alone time!" I pull him toward the hallway where our special closet is.

"Be good children." Jeremy shouts.

"Don't do anything I wouldn't do." Ash adds in.

I glance back and see Jeremy high five her. I smile because never in a million years would I think this is how my junior year would go.

Chapter Twenty-one

"I am so excited!" Ashley squeals, almost spilling her champagne. We are in the limo on the way to the prom. I glare at Jeremy.

"Hey don't look at me. The limo wasn't my idea. It was hers and she just invited me along."

"It's true. You can't go to Prom in anything else. Now drink this and get ready for some fun."

I take a sip and start to relax. We are each only having a glass to celebrate.

Logan left last night and I am already missing him. As if he knows I am thinking about him, I feel my purse vibrate.

Logan: *Your Mom sent me the pictures she took before you left. You look incredible and I am tempted to hop on a plane back there so I can dance with you. I miss you.*

Ash and I went shopping for dresses. She went for the scandalous red dress while I went for the more modest halter v-neck black dress. They both go to the floor but Ashley's has a slit up to her thigh and the top is low cut. I am afraid if she jumps too much she will be slipping out.

My dress is tight down to my thighs and then flares out. The top is a halter, low v-neck enough to make my chest pop but not so they're spilling out like a certain someone.

I text out my response and hit send.

Emma: *I miss you too! I wish I could dance with you tonight but we have next year. You need to go learn to make amazing films. I love you!*

Logan: *I love you! Tell my brother he better watch his hands and to treat you like a princess.*

I chuckle at his text and Jeremy glances over. "What's so funny?" I show him the text. "Tell him it's not me he should be worried about but every other guy at the Prom when they see you."

I blush but type what he said.

Logan: *Very true. Okay new mission: protect her from other guys.*

I show him the text and he gives me a thumbs up before turning back to Daniel.

Emma: *I could hold my own if some guy tries to do anything. Don't you worry. Now go back to your orientation and I will imagine dancing with you.*

Logan: *Text me when you get home so I know you're safe.*

He is always making sure I'm okay.

Emma: *Will do! Kisses*

Right as I am about to put my phone away, it vibrates again. He always has to get the last word.

Logan: *XOXO*

We arrive at the hotel where the Prom is being held. The theme is "Under the Sea" and they went all out. The entrance is decorated like the beach and there's a long bridge going through a tunnel. Once you reach the end of the bridge, you are taken miles underwater to the deep sea.

We find our table up front and set our purses down. We have about a half an hour till dinner is served and Ashley pulls me onto the dance floor shouting over her shoulder, "you can have her when I'm done."

We dance till our feet start to get sore. I am thankful Ashley did my hair in some crazy updo or it would have been a mess.

They make an announcement that dinner is being served in five minutes so we make our way back to our seats. I sit down next to Jeremy and grab my water. "You have fun out there?"

I sip my water. "Oh yes. I hope you brought your dancing shoes."

We eat dinner which consists of chicken and veggies. It isn't the greatest meal I have ever had, but what can you expect from a school function?

They set up a dessert bar thanks to the culinary club. They decorated sea creature shaped cookies and some sort of vanilla cream cake that looks like a sand castle. Once we have our fill, we head back to the dance floor. A slow song comes on. Jeremy takes my hand and pulls me a little closer.

I place my hand on his shoulder and feel his strong bicep. Logan has plenty of muscle but it's leaner, whereas Jeremy is pure muscle. He is taller than Logan, as well. Normally with heels on I come to Logan's chin but with Jeremy I'm at his chest. I consider myself tall at five-foot-eight but they are both well above six foot.

A few more fast songs play and they announce the Prom king and queen. Of course, Jeremy wins king and Mallory wins queen. They tell the king and queen to pick a partner for the royal waltz.

Jeremy comes over to me and extends his hand, "May I have this dance?" I take his hand and follow him to the middle of the dance floor next to Mallory and her date. I can feel the whispers around me. I am not used to being the center of attention and every girl here is wanting to dance with Jeremy.

A slow ballad starts and I whisper to Jeremy, "I don't know how to waltz."

"Just follow my lead."

Before I can say anything, Jeremy starts spinning around the dance floor. I concentrate on following his steps and try to anticipate what comes next. He spins me away from him and then back in, pulling me close again. We soon spin in a circle as we move around the dance floor.

He whispers in my ear, "In a second I am spinning you so your back is to me and I am going to lift your left leg. Hold around my shoulder with your left arm." I look at him like he is crazy. "Just trust me. You ready?"

I shrug, trying to remember what I am supposed to do. He lifts my left leg and I hold on. He whispers, "Bend your right leg a little and put your right arm out." I do as he says and feel like I'm flying. It's a good thing my dress is very flowy at the bottom or this never would have worked. My smile widens as Jeremy sets me back on the ground.

We dance around in one more circle before he dips me and we pose. I glance up and see him staring back at me intently. For a split second, I think he is going to kiss me but after a minute he lifts me back up. We take a bow and I run over to Ashley, mouthing "bathroom".

Ashley points to me, "we're going to go get a drink. Be right back."

When we get to the bathroom, Ashley checks the stalls as I splash water on my face. "Coast is clear now, what was that?"

"I didn't know we were going to do the waltz. I barely even knew the steps but Jeremy made it easy to follow."

Ashley crosses her arms looking at me closely. "You sure looked like you knew what you were doing. I don't know what was hotter; when he picked you up and spun you around or the dip at the end."

"Ughh, the dip." I think back to the almost kiss. Ashley looks at me questionably. "Ash, I thought he was going to kiss me. Worse than that, for a split second I wanted it to happen. I am the worst girlfriend ever. I love Logan with all my heart and he is the one I want to be with, so why am I thinking about kissing his brother?"

Ashley bursts out laughing. "That is his iconic move. For how long you had a crush on him I'm surprised you never heard about that. He always uses his waltz skills to pull off his signature move of lifting the girl up and dipping her. It makes the girl feel special."

"What? So that dance was something he has done before?" I hop up on the counter.

"Oh yes." She sits on the counter next to me. "I will admit though, you both do have chemistry when you dance. But off the dance floor you guys fight like brother and sister. It would never work. Logan is a better fit."

"Hey!" I shove her off the counter. "Well I am glad he does that dance with everyone. Who would have thought I would ever be dancing with him."

"It's a good thing I got it on video." Ashley pulls out her phone and hits play. I stare at myself in awe.

I point at the phone. "Is that actually me?"

"Yes it is. You could have been a dancer in another life." She locks her phone and grabs my hand. "Now we better get back to the boys before they send a search party."

Just as we are about to leave, in comes Mallory and Amber. Mallory glares at me.

"I thought you were dating Logan?"

Confused, I say, "I am. Why?"

"Well it sure didn't look like it on the dance floor."

"Jeremy and I are just friends. Logan couldn't go so Jeremy offered to step in."

"Well you better stay away from him. Jeremy is mine. He always comes back to me."

My jaw drops because last I heard Jeremy was so done with her. She makes me so angry that she can go around saying anything. I don't see her much but the few times I do, I want to punch her.

"Jeremy told me..." Ashley pulls me through the door before I can finish my sentence which is probably a good thing. "Thanks. She makes me so mad." I sigh. "Ashley, do you think Logan will get mad when he sees that video?"

She pauses before saying, "I saw the way you looked at Jeremy back when you had a crush on him and I see the way you look at Logan now. It is completely different. Your face lights up the second Logan walks in the room and the way you talk about him would make anyone fall in love with him. You are completely in love with Logan, and I see you spending forever together."

I sigh in relief and give her a hug before we head back to where we left the guys. We dance a few more songs before they call out the last dance.

The limo drops Ashley and Daniel off first.

We get to my house and Jeremy walks me to my door. "Thank you for being my date. You look beautiful if I haven't already told you tonight. I had an awesome time."

"I'm sure you would've had a great time with one of the many girls that wanted to go with you."

"Yeah but they wouldn't have been you. Now go call that brother of mine and tell him you're leaving him for me."

I give him an "Are you kidding me?" look.

"I am totally just kidding. Although if you weren't dating my brother, I would be kissing you right now." I stand there speechless.

"I had my chance, and let's be real — you and me could never work. You're like my little sister who I can tease." He bends down to kiss me on the cheek. "Goodnight Emma."

When my legs regain the ability to move, I go inside and run upstairs to call Logan. He answers after the first ring. "There's my love. So how was prom?"

"We had a blast and danced way too much. My feet are going to be sore tomorrow."

"So did my brother behave?"

"He fought off all those guys like a pro."

"I hope there weren't too many."

I have to tell him what almost happened. He is probably going to be mad but I don't feel right not telling him.

"No there weren't any. Logan... I have to tell you something..."

"Uhh ohh... that doesn't sound good. What happened?"

"Well, Jeremy won Prom king."

"That's awesome and doesn't sound bad."

"I wasn't done. They have the royal waltz and he chose me as his partner."

"Still not getting it."

I sigh and pause before continuing. "Logan the dance was very close, meaning our bodies were pressed up together. He did this spin move and then lifted me. Then he did more spin moves and dipped me at the end. I thought he was going to kiss me." I pause hoping to get the courage to say the next part. "Logan, a part of me wanted him to."

There is silence on the other end and I check my phone to make sure he hasn't hung up. It's still connected. I was right. He is mad. "Logan?"

Logan bursts out laughing. "I can't believe he used the move on you. I am going to give him such a hard time when I talk to him."

I'm shocked he knows his brother has a move. "Ashley said the same thing but I thought she was trying to make me feel better."

"Oh no, it's real and no girl can resist. Including you, it seems. But hey it's okay. I should have known he would do something like that."

"So you aren't mad?"

"Why would I be mad? Because you almost kissed him after I pushed you to go with him. Plus, you told me you once had a crush on him. I know you don't like him anymore."

I fall back on my bed. "I really don't. I am so happy with you. I think I'm just missing you. The whole time, I wished it was you I was dancing with." I sigh.

"What else, Emma?" He always seems to know when something is bothering me.

"He also said if I wasn't dating you he would have kissed me."

"Can you blame him?" I'm silent. "He's a flirt but he's my brother, and I know he would never do anything to hurt me. Same with you. That's why I didn't care about you two going together. He had his shot before I got here and I am glad he didn't do anything because now you're mine. So relax! I wish I was there right now to give you a kiss and make you forget everything."

"Me too, but only two weeks and I get to see you."

"Two weeks too long. Now get some sleep and dream about dancing with me."

"I love you so much!"

"I love you more. Goodnight my love."

"Goodnight."

We hang up and I let out the breath I didn't realize I was holding. I was so worried to tell him and he laughed it off. I'm not worried about us. He is always so understanding. I fall asleep dreaming of the night I had. Only instead of going with Jeremy, I went with Logan, the person I should have gone to Prom with in the first place.

Chapter Twenty-two

The summer goes by quickly. Coach has me swimming five hours a day.

Between that and the two classes I am taking at the local community college, I barely see anyone. Logan didn't come home until mid-July and Ashley got a job at the local pool as a lifeguard.

Jeremy had training for football this fall. He made the right choice to go to FSU. I told him Logan and I would be at as many games as we could, actually cheering for him instead of against him if he had chosen somewhere else.

Logan surprised me for my birthday in mid-June. My parents had a barbecue and bought me a beautiful blue car.

It was nice to have a day off and celebrate with the ones I love.

Coach gave me the week before school off and I spent most of my time with Logan. We enjoyed our time together chilling by the pool in the sunshine and spending time at what we now called "our park."

We both know this next year is going to be busy. So much for a relaxing senior year. I will be taking two classes at the community college in the morning and then going to the high school to take my regular classes in the afternoon. Coach has me swimming an hour and half in the morning before my college classes and then two and half hours in the afternoon. Saturday mornings I have to train from eight to twelve. Sunday is my only day off. I swear she is going to kill me.

She tells me if I want to be an Olympian that this is what I have to do. She also has me on a strict diet plan with Sunday being my cheat day, but even then, I am restricted.

I have always eaten pretty healthy but I really just have to be careful with sugar which is so hard because I love dessert. My mom and I found some good recipes where I can still satisfy my sweet tooth but with less sugar.

The first day of school, my alarm goes off at the early hour of 5 a.m. I reach to turn it off and slowly roll out of bed. I don't shower since I'll be getting in the pool anyway. I'll shower after practice. My backpack and swim bag with clothes for the day are already in my car. I change into my bathing suit with sweats on top and head to the kitchen. I make some peanut butter toast and grab a banana with some coffee to go. I don't like to eat a lot before practice so I don't get a cramp in the pool.

On my way out, I grab my giant lunch box from the fridge, which I packed the night before with snacks and lunch for the day.

When I get to the pool, I take my sweats off and dive in the water for warm ups. The cold water wakes me up.

Before I know it, my time is up and I have to get ready for class. I shower quickly and throw on some makeup. Thankfully, my hair dries straight so I don't have to worry about blow drying it. I change and hang up my bathing suit to dry for my afternoon practice.

My first class starts at eight at the community college. My class is two hours and then I head back to the high school for the last few classes of the day. My last class is a PE elective. Juniors, seniors and varsity sports students get to choose a sport to focus on. I chose swimming so I can be done with practice earlier and have time in the evenings.

Some days Coach makes me lift light weights and do other cardio such as biking and kickboxing. She wants to switch up my routine and get me stronger.

When 4:45 rolls around, I get out of the pool, rinse off and head to my car to go home. I start my homework, mainly from my college class, and an hour later my mom says dinner is ready.

After dinner, I help clean up. I prep my lunch and clothes for the next day, and then I finish homework and fall into bed exhausted.

This is only day one.

This routine is the same throughout the entire semester. I get used to the early hours and am usually in bed by nine so I can start the day over. I rarely see Ashley and Logan except lunch and our few classes together.

Logan and I talk each night and text throughout the day, but I can't help feel this distance between us. Jeremy has graduated but Logan still hangs with that crowd a lot and Amber is always around. I trust him and try not to let it bother me.

The weather starts to get cold so we eat in the cafeteria. It's the week of Thanksgiving and we have one more day till break.

"So what are you and Logan doing for your one year anniversary?" Ashley asks as she steals one of my grapes.

I pop a grape into my mouth too. "He hasn't told me anything. I do have to start studying for my college exams though.

The truth is we haven't talked about it. We haven't talked much other than our nightly phone calls, but even those are short because I am so exhausted.

"Emma, you study way too much. Plus, you're taking a computer class which can't be that hard and Trigonometry which Logan could help you do in his sleep. I thought this was supposed to be our year of fun. I barely see you between your swim practice and all your classes."

Just then Logan walks up. "You persuade her yet?"

"Persuade me to do what?"

"I was getting to it. Just building up to it and trying to get her to admit she needs to have some fun." Ashley looks at me.

I think back to the past weekend. "I do have fun. Just last weekend we went to the movies."

"Oh wow. Big plans."

Logan sits next to me. "What Ashley is trying to say is how would you like to spend Thanksgiving down in Tallahassee?"

"With you two? What about my family and your parents?" Logan loves to spend Thanksgiving with his family.

"They're coming too!" Ashley shouts. "My parents are going to visit friends up in Maine and I persuaded them to let me stay at your house, but then Logan brought this idea to me. Plus, some time away will do me good after my breakup with Daniel."

They broke up right after Halloween when she found him cheating on her with Mallory. Mallory is a freshman at the local community college so she is still around. He said he always wanted to know what it would be like to be with the Prom queen.

"Okay... but where are we going to stay?" I ask Logan.

"Ahh, that's a good question. My brother is currently living in the dorms and he hates it. Plus his roommate keeps stealing his stuff. He's been looking for a place to move into for the Spring semester. Since his birthday is in January, my parents decided to combine Christmas and birthday gifts this year. They bought a small house just off campus for him."

"A house? Wow, my parents got me a gift card and a new shirt for my birthday. I can't imagine a whole house." Ashley shakes her head amazed at Logan's family. "Must be nice to be rich."

"Ashley!" I shove her in the shoulder.

"What? It's true." She shoves me back.

"Believe me it isn't always amazing but that is beside the point. My parents are giving him the house early so he can start moving in. It has three bedroom and three and a half bathrooms. You two will have a room, my parents will have a room, and Emma's parents will have a room."

"What about you?" If I'm taking a vacation, I want Logan in the same house as me.

"I'll just be on the couch, and I'm sure Jeremy will take the other couch. Anything to get out of his dorm."

"No, you guys take our room. Ash and I will sleep on the couches."

"You are fine. Believe me when I say the couches my parents picked out will not only look amazing but will be just as comfy as a bed, if not better."

"Okay, I guess. So when do we leave?" I pull out my planner.

"Wednesday after your class, Emma. Our flight leaves at two."

I make a note in my planner. "Oh so you were sure this would all happen then?"

Logan shrugs. "I hoped, plus the flight times are pretty open."

I look at him suspiciously. "Well then it's settled. I am assuming my brother knows about this too?"

"Yes, he's coming over to the house on Thursday for Thanksgiving and then Saturday to watch the game. He said Friday he had something."

"I'm so excited!" Ashley squeals.

"Excited to get away for Thanksgiving or to see my brother?" I tease her.

"Wouldn't you like to know." She stands and walks off towards her locker.

"Oh she has it bad." I stand and Logan laughs.

"Know someone else that has it bad?"

"Who might that be?" I smile.

"Oh, just the luckiest guy on earth." He kisses me on the tip of my nose before kissing me on the lips.

We may not talk much lately but it's moments like this that I know we are okay. Plus, what other boyfriend plans a whole vacation for his family, your family, and best friend?

The bell rings and we break apart. "Guess we should go to class." I pull him to our lockers to get our books before class.

Chapter Twenty-three

As soon as my class ends on Wednesday, I run to my car and drive home. My bags are already packed but I throw a few textbooks in my backpack.

"Did I just see you put a textbook in your backpack?"

I turn around with a hand on my hip. "Yes, boyfriend of mine, I did. I need to pass this Trig class and I barely understand any of it."

He takes both my hands. "Okay, if you promise to not study the entire time and just relax and have fun, then I'll help you."

"Oh would you? That would be a lifesaver. I don't understand how this makes sense to you. Sin, cosine, and tangent? It is a different language."

"You didn't promise."

I roll my eyes. "Fine, I promise to have fun and not study the whole time."

"Good. Now give me a kiss. We have a flight to catch." I kiss him and he grabs my duffel bag.

"I thought the flight wasn't till 2pm?"

"Like I said, before the flight times are open. And knowing your best friend, she will still be deciding what to pack."

"Very true." I pick up my backpack and follow him out the door.

When he said the flight times were open, I wasn't sure what he meant. Now it all makes sense as I stand on the tarmac looking up at a private jet. "I knew they were rich, but not their own private jet rich." Ashley stares at the jet next to me.

Logan walks up behind us. "We share it with a few of my dad's coworkers so technically it isn't just ours."

"But you can use it whenever you want." Ashley is still staring at the jet.

"For the most part, yes." Logan hands our bags to one of the guys to put on the plane. I wondered how Logan was able to fly back and forth so easily this past summer.

We get on the plane and look around. I am trying not to freak out about how nice it is. I have only ever seen the inside of a private jet in movies, but to actually be standing in one now is crazy. I lean against a chair to make sure I don't fall over. They didn't exaggerate the inside in movies. From the huge leather white seats with tons of leg room to the flight attendants handing out champagne. "I feel like I am in some super nice first class."

It even smells rich like leather.

We sit and I am handed a glass of champagne. Ashley takes the seat across from me. Yes, they have seats that face each other.

She takes a glass of champagne and leans back, "I could get used to this."

Logan sits down next to me. "It has it perks."

I see my mom and dad enter the plane. My mom looks around amazed and almost uncomfortable. She never was one for expensive things, having had to work her whole life until she met my dad. She then became a stay at home mom raising my brother and I. Now she runs a very successful food blog. My dad sees Mr. Anderson and they begin discussing FSU football.

Mrs. Anderson comes up to my mom and they sit down next to each other. I hear her say, "We are so glad you guys and Emma were able to join us. Emma has talked non-stop about her amazing parents, and we're excited to get to know you all better."

I can tell my mom is embarrassed. She replies, "Oh, I'm sure Emma didn't say that much but nevertheless we are glad to be here. It'll be great to see the FSU campus again. I haven't been back in forever."

"That is where you and Emma's dad, Nathan, met, isn't it?"

"Yes we did..." She starts in on the story of how they met and I smile, glad my mom is enjoying herself.

I turn back to Ashley and Logan who are now in a debate over which is a better movie series — Star Wars or Star Trek. I lean back listening to my best friend and boyfriend go back and forth. Ashley may come off as the girly girl, always having to look perfect but deep down she is a huge nerd.

I look out the window at the rainy, overcast weather. I can't wait for the warm sunshine of Florida.

As we taxi down the runway, I can't help getting excited for the weekend. This semester has been very busy and stressful. A few days away will be perfect.

Before I know it, we are landing in Tallahassee. I have only been to Florida once when we moved my brother into college. Being a hardcore Seminole fan, I always wanted to attend a home game but I never had the chance. We go to tons of away games that are much closer to home in Tennessee.

I begin to wonder if Jeremy gets any free tickets. I'll have to ask him. He's after all the quarterback and if anyone should get tickets, he should.

We pull up to Jeremy's soon to be house. I remember Logan saying it had three bedrooms and three and a half bathrooms but this looks way bigger. My house back home has three bedrooms and three bathrooms and this looks double the size.

Mr. Anderson gives us a tour since they have been here before. We walk through the kitchen, overlooking the backyard. It still has a swing set from the previous owners. The living room has a huge ceiling with a loft and two bedrooms upstairs both with en-suite bathrooms. The third bedroom is the master. It is on the other side of the house separated by the garage. It is basically its own guest house. It even has its own mini kitchen, huge bathroom and side door entrance so you don't have to go through the main part of the house. You can live on that side and not even know you are connected to the rest of the house.

Mrs. Anderson turns to my parents, "We thought you all could have this bedroom. A romantic trip for you two being back to where you met. Give you all some privacy for a fun reunion trip."

My mom shakes her head. "Oh we couldn't take this room."

Mr. Anderson jumps in, handing her a key. "We insist."

My mom glances at my dad skeptically as she takes the key. "If you're sure."

"Yes, we're absolutely sure." Mrs. Anderson says.

My parents start unpacking and we head to the other side of the house.

Ashley and I take the smallest of the three bedrooms which has two double beds.

Mr. and Mrs. Anderson take the other bedroom with the king size bed. If I hadn't seen the room where my parents were staying, I would have said their room was the master. It is almost as big with a huge bathroom and a walk-in closet. Our room is big, just a little smaller bathroom and closet.

Once we are settled in, we order some Chinese food and watch a Thanksgiving movie together in the living room. Jeremy calls and says his conditioning is running late so he won't be able to make it but he will be there bright and early tomorrow.

Later, I fall asleep instantly on the softest mattress I have ever felt. It feels like I'm floating on clouds.

Chapter Twenty-four

The next day, I wake up at seven in the morning which is late for me since I normally wake up at five every day. I roll over trying to go back to sleep. After fifteen minutes of trying and failing, I quietly get out of bed. I change into some workout gear and tiptoe downstairs.

Logan is still asleep on the couch. I give him a kiss on the cheek. He stirs and looks up at me, still half asleep. "Hey, what time is it?" He reaches for his phone.

"Shhh... it is almost 7:30. I'm going for a run. You go back to sleep and I'll wake you up when I get back. Unless you want to go?"

"I think I'll sleep some more."

"You sure? It'll be fun."

"I'm good."

"Okay, I know you hate running but we can go check out the FSU gym later if you want?"

"Sure, and I only like running when I'm chasing you." He gives me another kiss. "You better wake me up when you get back."

"I will." I stand and go to the kitchen to grab some coffee and an apple. I find Mr. Anderson in the kitchen drinking coffee and reading the paper. He looks up as I enter. "Good morning Emma. What are you doing up so early?"

"I couldn't sleep. Normally I get up at five. I'm surprised I slept in this late."

"Ahh yes. I know what you mean. Can't sleep past six anymore myself. Are you heading out for a run?"

"Yep, I tried to get Logan to go with me but him and running don't mix. We might go check out the gym at FSU later though."

"He never has liked running, but get him in a gym and he will stay there all day."

"He's pretty funny with that. I'd much rather be enjoying the outdoors during my workout."

"Well, Jeremy is headed over now if you want to wait for him. I am sure he would love to go for a run."

"Sure I might do that." I sit down and take a bite of my apple.

As I wait for Jeremy, Mr. Anderson and I discuss FSU football and how they haven't done as bad as we thought for being a complete rebuilding team.

"I think it's that quarterback they have. He has one arm on him."

"You're just saying that because you are my dad." We hear from the kitchen door. Jeremy walks in and gives his dad a hug. He bends down to give me a hug as well. He notices my running gear. "You going for a run?"

"I was planning on it but your dad here thought you might want to go so I was waiting."

"Sure, let me go change. Umm... where is the bathroom?" His dad points to the door near the stairs. A minute later he's back. "Now Dad I have awesome receivers so it isn't just me. The defense helps out too."

"Oh I know son, but a dad can still be proud."

"Of course." He smiles at his dad and then turns to me. "You ready?"

"Sure." I rinse out my cup and grab my sneakers. After five minutes of running, I take off my jacket, already feeling drenched in sweat. "How is it this hot so early in the morning?"

"Welcome to Florida. It is always sunny and warm. I do have to say I miss the blustery cold mornings and that slight chance of snow."

"Yeah but this is like heaven. I can't wait to come here next year."

"Oh did you get in?"

"I haven't heard back yet but fingers crossed." Jeremy holds up two crossed fingers as I take off. He immediately catches up to me and he points to take the next left.

As we get closer, I see the brick buildings up ahead and know we are officially on the FSU campus. As we run by, I gaze at each building and fall in love with the school all over again. We head back to the house and I push myself to keep up with Jeremy.

We enter the kitchen and smell the turkey in the oven. I love the smells of Thanksgiving.

I chug a big glass of water and turn on the faucet for more.

"Whoa there, you a little winded from all that running?" Jeremy bumps my shoulder as he reaches over to fill his glass.

I glance at Jeremy as I finish my water. "I don't do much running in the pool. It is a different cardio, so yes, I am winded keeping up with you."

"I bet I could beat you in the pool now."

"No, she can definitely still beat you. I bet even more than last time. She's been training nonstop and it's been paying off." Logan pours himself a cup of coffee. I walk over and kiss him on the cheek.

"Good morning sleepy head. I was just coming to wake you".

"Good morning. Did you have a good run? I see you found a stray along the way?" He nods to Jeremy and takes a sip of his coffee to hide his smirk.

"Yes, he took me over to campus and everything was so quiet and peaceful. I can't wait to come here next year with you."

"We still have to get in."

"I know, but I have faith."

We both sent in our applications and FSU is our first choice. We can't wait to come here together next year.

He leans down to kiss me. "So when is this race happening where you beat my brother again?"

I glance at Jeremy. "How about this afternoon? Logan and I were thinking about checking out the gym. If the pool is open, we could go then."

"Sounds like a plan. Now where can I shower? The one down here didn't have a shower." Mr. Anderson who has been sitting at the table the whole time looks over, "Your mom is just finishing up and then you can use ours. Can anyone come to this race later?"

"Sure, Dad. By the way, what kind of deal did you get on renting this place? I can't take my roommate anymore, and I am so ready to move out."

Mr. Anderson freezes for a second but recovers quickly, "You'll have to ask your mom."

"Okay." He heads outside to grab his bag.

Logan asks his dad. "He doesn't know this is his yet?"

"No, we were going to tell him at lunch."

"He is going to be so surprised." I drink the rest of the water before putting it on the counter for later. "I'm going to take a shower."

When I get upstairs, I hear the shower running. I grab some clothes while I wait for Ashley to be done. Five minutes later she comes into the room with a robe on and a towel on her head. "Hey, where were you?"

"I went for a run. Have to keep up with my workouts or Coach will kill me."

"True. Is their coffee downstairs?"

"Yep. Mr. Anderson and Logan are down there too. My mom must have put the turkey in the oven while I was gone. I am going to shower and then go find her to start the rest of the dishes."

"Okay. What time is your brother getting here?"

"I'm not sure. We aren't eating till two, so probably right before that. Why do you ask?"

"Oh, just curious. I am going to change and get some coffee before I do my hair. I need caffeine."

I shake my head at her, knowing full well why she wanted to know when my brother would be here. She doesn't want him seeing her without makeup on and her hair done. I head into the bathroom to shower and get ready to help my mom prepare the Thanksgiving meal.

When I get out of the shower, I see Ashley hyperventilating on her bed. "What's wrong?"

"I thought you said your brother wasn't here yet?"

"He isn't."

"Oh he is. I was getting coffee and he came in with bagels for everyone. He saw me looking like this."

"You look beautiful. Plus, it's not like he hasn't seen you without makeup."

"Yeah, when I was younger, but not recently."

"Ashley, you look great without makeup. But if you really have to wear some then go. He'll still be downstairs when you're done."

"You know most girls would be weirded out if their best friend liked their brother."

"Yeah well I'm not most girls am I?"

"You most definitely are not. Now give me fifteen minutes and I'll meet you downstairs."

"Sounds good." I quickly brush my hair and put on some light eye makeup before making my way downstairs. I run up to Ty and give him a big hug.

"Was that Ashley I saw? I didn't know she was coming".

"Yeah! I'm super happy she was able to come."

"I thought it was her. She was getting coffee when I walked in. She saw me and was gone instantly. She didn't even take her coffee." He points at the full cup on the counter.

"Oh yeah, she must have forgotten something upstairs." I was not about to tell him the real reason she had taken off running and get in between whatever they have going on.

"Hmm... girls are confusing. Anyway, I brought you some low-fat cream cheese over there and an everything thin bagel."

"Yes, you are the best."

"Gotta look out for my future Olympian sister." He messes my hair.

I push him away and grab my bagel.

My mom comes into the kitchen a few minutes later and we start cooking. Mrs. Anderson tells us to put her to work too. She talks about wanting to learn to cook more meals and what better way than with the biggest meal of the year. We put her to work peeling the potatoes. My mom and I start on the pumpkin and apple pies.

When Ashley comes down, she starts the green bean and sweet potato casseroles.

When Mrs. Anderson finishes the potatoes, she cuts them and puts them in the pot to boil. I help her with the stuffing and before we know it, we are almost done.

While everything is cooking, we sit down at the table, relaxing, and enjoying some girl time while the guys are outside. The kitchen is already smelling delicious!

Chapter Twenty-five

About an hour later, the guys come inside cheering and grab the hors d'oeuvres. We laid out a variety of meats, cheeses, and crackers along with a spinach dip and buffalo dip.

They have been playing basketball — sons versus dads. The boys won but the dads definitely gave them a challenge, or so they claimed. They ask if any of us want to play two-hand touch football. Ty and my dad come over and pick me up from my chair.

"Emma will play." My dad says.

Ashley jumps in. "I'll play." I grin at her, knowing the only reason she wants to play is the chance that Ty will tag her.

We make Jeremy the all around quarterback with Logan and Ty as captains. The first to five touchdowns wins.

To Logan's dismay, Ty picks me first so Logan picks Ashley. Ty then picks our dad and Logan selects his dad. We have the ball first and we jog over to Jeremy.

"Okay so how do you guys want to do this?"

Ty points at me. "Emma is the fastest, so if we're running the ball I vote for her." My dad nods in agreement.

"Okay, let's do a running play first. I will fake to you Mr. Collins and hand the ball off to Emma. Ty, I want you to run to the left. Ready?"

We put our hands in and say, "Goooo, Collins!"

We line up against the others. Jeremy yells "ready, set, hike" from behind us. My dad and Ty take off running as Jeremy fakes to my dad. I run forward and before Logan realizes, I circle back and take the ball from Jeremy. I run towards the other end of the field. With me having to circle back, Logan is already in front of me. He touches me right before the goal line.

We line up again and this time we choose a pass play. Jeremy is going to pass to Ty but fake a hand off to me. We run the play and Jeremy throws a high ball that Ty easily catches. Ashley makes a good attempt jumping up to get it. I think she was scared to jump on my brother. We score and swap sides.

They run a few plays before they finally score. Logan has a good maneuver move around me, but I catch him. We end up winning 5-3.

Mr. Anderson sits out the next game, to watch with his wife and my mom. We switch up the teams, keeping Logan and Ty as captains. This time Logan picks first. He looks at me. "Sorry Emma, you're good, but I have to win this time." He points to Jeremy. "Big bro, get over here."

Ty points at me. "Are you ready to put that throwing arm to use?" I nod.

Logan picks my dad and we get Ashley. Since we have two girls on our team, we get the ball first.

We start with a running play. I fake to Ty but hand the ball off to Ashley who takes off running. Logan tags her halfway to the line.

Next is a pass play. I plan on throwing to Ashley. I say hike and they take off running. I see Logan blocking Ashley and my dad blocking Ty. Jeremy comes running at me just as I see Ty move to the left and get open. Ashley is still blocked so I throw a spiral to Ty. Right after I release the ball, Jeremy makes it to me and looks back as Ty catches it in the end zone. "Wow, I didn't know you had an arm like that."

"There's a lot you don't know about me." I laugh and Jeremy shrugs.

We switch sides and they score instantly. In our next round, Ty plays quarterback.

A few more rounds go by and the score is 4-4. We somehow manage to keep up with them but I think they are just taking it easy on us. Either that or we're just sneaky.

We are on offense again and I am back to playing quarterback.

We slowly make our way down the field till we are right by the goal line. This is our last attempt at scoring and we are doing a running play. Ty will fake running into the end zone, then circle back and I will hand him the ball.

I say hike and he takes off. He is circling back when I see Jeremy nod at Logan.

Next thing I know, they are both running at me yelling "Blitz". I see a gap in the middle and take off running with everything I have. My dad is busy covering Ashley before he can make it to me.

Right as I cross into the end zone, Logan catches up and tackles me to the ground. I gaze up at him and smile. The sun is shining down around his face making him look like he is glowing. "You aren't supposed to tackle me."

"Well maybe I just wanted an excuse for you to be in my arms."

"You never need an excuse for that, but thanks for the path to the end zone."

He gazes back at me. "Where did you learn to play like that?"

"Well if you remember, my dad is a retired NFL wide receiver and the coach at our high school. I've been playing football with my dad and brother since I could walk. Just one of my many talents. If you stick around, maybe you'll see more." I wink at him.

After washing up we sit down at the table and dig into the food. As a Thanksgiving tradition, we go around the table saying something we're thankful for.

I mention I am thankful for my coach, even though I feel like sometimes I am going to die from how hard she pushes me. I know if I get to the Olympics, it will be because of her.

Mrs. Anderson says she is thankful that she got to help cook this meal and learn some cooking tips. She looks over at Mr.

Anderson and he urges her on. "This is a better time than any. We are so proud of our boys, and with Christmas coming up we wanted to give one of them an early gift. Jeremy, you have been working hard and doing an awesome job at football, so we thought you might want your own space. Your dad and I bought you a house."

"What? Are you serious?" Jeremy jumps up from the table to give them hugs. "When do I get to see this house?"

"Well you're currently in it." Mr. Anderson gestures to the house. "There are a few rules though. 1. This is a family house, so you better make room for us if we come to visit. 2. If your brother goes to school at FSU next year and doesn't want to stay in the dorms, he'll be allowed to stay here."

Jeremy high fives Logan. "Of course, my little bro can be my roommate if he wants. Any other rules?"

"Last rule, if something breaks, during let's say a party, which we do not condone but we were also in college once upon a time, then it is your responsibility and under your expense to fix it."

"I will! Ahh... thanks so much Mom and Dad. I can't wait to start moving in. This house is amazing. I'm taking the room you all are in. That is one master bedroom!"

"You don't want the room on the other side of the garage?" Logan asks surprised. "If I come here next year, I call that room." I am just as surprised that Jeremy didn't want that room.

"That is a cool room, but I like having access to the full kitchen. Plus, I figured that would be a good room if I decide to have a roommate. Then they can have their own space."

We finish up our meal and the guys clean the kitchen. "Are you two still up for checking out the gym?"

I nod and Logan looks at Jeremy. "Are you ready to be beat for a second time today? First football and next swimming?"

"I doubt she'll beat me again but I am down. I have to run to my apartment first but I will meet you there in let's say an hour?"

"Sounds good. And get ready to eat my waves." I grab a bottle of water and go upstairs to get ready.

As I get halfway up the stairs, I hear Jeremy tell Logan, "You might want to start prepping her for a loss, little bro." I just laugh and continue upstairs.

Chapter Twenty-six

"Wow, this place is amazing." I gaze around at the FSU rec center. I could do without the smell of sweat but that is just from the gym.

"Wait till you see the best part!" Jeremy gestures to the doors ahead. I take Logan's hand as we follow Jeremy. On the other side of the doors is the pool hall. I breathe in the chlorine scent.

"Yes, this place is officially the best. All I know is I better get that acceptance letter sooner rather than later. I can't wait to find out if I got in."

"You will get in. They would be crazy not to. Plus, you already got early admission to Brown and Yale. I don't know why a non-Ivy league school would deny you." Logan kisses me.

"Alright, lovebirds." He lightly punches Logan. "Are you ready to see me kick your girlfriend's butt in swimming?"

"Good luck bro." Logan slaps him on the shoulder as our parents walk in.

"Where are Ash and Ty?" I look around for them thinking maybe they are just slow.

"Ashley wanted a tour of the campus and Ty volunteered." My mom gives me a knowing look. I shake my head thinking of Ashley and her tactics to get Ty to spend time with her. Although my brother volunteered to show her around campus so that is interesting.

"So is this race happening?" Mr. Anderson walks over to us. "I'm cheering for this one right here." He places his hands on my shoulders. "You ready Emma?"

"Thanks for the support Dad." Jeremy takes off his shirt.

"Anytime son. You know someone beating you in something once in a while is good for you, especially a girl." He pats him on the shoulder as he goes to sit on the bleachers along the side of the pool.

Logan massages my shoulders. "You ready?".

"Oh yeah!" I hand Logan my bag and take off my sweats. I do some quick stretches. "Okay, we're going to test out that endurance. This is twenty-five yards one way?" Jeremy nods. "Okay, close enough to twenty-five meters. We are going to do a 400-meter race or in this case, slightly under."

Jeremy looks out at the pool, mentally calculating the distance. "That is eight laps correct?" I nod. "Okay sounds easy enough. Being on the football team, I have built up plenty of endurance. You can ask the cheerleaders about my endurance too." He winks as he stretches his arms above his head.

"Gross. I did not need to know that."

"You ready?" Logan asks. We both step up to the edge of the pool. "Okay on my mark. Eight laps and first to touch my hand wins." We put on our goggles and prepare to dive in. "On your mark, get set, go!"

We dive in. The second I feel the warm water, I am in my element. It feels good on my sore muscles from all my training. It is nice that they heat the pool. The cold water is always a shock and takes a minute to get used to. This water is warm and feels great.

Stroke, stroke, breath.

Stroke, stroke, breath.

I see Jeremy ahead of me. I'm not worried. We are only on lap one of eight. If he keeps going like that he is going to burn out before the end. I save my energy for the end and keep swimming.

I flip around and start on lap five. This is the point I start gaining on whoever is first, in this case Jeremy. We are neck and neck. As I flip around for lap six, I pull ahead of Jeremy. By lap seven, I am a good ten strokes in front and on the last lap he is only halfway back before I hit Logan's hand. When Jeremy finally gets to the end, he is out of breath.

I can't help saying, "who is a little winded now?"

"Yeah, yeah. I run, not swim." Jeremy splashes me.

I splash him back. "The thing with the longer swim races especially the 400-meter and 800-meter is that you can't put all your energy into the first few laps or else you'll never make it by the end."

"Yeah, I started realizing that about halfway but it was already too late. Good race though. I guess you're officially the swim champion." He lifts himself out of the pool and grabs his towel. "This is definitely some serious cardio and stretching for your arms and legs. I am going to talk to my coach about incorporating more swimming into our workouts."

I hop up next to him. "Why do you think I love swimming?"

Logan wraps me in a towel and gives me a quick kiss before pulling away. "What, you don't want to give your girlfriend a hug?"

Logan backs up. "Don't you dare! I am dry and plan to stay like that." I inch towards him and before he can get away, I pull him into a hug. When I let go, I see a huge wet spot on the front of his shirt.

He glances down at his shirt. "Thanks a lot. Guess I will have to take it off."

"I won't complain." He slowly inches his shirt up almost to his chest before dropping it. Only giving me a peek at his abs.

"You would like that wouldn't you." He picks me up and gives me another hug.

Our parents walk over to congratulate me and tell Jeremy he put in a good effort.

Mr. Anderson walks over to Jeremy. "Good job son."

"Thanks Dad. Emma is a great swimmer and she deserved that win. I'll get her next time."

Upon hearing my name, I say to Jeremy and his dad, "name the time and place."

Logan wraps his arm around my shoulders. "You go change and then let's check out the rest of the gym."

"Sounds good. Did you bring another shirt?"

Logan glances down at his shirt once again and shakes his head. "Nah, this should dry pretty quick."

We explore the rest of the gym and it only cements my desire to come here. I can't wait to hopefully spend the next four years here with Logan, Jeremy and my brother.

"You would think all the training I have been doing would prepare me for hours of shopping, but I swear my legs are more tired than after a week of swim practice." I fall onto my bed.

"You say that every year. I'm just mad that the guys wouldn't go with us." She falls next to me.

"You know the guys and football. Like they would ever give up a chance to watch an FSU practice. Speaking of guys, how was that tour with my brother?"

"Oh you know your brother. He was nothing but a gentleman, holding doors open, pointing to all the different buildings and flirting with every girl except me."

"Ash, he is a sophomore in college. You can't expect him to not talk to girls or date, or whatever else he does. I don't ask because I really don't want to know."

She rests her head on my shoulder. "I know but it is hard. How did you get over your crush on Jeremy?"

"I fell in love with his brother."

"Right..." She looks at me hopeful. "Do you have any long lost brothers?"

"I hope not. I can barely handle one. We just need to find you a man that isn't a cheater or a sophomore player in college, but first I need to study." I open up my book to read over some Trig formulas.

"Fine, Miss obsessive studier. I'm gonna go talk to Jeremy. Maybe he'll start to like me."

I throw a pillow at her. "Good luck with that. Pretty sure he is about as close to settling down as my brother is."

She shrugs. "Fine, I'll talk to Logan instead." She closes the door before I can throw another pillow. I really hope one day she will find someone amazing. Maybe it will be my brother, but that would require him to want to settle down and I don't see that happening for a while. She jokes about Jeremy but I know they have zero chemistry so that would never work, unfortunately.

I turn back to my notes, hoping to get some studying done. After a few minutes of reading the same formula, I am already bored. How does Logan like this?

Chapter Twenty-seven

Saturday morning, I roll over to see the clock says ten. I realize I don't have much time to help my mom make our leftover Thanksgiving tailgating snacks before the annual Seminole/Gator game. I take a shower and go downstairs to get some coffee.

When I get to the kitchen, everyone is already up. "Hey babe." Logan gives me a kiss. "I was about to come up and see if you were alive."

"You never sleep in this late." My mom sets a bowl of yogurt with mixed fruit in front of me.

"I know. It was probably that Trig homework that put me into a deep sleep."

"I can help you later." Logan sits down next to me stealing a raspberry.

"Hey!" I swat at his hand. "I've been eating terribly these past few days. I need to get back on my training diet and this is all mine." I wink at him and turn to my mom. "Have you already started on the tailgate foods?"

"Uhhh..." She glances at Logan. He shakes his head. *What is that about?*

"We decided this year that we were going to order in. Figured you would want something cleaner to eat. The guys want chicken wings but Logan said they have wraps too."

"Okay..." I look back and forth between my mom and Logan. "What time is Ty getting here?"

My mom turns around so I can't see her face and a good minute passes before she answers. "He had some errands to run this morning so he was going to get here right before the game." I know something suspicious is going on with my mom and Logan but I don't know what.

I ask Logan. "What should we do till the game starts then?"

"Well when you're done with breakfast I thought you, me, and Ashley could go drive around Tallahassee to see what game day looks like. Plus, we have to pick up the food and be back here before game time."

"Sounds perfect." I finish my bowl of fruit and yogurt.

I dress in my Anderson jersey #13. Jeremy bought jerseys for Ashley and I with his number on them saying we have to wear them so everyone will know he is the best. Him and his big ego.

When Ashley is finished in the shower, we put black lines under our eyes. We even add a #13 on our cheeks. Since we are watching the game here, I figure Jeremy will never know or be able to use it to feed his ego.

There is a car waiting for us outside. We drive around for a bit, taking in all the fans making their way to the game and booing Gator fans.

As we get closer to the stadium, all I want to do is go inside and watch the game. Jeremy said he didn't have any extra tickets. He'd promised them to some friends before he knew we were coming. We tried to buy tickets but they were all sold out. I am not surprised as this is a huge rivalry game every year.

I notice the time in the car and nudge Logan. "Hey we should probably get that food and head home so we don't miss kickoff."

"I want to show you something first." The driver pulls up to the stadium.

We walk to a side entrance and Logan shows the security guard his driver's license. We walk through a hallway before entering a tunnel. At the end of the tunnel, I realize we are on the field. I look around in awe. I can see the clean white lines on the field. The smell of freshly cut grass mixed with concession food fills my nose.

We walk up a set of stairs and make our way to the 50-yard line. I stumble back when I see my family and Logan's parents seated in the third row. "What's going on?"

"I thought you might want to watch the game in person versus at home on a TV."

"Seriously?" Logan nods and I jump up and down. I throw my arms around him before running over to my parents and my brother. "Did you guys know about this?" They nod and I turn back to Ashley. "Did you?"

She nods too. "I just found out about it this morning though."

We take our seats and I squeeze Logan's hand. "Have I told you how thankful I am for you?"

"Are you thankful for me being amazing or for my connections?"

"Both!" I nudge him, jokingly. "This is awesome."

We watch the Seminoles destroy the Gators, once again. Jeremy does amazing as the quarterback and I am truly impressed.

After the game is over, we stay in our seats waiting for Jeremy to come back out.

"Hey everyone! I'm glad you all made it." He talks to his dad who congratulates him and starts talking about different plays they ran. My dad joins in and mentions some play from when Jeremy played for him in high school. I always forget that my dad coached him. I still go to the football games every Friday night and I am just so used to my dad being down there that I don't really pay attention. I just like the game.

He eventually makes his way over to us and Logan gives him a hug. "Awesome job bro."

"Thanks little bro." He turns to me. "Nice number on your cheek Emma. Are you a fan?"

I rub my cheek, totally forgetting I put it on as a joke. Now I probably have a big smear across my cheek.

"Please don't get a bigger head than you already have." I punch him in the shoulder. "But nice job keeping those Gators back. We can't have them winning."

"Anytime. Well, I best be getting back to the locker room to change. A bunch of the guys and I are going to a party tonight to celebrate. You four wanna come?" He points at Ashley, Ty, Logan and I.

Ashley shouts "yes". We laugh and Logan adds, "guess we are going." My brother agrees too.

We meet up with Jeremy later at the house party. Walking in, I see beer kegs and people everywhere that we can barely get in the door. The music blares some pop song.

Ashley and Ty go to get drinks. They come back and Ty hands Logan a beer while Ashley hands me a red solo cup with some blue concoction in it. "Ashley what is this?"

"I don't know. Just drink it." I take a small sip and gag at whatever is in the cup. It reeks of alcohol and is so sweet, I might throw up. I knew it would have alcohol but the smell is like straight rubbing alcohol.

"Right, I'm going to go search for some water." I give Logan a kiss on the cheek.

"Do you want me to go with you?"

I shake my head. "I'll meet you back here."

In the kitchen, I bump into a couple making out. "Sorry." I start to walk away when the couple pulls apart.

"Hey Emma. I didn't know you all were here already." He pushes back his hair that has fallen on his forehead. The girl he was making out with tries to get his attention back.

"Jer bear, come back here." He holds up his finger signaling her to give him a minute.

"Where is everyone else?" Jeremy looks around for the others.

The girl looks at me with a death glare. I grab onto Jeremy's arm and pretend to whisper but really shout my words. "I got you that ointment for you know... that problem you have." I quickly glance down.

Jeremy's jaw drops for a brief second before he recovers. "Yes, Emma. I thought we weren't going to talk about that here." He looks around, hoping no one is listening but, of course, they are.

I kiss him on the cheek. "Okay. I'll be over there with your friend." I glance back over at Logan who is standing there snickering.

I walk over to Logan and feel Jeremy come up behind me not even ten seconds later. He wraps his arms around me and gives me a sloppy kiss on the cheek. "Emma, I don't know whether to kiss you or kill you right now. That was brilliant but now every girl is going to think something is wrong with me. Thankfully most of them don't care and just want a piece of this."

I punch his arm. "You are so full of yourself. I was trying to help and thought it would be funny."

"Bro, you should have seen your face when she said that." Logan adds.

"I was not expecting that from Emma. Thanks again for saving me. That girl always finds me."

"You're the big quarterback superstar. Anyway, I think we are going to head out but we are looking for Ash."

"Last I saw her she was on the balcony. Here I'll help you find her." He throws an arm around each of our shoulders and steers us to the balcony.

Out on the balcony, we see Ashley talking to some guy. I can tell from here that she is putting on all her moves. As we get closer, she sees me and winks. She excuses herself from the guy and walks over to us. "Hey what's up?"

"We were going to head out. You ready?"

She glances back at the guy. "I kinda want to stay. Do you mind?"

"I'll make sure she gets home safely." Jeremy says.

"I'll see you at home." Ashley gives me a hug.

"Be safe." I then look at Jeremy. "I'm trusting you with my best friend."

"Scouts honor, I will bring her home safe." He signals with his hand.

"Go have fun but don't do anything I wouldn't do." She laughs as I push her back to the guy. She knows I would never do anything with a guy I just met but Ash is definitely not me. I'm sure she will at least make out with him.

I give Jeremy a hug. "Thanks for keeping an eye on her."

Logan pats him on the back. "Please watch her. She can be a little crazy." Jeremy nods as we head out.

As the driver pulls away from the house, I can't help but watch it get smaller and smaller. I ask Logan, "Can we trust your brother? I found him in the kitchen earlier making out with that same girl he wanted saving from."

"Yes, we can trust him. If I could choose anyone to trust the most, I would pick my brother. He may be crazy, but he always has my back. Plus, I have already trusted him with what I hold most dear."

"What's that?"

"You." He kisses me deeply, pushing every worried thought out of my head. He pulls me close as I cuddle next to him thinking I wouldn't want to be anywhere else.

Chapter Twenty-eight

The Senior Winter Ski Trip is three days between Christmas and New Year's. Ashley is coming over to help me pack. She says I have to be fashionable and warm. Since Logan is going, I have to look good. If it were up to me, I would just have my bibs, jacket and snow boots. Knowing her, I am going to be wearing an assortment of sweaters and some sort of cute snow pants. Do they even make those?

"Hey you. Are you ready to pack for this epic trip?" I look up to see Ashley standing in my doorway.

"Yes! I have been dreaming about this trip since we were freshmen."

It's a special trip the seniors take to an exclusive ski resort. They have huge fireplaces to cuddle up in front of, hot tubs to chill out in, rooms with amazing views, and then there are the highly rated ski slopes.

"Oh this was at your front door." She tosses me a small box.

I open it and immediately close it.

"What is it?"

"Nnn...nothing." I put the box next to me out of reach. "Let's pack."

I was half right about what clothes Ashley would make me wear. She is good about that which I should have known. She gives me a good mix of clothes I feel comfortable in and a few things that I would never wear but are surprisingly comfortable too. One in particular are these leggings. She says they will give me more flexibility to move on the slopes but still keep my legs warm.

I go into my bathroom to gather the toiletries I will need. As I come out, I see Ashley pick up the box. Before I can grab it from her, she opens it.

"Whoa. What is this?" She pulls out the dried red rose and the note underneath. She reads it. "Roses are red, violets are blue, this ski trip will be a new start for me and you."

She flips it over looking for more. "Is this from Logan?"

"Umm yeah, maybe." I take the box and note from her to put it in the secret shoebox in my closet. Ashley followed me and peers over my shoulder. I quickly close the shoebox but not before she sees other notes and trinkets in it.

"Have you been holding out on me with the cute notes Logan has been sending?"

"They're private, and I wanted to keep them to myself."

"Now you have to show me."

"Fine." I pull out the shoebox and open the top, pushing it towards her.

She starts pulling out different notes. "You said these are from Logan?" I shrug and busy myself with other items I might need.

"These are really creepy. I didn't know Logan could be so dark. Like this one, "I have watched you in the halls, smiling, laughing. One day those smiles and laughs will be all mine."

I shrug again. "He's a filmmaker. Probably just going with his different stories and ideas."

"You two have fun with that. He almost sounds like a stalker."

I quickly turn so she can't see the nervousness on my face. I have been getting these letters and little gifts all semester. At first, I didn't think anything of it but then they started to get darker. I put those at the bottom so hopefully Ashley doesn't get to those. Especially the one that said, "All I want to do is love you forever and keep you safe. I will tie you to a chair, so you will never be able to leave me again."

I should tell her the truth, but I'm hoping one day they will just stop. I take the box from her and put it in the back of my closet with the new note inside.

"Let's go get something to eat. I'm starving."

"Sounds like a plan. Emma, you know if anything were ever going on, you could tell me."

I nod. I know she would go to the ends of the earth to destroy anyone that threatened me and I would do the same for her, but this seems different. It has only been a series of notes and small gifts like the rose or a mini figurine of an Olympian. If anything, they are kinda cute.

The next morning, we arrive at the school bright and early. Well for me it's almost a normal time. Everyone else is still half asleep or chugging cups of coffee.

I hand my duffel bag to the guys loading the bus. Ashley does the same and then practically falls on me. "4 a.m. should be banned. Why do we have to be here so early?"

"So we get there at a decent hour and have time to do something today. We are only there for three days so they want to give us as much time as possible. Would you rather get there super late tonight and have a whole day shot?"

"No." Ashley rests her head on my shoulder. "I need coffee though."

I pull out a big thermos of coffee. "That I do have, but you also have a five hour bus ride you could use to sleep and then have the coffee."

"That sounds like the best idea you have ever had. I'll go find seats."

"Don't forget L..."

"Yes, I won't forget your boy toy stalker." I feel arms wrap around my waist and a head rest on my shoulder.

"What is this about a boy toy stalker? Sounds like the beginning of a great movie."

I turn my head to give him a kiss. "Oh nothing. Ashley just thinks she's funny, and apparently, she's still asleep."

"What? I thought the notes were cute even if they were kind of stalkery." She makes her way to the bus.

"Notes? What notes?" He turns me around so he can see my face.

"I don't know what she's talking about. Like I said she is still asleep or it might be the early hour. Either way, let's go get seats before the good ones are gone."

He gives me one last look and nods. I have a feeling we're going to be talking about this later. He links our fingers, grabs my backpack, and we walk towards the bus.

The bus is one of those super nice coach ones with the slightly reclining seats and actual room for your legs.

Five hours later, we reach the ski resort. Everyone is awake and ready to be off the bus. We stopped about three hours in but most people were asleep.

Everyone files off the bus and finds their bag. We get our room assignments. Boys are on the second floor and girls are on the third. I am rooming with Ashley.

We open the door to our room and both our jaws drop. It has two double beds with end tables, a dresser, a giant flatscreen TV, and a closet. That is where the regular hotel room ends. Then there is a mini kitchen, complete with a fridge, microwave and breakfast bar.

Underneath the TV is a fireplace. It is one of those that can be seen from both sides in the bathroom and bedroom. Next to it in the bathroom is a giant whirlpool tub and a massive walk-in shower.

We go back into the main room and open the doors leading to the balcony. The view is one of the most amazing ones I have ever seen. Mountains extend as far as I can see, all covered in snow. The sky is blue and the clouds are perfectly puffy and white.

"Well look at that view." I hear from below me.

"Logan?" I lean over the side of the railing to see him staring up at me.

"Looks like I have the room right below you."

"I will make sure to stomp around a bunch." I tease.

"Maybe I can pull a Romeo and climb up there, late at night."

"As much as I would love that, I don't want you to slip and fall. I will, however, meet you down in the lobby in five minutes."

Logan laughs and agrees as I see him disappear. I go back in and find Ashley lounging on the bed reading a pamphlet.

"Did you know these are only the basic rooms but there are higher tiers that have a full kitchen, a hot tub on the balcony with full privacy, and twenty-four hour room service? I guess ours only has twelve hour room service from 7 a.m. to 7 p.m. No late night snacks."

"I heard the lobby has twenty-four hour snacks though. I was actually going to meet Logan down there in five minutes. Wanna join?"

"Sure, let's go." We each grab a room key and make our way down to the lobby. Logan is already there.

We find a table and order lunch. We need our energy before we head out on the slopes this afternoon. The nice thing about this place is all the meals are included so we don't have to worry about extra costs. We get breakfast, lunch, dinner, and two snacks throughout the day.

"Who are you rooming with?" Ashley asks Logan.

"I'm not sure yet. He wasn't in the room when I got there. Maybe when I go back up, he will be."

"So the rooms, they're pretty amazing, aren't they?"

Logan agrees. "Emma and I are going to come here for our honeymoon."

My jaw drops for the second time today.

"Yes and you can get the room with the hot tub on the balcony."

Logan is still staring at me. "Yeah we can. How does that sound Emma?"

All I can do is nod. We've talked about the future before but this is the first real time he has said it out loud in front of someone else.

Before anyone can say anything else, our lunch arrives. I ordered a buffalo chicken wrap with a cucumber, tomato, and onion salad on the side. I may be on a mini vacation but I still have to watch what I eat or training will be a nightmare when the semester starts back up. I can still indulge once in a while.

Logan laughs before digging into his burger. We finish and then head back to our rooms to get dressed for the slopes.

In our room, Ashley starts getting changed but my focus is on the red rose in the center of my bed with a note attached.

Meet me by the gazebo tonight at 10 p.m.
where we will start our forever.

I feel my forehead start to sweat and my pulse quicken. I immediately throw it in the trash before Ashley can see.

"Why did you just throw a rose in the trash?" Of course, she saw.

"I don't need it."

Ashley takes it out of the trash and removes the note before reading it. "Oh my gosh. Is this from Logan? This is so cute. Are you going to go? We need to make sure you wear something super cute."

Before I can say anything, there is a knock on the door. I open it to find Logan bundled up in his snow gear. He walks in and sits on the bed.

I go into the bathroom to change. As I come out, I see Logan grab the rose.

"Who's this from?" Logan asks.

"From you silly." Ashley laughs with the note still in her hand. "Don't worry, I'll cover for Emma tonight if they do any late night checks."

"What are you talking about? I didn't send this. Emma?" He stands up and comes over to me. "What's going on?"

I know I am caught at this point so the truth is the best. "I should have told you. I've been getting these notes and little gifts since the beginning of the school year. I thought they were harmless — or well they still are. This is the first time I've been asked to meet."

"Wait... I thought you said they were from Logan?" Ashley asks, hurt that I didn't tell her the truth.

"I didn't want to face the truth. I am sorry I didn't tell you. I was planning on ignoring it."

"I think that's best." Logan adds. "Now if they continue, please tell me so we can figure it out together."

"Okay. I'm sorry for not telling you either. Let's just forget about it and go to the slopes. I'm ready to kick some snow in your face because you won't be able to catch up."

"Oh is that right?" Logan tackles me to the bed. "I think a bet is in order." He links our hands and stretches them above my head while above laying me. "How about the winner gets to pick our next date night."

"Done." I give him a quick kiss before rolling him over so I am straddling him. "Last one there gives a foot massage."

I grab Ashley on the way out and we run down the hall laughing with Logan not far behind.

Chapter Twenty-nine

The next few days of the trip pass too quickly.

"It feels like we just got here. How are we already leaving tomorrow?"

"I know. I could stay here forever." I lean back in my chair.

"Don't lean back. You're going to mess up your curls."

Ashley is putting makeup on me. She curled my hair and helped me pick out my outfit for tonight. Logan are I are going to a restaurant on the resort grounds. It's a reservation-only restaurant that isn't included in the daily meals but he said he wanted to have a special night.

I actually learned a lot about Logan this week. It turns out Logan was hiding his skill on a snowboard because he had beaten me all but once. I think he let me win that time though.

He won our bet but he insisted this wasn't his date he was choosing. He had something else in mind when we got home. I didn't fight him too much because he always picks the best dates. I was just impressed at how good he was on the snowboard.

When Ashley finishes my curls, she grabs my outfit. She selected a deep red off the shoulder long sleeve dress that goes to mid-thigh. I have tights on underneath and knee-high boots.

A few minutes after I finish getting dressed, Logan knocks at the door.

"Emma, you look beautiful." He says when I open the door and immediately kisses my cheek.

"You look very handsome yourself."

He has on dark jeans and a deep blue button up shirt. I can't help staring. His jacket is slung over his shoulder.

"Here's your coat Emma." Ashley says, tearing my gaze away from Logan and his giant smirk. He knows I was checking him out. She hands me my coat and a scarf.

Logan takes my hand and leads me down the hall to the elevators.

Ashley yells down the hall. "Make sure to bring her back at a reasonable hour, and don't have too much fun."

I laugh as the elevator doors open.

The restaurant is on the top floor of the resort. The entire wall opposite the elevators and kitchen is made of glass to give you a stunning view. The sun will be setting soon and you can already see how beautiful it will be when it drops behind the mountains.

The hostess asks for our name.

"Anderson," replies Logan.

She jots something down and then says, "Right this way."

She leads us to a table right in the middle of the giant window. I lay my coat on the back of my chair. I haven't needed it yet but I didn't know if Logan would want to go outside for a walk after.

She hands us menus and lets us know that our waiter would be right with us.

Everything on the menu looks delicious. It is laid out in three courses, and we each pick an appetizer and entree. The desserts have mini selections that each of us can select from or a larger dessert that we can share.

We start with a honey BBQ flatbread made with a cauliflower crust and a caprese salad. The flatbread has the option of regular crust or cauliflower crust, I assume for gluten free but Logan chose it because he knows I am trying to eat healthy. One of the many reasons I love him.

For my meal, I order a Mandarin Chicken salad. Logan gets steak medallions and a baked potato because what else would he get. I swear he is going to turn into a steak and potato.

Our waiter brings out the flatbread and salad. We share them and they are delicious. You wouldn't even be able to tell the crust is cauliflower. Logan can tell though, because he makes a face but continues eating it. He is so good at sticking with me and my crazy meal plan.

Before our food comes out, our waiter asks which dessert we would like since some of them take longer to make. We agree on the molten chocolate lava cake to share.

Our main course comes out and I dig into my salad. There is something about the sweetness of the oranges mixed with the grilled chicken, the crunch of the little breadsticks, and the nuttiness of the almonds topped off with the delicious honey sesame dressing. I am betting this salad has more calories in the dressing alone than the chocolate cake we ordered. Good thing we got the cauliflower crust with our flatbread.

"Any more notes?"

"No. Nothing since that one when we first got here."

"Good. Let me know if anything else appears."

"I will. So any word on your mysterious roommate? It's so weird that you haven't seen him."

"It is. He comes in late at night when I am already asleep and leaves super early in the morning. The only time I saw him was in the middle of night when I got up to go to the bathroom, and even then, I couldn't really see him in the dark. Just saw a body under the covers."

"Don't you think that's weird?" Logan shrugs.

Our waiter collects our plates and lets us know our dessert will be out in a few minutes.

Outside, the sun has just set below the mountains and the view is spectacular. The oranges, purples, and pinks highlight the mountains. It will be sad to leave this place.

"I don't want to leave tomorrow."

"I already promised that we'll come back here on our honeymoon," says Logan.

"Oh are we now?" I tease him.

He looks very serious. "Yes, we will. Emma, I want you to know…"

Our waiter shows up cutting off whatever he was going to say. "Your dessert."

He pours hot chocolate syrup over the cake and then adds a scoop of vanilla ice cream on top. It instantly starts melting into the top and then the chocolate in the center explodes out the top. Maybe explodes is the wrong word, but it is a mini volcano erupting like that science experiment you do mixing baking soda and vinegar. It is the craziest chocolate lava cake I have ever seen.

"Enjoy."

"What kind of magic cake is this?" Logan has already taken a bite.

"I don't know but it's delicious. Try some." He scoops another piece onto his spoon and lifts it to my lips. I close my lips around the spoon and let out a moan. It is the most delicious thing I have ever had. Between the warm chocolate, the moist chocolate cake and the cold vanilla ice cream, it is an explosion in my mouth which works since it was just exploding on the plate.

After we scarf down the cake, Logan asks me if I want to go for a walk. I put my coat on and take his hand. We head towards the gazebo. The resort still has their Christmas lights up and the gazebo is covered making it glow.

Logan leads me to the center and offers me his hand. "Can I have this dance?"

"We have no music." I laugh.

Logan pulls out his phone and puts on a slow song before pulling me close, and then we begin to dance. I feel like we are in a cheesy romantic movie right now. Now that I think about it, most of our relationship has these moments and I love it. I rest my head on his shoulder.

"Logan, what were you going to say before the dessert came?"

He pulls away slightly so he can look at me. "I was going to say I want you to know how serious I am about you. When I said I want to come here on our honeymoon, I was serious. I want that with you, Emma. I want the wedding, kids, and forever. I'm not proposing now but I will one day soon. I hope that doesn't scare you but I want you to know how I feel. I have never felt like this before."

I take a deep breath. "That is all very scary, but the crazy part is that I feel the same way. I love you, Logan. I love you so much. I know we're only seniors and most high school relationships don't last, but I want forever with you too."

Logan pulls me into a kiss that sends a warm surge through my body.

"Good. Now let's go inside before we freeze and don't make it to forever. It is till death do us part, right?"

I laugh and grab his hand. "Right."

Logan walks me to my room and kisses me good night. "See you tomorrow."

"Tomorrow." I repeat and enter the room. I fall onto the bed.

"Good night?" Ashley asks from her bed.

"The best!" I can't help the grin spreading across my face.

The next morning, I am up bright and early. We are planning on hitting the slopes and then grabbing brunch before we have to leave. The buses are loading up and leaving at 1 p.m. so we have some time.

I get dressed for the slopes and find Ashley still getting ready. "I am going to go grab Logan. Want to meet us down in the lobby in fifteen minutes?"

"Sure, but if you aren't down in thirty minutes, I am coming up there."

I laugh as I leave the room. I get to Logan's room and knock. No one answers so I knock again. I hear a loud thud. "Logan?"

The door is slightly ajar so I peek in but I don't see anyone. I call out for Logan again as I enter the room. The door closes behind me and the swing guard is latched. I see Sam. My ex-boyfriend from sophomore year.

"Sam? What are you doing here?"

"Oh didn't you hear? I'm your new boyfriend's roommate. Don't worry though, he won't be a problem much longer. Come have a seat."

"Sam, what are you talking about? Where's Logan?"

"Logan is a little tied up at the moment. Come over here. I want to talk and catch up."

I glance around the room and don't see Logan. I see the bathroom door is shut. I could always go lock myself in there if I needed to.

I sit on the bed across from Sam. "So what did you want to talk about?"

"I was wondering what you see in him? All I see is a stuck-up jock that goes around talking himself up by posting his films all about himself."

"Most of his films aren't even about him."

"Not the ones I have seen. I just don't think he's your type. You deserve someone more like me that will actually care about you." He moves over to the bed I am sitting on and takes my hand. I scoot over but he scoots over as well and grabs my waist so I can't go anywhere. With his other hand, he links our fingers and slowly caresses the top of my hand.

"We were so happy together Emma, and then you broke up with me. I gave you the summer to have space. Then junior year I was going to show you how great we were together, but then he showed up. So I decided to let you have some fun and see what you don't want in a guy but then you got closer. Fast forward to this year, I wanted to show you how much I cared. Did you get all my notes and gifts?"

I think about the shoebox in my closet at home. I am going to burn it as soon as I get home. "Those were from you?"

"Yes. Didn't you like them? It shows how much I know you, Emma."

He takes my hand and puts it to his face as if he is petting himself.

I feel like I am going to puke.

"Don't you feel this spark?" He kisses my hand. I try to pull it away but he grasps it tighter.

"Sam, I'm sorry we broke up. But I just don't have those feelings anymore. Can you please tell me where Logan is?"

I hear another thud like the one I heard when I was outside the room.

Then it clicks. "Sam, is Logan in the bathroom?"

"I told you he was tied up. I needed you to listen to me without him. Emma, I love you. I want you to come back to me." He says, the anger rising with each word then in a completely calm voice he adds, "Please, will you come back to me?"

I am not sure what is going on with him. This is not how he was when we were dating. He seems almost out of it.

"Sam, we are going to get you some help, but you have to let me get Logan. Can you do that for me?"

"Emma, I just want you to want me. Please let me just hold you." He pulls me into him and wraps his arms around me, resting his head on my shoulder. I think he is actually crying.

"Alright Sam, I'm going to stand up now. Will you let me?"

"Will you come back to me?" He sounds on the verge of tears.

"Yes, Sam but you have to let me stand up so I can help you."

"Okay." He stands up and his eyes go wide in shock as he sees something over my shoulder. Logan comes running over and punches Sam in the nose.

"Logan!" I shout.

Logan looks at Sam. "That's for touching my girlfriend."

Sam looks over at me. "Emma, I'm sorry. I just want you to want me. We're so good together."

Logan looks ready to punch him again. It doesn't look like he broke his nose the first time, despite the blood coming out but another punch and he might.

"Logan, stop. I think he's sick."

"Yeah sick in the mind. He knocked me out and then tied me to the toilet. I had to work the ropes off me. I had just woken back up when I heard you come in."

"Let's just call a chaperone and explain it."

I pull out my phone and call the chaperone line. They have a phone specific to whoever is on watch during the trip. Mr. Stephens, our English teacher, answers the phone. "Hi sir, can you please come to room 205. We have a situation. We'll explain when you get here. Please hurry." I undo the swing guard and use it to prop the door open.

Logan is still eying Sam who has his face in his hands. I walk over to Logan and link my arm with his.

"Mr. Stephens is on his way now."

Sam looks up and zeroes in on our linked arms. His face goes from sad to very angry. He leaps at Logan and tackles him to the ground. Not even a few seconds later, Mr. Stephens comes bursting through the door pulling them apart.

I pull Logan over to me as Mr. Stephens holds Sam back.

"Can someone explain to me what is going on?

"I came looking for Logan this morning because we were planning on hitting the slopes, but when I got here Logan wasn't anywhere, just Sam. He said he wanted to talk. It turns out he had knocked out and tied up Logan in the bathroom.

Sam and I used to date back in sophomore year and he wanted to talk about our relationship."

Sam has stopped fighting Mr. Stephens and is back to being sad and confined.

"Mr. Stephens, I think Sam is sick. One second, he was super angry and the next he was sad. I've never seen him like this."

Mr. Stephens nods like he knows. "I will take care of this. Are you both alright?"

I nod. Logan looks like he is ready to go after Sam but I squeeze his hand and he nods as well.

"Very well. Dare I ask why Sam's nose is bleeding?"

"I punched him because he was touching Emma."

"Emma, is this true?"

"Yes. He was holding me. It was uncomfortable but I realized that he was sick and didn't want to make the situation worse. Logan was only defending me."

"Emma, that was smart. Logan, we will discuss punching later."

"But he tied me--"

"I understand, but that doesn't give you the right to punch him. Now let me take him to the other chaperones so we can figure out what to do. You two still have time to hit the slopes. Go have fun and I will see you on the bus at one."

He turns toward the door with his arm around Sam's shoulders. Ashley appears in the doorway as they leave.

"Was that Sam?"

"Yes, now let's go before we waste more time on sick ex-boyfriends."

"What happened?"

"I'll explain at brunch. Logan can fill you in on how he was tied up to the toilet all morning though." Ashley looks between us confused and shocked.

I say to Logan, "Put ski clothes on. You can burn all that adrenaline on the slopes."

The rest of the day is uneventful and I am surprised to see that Sam is not on the bus ride home. That was really scary but I hope he gets the help he needs. We learned all about illnesses in AP Psychology and I recognized some of the symptoms like the instant mood change. The biggest thing is to not overreact and cause another emotion.

Ashley and Logan are both asleep but I am too worked up to sleep. I look out at the mountains we pass. My life was always simple and normal. Enter Logan. He has made it exciting and always makes me guess what comes next. Well Logan, I can't wait to see what comes next.

Chapter Thirty

A few days after we get home, the Andersons have their annual New Year's Eve party and this year I persuaded my parents to go. It was great to see them dancing and enjoying themselves.

The new semester starts too soon but I am excited to no longer have Trig. I somehow passed with a B and I never would have been able to do it without Logan's help.

This semester, I have two different college classes. One is an anatomy class which I am excited about, and the other is a speech class which I am not looking forward to. I have never been good at speaking in front of people. However, it's a requirement for most majors and I figure it will help in the future. If I do make it to the Olympics, I am bound to have to stand in front of an audience and speak. Or maybe just do interviews, but either way it should help.

I found out about a week into school starting that Sam is bipolar. He has medicine that he was supposed to be taking. I guess he had been taking it up till this past summer. It would explain the weird stalker notes and gifts that started last semester.

Speaking of which, I immediately threw that box away when I got home from the trip. I only kept it in case it was needed if things escalated. In a way they did, but it got him the help he needed. He is in a program to help him get back on track. I really do wish him the best. People probably think I am crazy for saying that but he was sick.

Logan is still not a fan and gets mad anytime his name is brought up so it is a subject we tend to avoid. While he got off with a warning for punching him, he also got a lecture from Mr. Stephens which could be considered a punishment in itself. Especially when he gives you a 1000-word essay on "other ways to defend your girlfriend besides resorting to violence". I laughed when I heard the topic.

February rolls around and I am headed home from swim practice. I go inside my house and my parents are waiting for me with an envelope in their hands. "Is that what I think it is?"

My mom nods and I drop my bags, running to her. I take the envelope and examine it. "It's kinda small for an acceptance."

"That doesn't mean anything anymore. Most of the information is online anyway. I'm actually surprised they still send snail mail out." My dad reassures me.

My dad is the only one that still calls it snail mail.

"I guess. Okay here it goes." I slowly open the envelope, sliding my pointer finger under the seal. My fingers shake as I pull out the folded piece of paper. I unfold the letter and close my eyes, too scared to look. I take a deep break and open my eyes scanning the letter. I read the first sentence. "Congratulations!

We are pleased to inform you that you have been accepted into Florida State University beginning in Fall."

I scream and jump around. My parents join in and soon we all fall to the ground laughing.

My dad leaps up and grabs his keys. "Grab your coats, we're going to celebrate."

I call Logan and the second he answers, I shout, "I GOT IN!"

He laughs. "I never thought you wouldn't. Congratulations. I am so proud of you!"

"Did you get your letter?"

"Yes, and I got in too."

"Ahhh... this is so great. I can't wait till next year." It will be the perfect year with him. Add in the fact that both our brothers go there too.

"Me too." His voice lacks the enthusiasm I assumed he would have. I remember the last time when he got into his film program and he had to miss prom. He was super quiet then too. I know I shouldn't worry but I can't help it. I decide to brush it off because this night is about celebrating. I invite him to dinner.

"Sure. I'll see you there."

"Sounds good. I love you."

"Me too."

We have a delicious dinner at my favorite steak place celebrating both our acceptance letters.

Logan is unusually quiet throughout dinner. Last time we went to get steak, he devoured his plate but tonight he slowly eats it as he pushes it around his plate.

When we walk out to the parking lot, I tell my parents I am going to say goodbye to Logan. "Hey is everything okay?"

"Yeah, sorry. I have just been stressed with school and waiting to hear back about schools. I'm just tired I guess but I'm glad I was accepted."

"True. Well, hey, we did it and we are going to have an awesome time next year. Our brothers are both there too!" I can't help grabbing his hands and jumping but he doesn't join in. He seems to be looking right through me.

"Very true. It'll be fun. I will see you tomorrow at school. Love you."

"Love you too." He lets go of my hands and gives me a quick kiss on the forehead before turning away. He never kisses me on the forehead and he didn't even say goodbye.

Maybe he really is stressed.

It isn't till the beginning of March that I realize something really is up with Logan. I am sitting at lunch with Ashley. Logan has a film project he is working on through lunch so it is just us.

"Hey Ash, have you noticed anything weird with Logan recently?"

"Not really. He has been quieter lately, but I figured that had to do with the last semester of high school. I know our classes have been stressful."

"Yeah that's what I thought but it seems anytime I bring up the future or college he gets quiet. Ashley, what if he is planning on breaking up with me?"

"Em, I highly doubt he is going to break up with you. That boy loves you so much it's sickening. I'm telling you he is just stressed with school. If it is bugging you so much, why don't you ask him?"

Because I am scared he is going to break up with me and asking will make it happen sooner. I wonder if he is still fed up with the Sam situation. Maybe he thinks I'm too much drama.

"You're right. I am probably freaking out about nothing but I will talk to him."

I don't get to talk to him till that weekend. Between swim practice and AP exams only a month away, we are all stressed.

Saturday night we go to the Spanish restaurant we went to when he was helping me practice for my exam. I have all happy memories here and I am worried that is about to change. I will probably never be able to come here again.

After we order, I come out and ask him. "Are you planning on breaking up with me?"

Logan practically spits his chip out. "I'm sorry what?"

"I asked if you are planning on breaking up with me?"

"No. Why would you think that?" He looks completely dumbfounded.

"You have been so distant lately and anytime I bring up college next year you change the subject."

"I've been stressed with school but I am definitely not breaking up with you. I do have a question for you." I am still expecting the worst because maybe he is going to ask for time or a break. My heart is pounding.

"What would you say if I didn't go to FSU next year?"

"What do you mean? Would you not go to school at all?"

He looks down at his plate, unsure of how to continue. "No, I'd go. It's just, I got into the NYU Film program, specifically the Tisch School of the Arts."

"That's amazing! I didn't even know you applied there." Why would he not tell me about it?

"I didn't tell anyone but my parents. I honestly didn't think I would ever get in. I figured it would be better to let myself down easy by not telling anyone."

"Well, I am mad at you for not telling me but I can get over it because I am so proud of you. That is one of the top film schools. You have to go."

"What about FSU and us?"

He takes my hands, making circles on my thumbs. I feel goosebumps rising up on my arms and it makes me realize how much I am going to miss seeing him every day. Just like with missing Prom last year for his film program, I know I have to make sure he goes. He will always regret it if he doesn't.

"I'll have my brother and your brother to annoy at FSU. Plus, I'll have a boyfriend to brag about to everyone."

"Are you sure?" He searches my eyes trying to find the truth.

I smile at him, giving his hands a squeeze. "Yes, I am sure. I'm not worried about us at all. Well, I was worried so if something like this happens again, please just tell me right away."

"Deal."

"Plus, we still have holidays and if I remember correctly, doesn't your dad still have that private jet?"

"He does."

"Then we can still visit each other. You can't turn down this opportunity."

"I was so scared to tell you because I know how much you wanted to go to FSU together."

"I do but I'd rather you have told me than you pulling away. If this long distance is going to work then we need to be honest with each other. Okay?"

He squeezes my hands and releases them. "Yes I agree."

"Plus all the time I'm not in class will be spent training for the Olympics. I have about two years before the trials and I still have plenty of work to do."

"You will do great. Have I told you how amazing you are? Not just swimming but as a girlfriend and a person?"

"Oh I know already." I stick my tongue out at him.

Logan throws a chip at me. "Hey."

I throw one back at him. "Don't they say absence makes the heart grow fonder?"

He leans over the table to give me a kiss. "That they do."

Chapter Thirty-one

Over Spring Break, I have the opportunity to not only visit FSU for a swim meet but swim with the women's team. Since I received a scholarship for swimming and academics at FSU, they want me to come participate in their pre-season meet. I am thankful it falls during my Spring Break so I can join.

They are even putting me up in the dorms so I can experience them before next year. The week will be full of training with the team and then a meet on Thursday and Friday.

Logan is flying in on Wednesday night to come watch the meets. He has to work on his final film project earlier in the week. He has been keeping it a big secret and won't tell me anything about it.

I enter the FSU gym on Monday morning to meet the team. They all introduce themselves and welcome me onto the team.

The coach, Mr. Grayson, is young, probably late-twenties. He has dark almost black hair, dark brown eyes and the thickest Italian accent. I've heard he is very tough. He even tells me that since I am basically on the team, I will be treated like I am on the team. It makes me feel good but also a little scared.

We do warm ups and then run speed trials. I definitely feel like part of the team when he is yelling at me to fix my stroke or flip sooner.

By the end of practice, I am beat but I am also used to long hard practices. His accent took some getting used to but once I understood what he was saying, I took in his feedback.

A few of the girls on the swim team invite me to dinner and I gladly accept. My roommate is on the swim team so after we shower, we head back to the dorm. I got in the night before but we didn't have much of a chance to talk.

Her name is Danielle and she is a freshman. She has dark brown hair, almost black and the brightest green eyes. They look like two emeralds.

I ask her if the coach is always that hard. She tells me he was nice today. I look at her shocked. "Don't worry you'll get used to it. Plus, he is the best. You are really good though so you shouldn't worry. Aren't you headed toward the Olympics?"

Where did she hear that? "I am trying. It has been a dream of mine since I can remember."

"Well Coach Grayson can help you get there. He actually coached Natalie Coughlin for a few years before he came here to FSU."

"Really? I didn't know that. I am just honored to be able to swim with you all this week." She is my idol and the fact that I didn't know that makes this so amazing.

We meet the rest of the girls at a place called "Shake and Salads". They have salads and shakes in a buffet style. You pay for whichever you want and then add in your toppings and mix-ins. At the end of the line, they will toss your salad or blend your shake. Once we all have our salads, we head over to a table.

As we finish up, all the girls go silent. I look behind me to see Jeremy walk in with a few guys from the football team. All the girls are staring at him. I laugh at the fact that no matter where he goes, he is always the talk of the group. Why would college be any different?

A few minutes later, I feel arms snake around my shoulders and a hand reach out to steal a cucumber from my bowl. "Thanks Em." He kisses my cheek, standing up and placing his hands on my shoulders.

"My pleasure Mr. Ego."

"I forgot you were going to be here this week. I remember your brother mentioning something a few weeks ago. Who are all your friends?"

"These are all girls from the swim team. I'm swimming in the meet on Thursday and Friday."

"No way. That's awesome. I'll definitely be there to watch after practice."

"My brother and I are going out to dinner on Thursday if you want to come?" I glance up at him.

"I don't want to intrude." He shrugs.

"Oh well, Logan will be there too."

He agrees to go. "How is my baby brother these days? Are you ready to graduate?"

"We sure are!"

"Well, how about you come to my place tomorrow night? My roommate is out of town so it is super quiet for once. We can have some dinner and catch up before my brother gets here and hogs all your attention. I miss my best girl!"

I laugh at his antics. He is probably trying to hype me up to the other girls but I could care less about that.

"Sure."

"Perfect. I'll text you the deets."

"Okay but, Jer, no one says deets anymore."

"Yeah whatever Miss Know It All." He gives my shoulders one last squeeze and looks at the rest of the girls. "It was nice meeting you all. Take care of my Em here." He then heads back over to his football buddies.

Almost immediately, all the girls are asking me how I know the quarterback and if we are dating and a whole bunch of other questions.

"We're not dating. We're more like siblings. I have been dating his brother for almost a year and a half, so I've hung out with him and his family a bunch. We also went to high school together."

"Is he dating anyone?"

"Ummm. I'm not sure. I don't think he dates or well long term anyway. Honestly, I don't know who would want to date him. He is so annoying."

Just then my phone chimes alerting me of a text message. I see it is from Jeremy.

"Oh is that him?" Danielle jumps in her seat, clearly way too excited.

"Read it out loud." Another girl shouts.

Jeremy: *My house tomorrow night. 7 p.m. Bring a bathing suit.*

Almost immediately another text pops up.

Jeremy: *A sexy two piece, not a one piece ;)*

I grimace at Jeremy and see him smirking at me. I text back.

Emma: *You wish!*

Danielle leans over to me. "You say you are dating his brother but you and Jeremy have some serious chemistry. I can feel it even with him across the room."

"We basically can't stand each other. Plus, I am absolutely in love with his brother, Logan, who you will all meet on Thursday. He is amazing!" I look each one of them in the eyes, making it clear there is nothing between Jeremy and I.

"He sure flirts with you like there is something."

"He flirts with everyone. You're all more than welcome to him, just be careful because he doesn't believe in relationships."

They all seem satisfied with my answer and go back to asking what he was like in high school, along with every other question they can think of.

Chapter Thirty-two

The next day at practice is the same as before. Coach Grayson pushes us to our limit in the morning at the pool. In the afternoon, he has us lifting weights.

As Danielle and I walk back to her dorm after practice, I feel my shoulders tense up. I reach behind to rub them. "If we have one more day of practice like that, I don't think I will be able to race on Thursday."

"Don't worry. Usually the day before a meet, Coach Grayson just makes us run around the track and do light conditioning in the afternoon."

"Oh good. I'm used to the weights and conditioning but I guess I just got used to my routine. Shake it up a little and wow, it works you."

"That's why Coach Grayson is the best."

We enter her room and she says I can take a shower first. Both her roommate and suite-mates are gone for the week so we have the place to ourselves. The four of them share one bathroom which is much better than a community bathroom. I quickly shower and then change into shorts and a lacy tank top.

Back in the room, Danielle sits on her bed flipping through a magazine. "Are you excited for dinner with Jeremy?"

"I guess." I think she assumes there is more to our relationship than I let on. "You know we're just friends right?"

"If you say so." She doesn't look up from her magazine.

"I'm serious. I will be honest, I did have a crush on him when I was a freshman in high school, but he completely ignored me. I'm pretty sure he didn't even know who I was till I started dating his brother. We have a very friendly relationship but that is all we are — friends, nothing more."

"Okay, okay I get it. I just... if I was in your position... you are just one lucky girl the way he hangs on to your every word."

"Yeah well like I said before, you can have him. Just be careful." I pull out one of my one piece bathing suits from my duffel and throw it in my bag. Too bad for him, I don't have anything else with me. I am assuming he wants to go in the hot tub which is fine by me. I can't wait to soak my sore muscles.

"I am just going to fix my hair and I'll be headed out."

When I come out of the bathroom, Danielle has switched on the TV. "Have a great time!" She smiles at me suspiciously. I guess she still doesn't believe me about Jeremy.

I grab my bag and wait for my Uber. I pull up to Jeremy's house remembering the last time I was here over Thanksgiving. I am interested to see what he has done with the place since moving in.

According to Logan, the hot tub was one of the first things Jeremy added when he moved in.

I walk up to the door and am about to knock when the door swings open.

"Emma!" Jeremy pulls me through the door and gives me a hug. My nose is instantly filled with a sweet aroma of something I can't quite figure out.

The living room is pretty much the same other than the added bookshelf of DVDs, video games and the Xbox under the TV.

We enter the kitchen and I see a ton of toppings spread out across the counter. "What are you making?"

"Make your own pizza night. What else?" That's what the smell is — dough.

While our pizzas bake in the oven, Jeremy pulls out a bottle of red wine. "Want some?"

"I probably shouldn't."

"You took an Uber didn't you?" I nod. "Just one glass. I promise I have the best intentions."

"You better, or your brother will beat you up. You may be bigger but unleash the monster and I don't know what will happen. You heard about what happened on the Senior Ski Trip, didn't you?"

Jeremy pours two glasses of wine and passes the glass to me. "I didn't think he had it in him. Glad you're okay. Who knew you would end up with the stalker? So is that a yes on the wine? If not, I will totally drink it."

I take the glass from him. "Just one." We sit down at the counter and I take a sip. "So what's new with you Mr. Hot Shot Quarterback? And when did you start drinking red wine?"

"Not much. Preparing for next season and enjoying our Spring games. We have a game on Saturday if you'll still be here. The wine is for you because I know you like it, but I'm also not opposed to a good red."

"Logan and I were planning on going actually. We don't leave till Sunday. College is making you fancy."

"Yeah, yeah. So how have you been, Miss Soon to Be Olympic Swimmer?"

I finish off my glass of wine and Jeremy refills it. Whatever kind of wine this is, it tastes like grape juice. I didn't realize I had basically been chugging it. For some reason I am nervous even though this is Jeremy. I guess one more can't hurt. "I've been busy between finals coming up and my crazy training schedule that is only bound to get more intense when I come here. Prom is coming up too. I have a great date this year."

"Can't be better than your date last year."

"Right...And those famous moves."

"Oh yes." Jeremy hops off his chair, takes my glass from my hand and sets it on the table. "I believe it was something like this." He pulls me off my chair and spins me.

"Jeremy, what are you doing? First off there is no music and second off..."

"Second off what? Two friends can't share a dance? We danced all night at Prom last year."

He grabs a remote off the counter and pushes a button. A slow waltz comes through the speakers. It isn't the same one we danced to but a different slower tune.

He pulls me close and we sway to the music. Halfway through the song, the music picks up and he spins me out. "Remember this." He lifts my leg up and I extend my arm out like that night almost a year ago. Both of us burst out laughing. He sets me down and spins me one more time before dipping me as the music ends. I look up at him and see him moving his head closer. This time there is no audience. I close my eyes and feel my heart beat pick up. The wine must be getting to me because I can't think of anything else but feel his breath on my lips as they inch closer.

Just then the timer for the oven goes off. I shake my head and stand up, twisting out of Jeremy's grip.

I need some water. I walk over to the faucet and fill a glass with water.

Jeremy takes the pizzas out of the oven. "I'm so sorry. I got carried away and shouldn't have tried to kiss you." I don't turn to face him. "Emma, please turn around."

I finish my water and slowly turn around.

"It's fine, but I should probably go." I turn to leave when he reaches out to grab my arm.

"Emma the pizzas just came out. Let's eat and forget whatever almost happened. We can go back to enjoying each other's friendly company. I am an idiot."

"Fine, but you sit over there." I point to the far chair at the counter.

I grab my pizza and sit at the chair on the opposite end. I lift a piece to my mouth and can't help but moan at how good it tasted. I added a pesto base with onions, chicken, artichokes, and feta cheese on top. I see Jeremy out of the corner of my eye who has his mouth open staring at me. "What? I make a great pizza."

He laughs and digs into his own pizza. He goes with his version of a tomato sauce meat lover's pizza.

After we clean up, it is only 8:30 and Jeremy asks if I want to go in the hot tub. I quickly say yes because I have been dreaming about this hot tub. The dance earlier in the night is long forgotten. We had a great conversation while we ate our pizzas and things are like they used to be — completely friendly with Jeremy's normal flirtation thrown in.

I grab my bag and excuse myself to the bathroom but not before saying, "no funny business in the hot tub or I will have to tell your brother you tried to kiss me."

I close the bathroom door behind me and look in my bag for my bathing suit. Instead, I see a bag from "All Things Water". Inside I find a tiny black string bikini with the tags still on. There is a note.

Just in case. Have fun! Danielle

I am going to kill her when I get back to the dorm. She reminds me a lot of Ashley.

I double check my bag, hoping she forgot to take out my one piece. No such luck. I put on the bikini and glance at myself in the mirror. It barely covers anything but I can imagine Ashley telling me how hot I look. I grab a towel and wrap it around my body. I plan on taking it off right before I get in.

Jeremy is already in the hot tub when I get outside. I walk over to the steps leading up to the hot tub. I set my towel on the back of a chair and climb the stairs. I get in as quickly as possible and sink into the water.

I hear Jeremy groan. "Man, Emma, why do you have to be dating my brother?"

"Because I love him."

"Well that is one sexy bathing suit. I didn't think you would take my text so seriously."

"Seems I have a new friend who thought it would be funny to steal my bathing suit and replace it with this one."

"You won't see me complaining." He throws his hands up.

Feeling embarrassed, I sink lower into the water enjoying the hot water on my sore muscles. I look up at the twinkling lights that he hung above the hot tub, which extend into the backyard. I can't wait to see the backyard in the daytime.

"Change of subject. This water feels amazing. I swear my swim coach is trying to kill me."

"I've heard he is a tough one. Although he has worked with past Olympians so he is your best bet at getting there."

"That is what I heard. I am excited to work with him but it might take a while to get used to his conditioning methods." I massage my neck hoping to get some of the kinks out.

Jeremy slides over and turns me so my back is to him.

"What are you doing?"

"Just relax. I'm just giving you a friendly back massage. I promise!"

"Okay but nothing lower than my shoulder blades."

"Deal." He massages my shoulders and neck. I let out a moan as his hands work through my stiff muscles.

"Your hands are like magic on my aching muscles."

"I'll show you what else these magic hands can do."

I look back at him making sure to make eye contact so he can see I am serious. "Don't make me slap you."

"Am I interrupting something?" A voice says from behind me. I turn around to see Logan standing there. Jeremy drops his hands and scoots over to where he was sitting before.

I leap out of the hot tub and run over to him. I throw my arms around his neck not caring that I am soaking wet or in a tiny bikini. He doesn't return the hug but instead tenses at my touch.

"I thought you weren't coming till tomorrow?" I say excited to see him.

"Clearly. I wanted to come early to surprise you at practice tomorrow but it seems I interrupted something. Maybe I should just go and not come back."

"Logan no, you're not interrupting anything. We were hanging out and Jeremy was getting a kink out of my neck. You wouldn't believe the coach FSU has. He's very intense."

I see Logan glaring at his brother over my shoulder. "That is not what it looked like."

It suddenly clicks why he thought something else was going on. "Please Logan, you know me and your brother. We would never do anything like that. I love you and only you."

"Yeah I thought I knew you both too." He unwraps my arms from his body. He glances down and sees what I was wearing. There is a brief break in his angry exterior but it doesn't last long. "Put some clothes on."

He turns to go but right before he goes through the door he says, "I'm going to bed. Don't follow me."

I grab my towel from the chair and start after him until I hear Jeremy behind me. "Don't Emma. He needs space."

I face Jeremy. "You know what Jeremy, I am done listening to you. What is this? Some kind of game to you? Flirt with your brother's girlfriend and see what happens? Well wake up! I am in love with your brother, not you. I could never love someone like you."

I run inside before Jeremy can say another word. I grab my wine glass off the counter and down the rest of the contents. I then make my way upstairs to the guest room hoping Logan will listen to me.

"Logan! Please let me in so I can explain. You have to believe nothing happened. I would never do anything to mess us up." I knock on the door and there is no answer. I try the handle but it is locked. I hear shuffling inside and then hear his voice.

"Emma, please just go away. I need space."

I place my hand on the door hoping he is right on the other side. I feel the tears come and I don't try to brush them away. "Logan. Please. I love you."

"Emma... go."

I slide down the wall next to the door and let the tears fall. I wrap the towel tighter around me. I know I should get up and go back to the dorms or at least let Danielle know I'm not coming home but I can't make myself get up. Instead, I sit there and sob until I eventually fall asleep.

Chapter Thirty-three

I wake up to find my head on a pillow and I am covered by a blanket. I am still in the hallway but Jeremy must have given me the pillow and blanket the night before.

I slowly get up and see Logan's room is open. I run inside but don't see him anywhere. I hurry downstairs hoping he is there, but it's just Jeremy sitting at the counter drinking coffee.

"Hey Emma. I made coffee."

"Hey." I feel bad for what I said last night but I am not ready to apologize yet. Instead, I pour myself a cup of coffee. "Have you seen Logan?"

"He went out for a run." I practically spit out my coffee.

"I am sorry, did you say a run?" He hates running unless it is around the bases on the baseball field.

"That's what he said. I didn't try to question him. Listen Emma, about last night, I'm sorry. I wasn't trying to mess anything up with you and my brother. Honestly, you two are perfect together. I have never seen anyone more perfect for each other. I missed having you around, and I was just jealous of what you two have but nothing more. I won't get in the way anymore. I just want us to get back to where we were before."

"It's fine. I want us to get back to where we were too but it might take some time. I need to make things right with Logan. I don't want to lose him."

"Emma, can I tell you something? Something you have to promise you won't tell Logan I told you."

"Jeremy I don't know." I don't think I can take him confessing he likes me or something like that. He says he wants things to go back to normal but that's not going to happen if he has feelings for me.

"It's nothing bad. It's just... a big reason Logan came back from Europe was because of a girl. A girl he was crazy about and she cheated. You need to ask him for the full story but he was pretty torn up about it the summer before your junior year. Just talk to him."

"I didn't cheat on him. Nothing happened between you and me. And nothing ever will."

"I know, but just talk to him." He looks like he wants to add more to his comment but won't.

I nod. "Jer, I am sorry about what I said last night. I didn't mean any of it. I was just angry Logan wouldn't even look at me and I took it out on you."

"I know, Em, I know. Now go change out of that bikini before I throw you over my shoulder and take you upstairs." I look at him shocked and before I can get mad, he smirks. "Too soon?"

"Jeremy Anderson, what am I going to do with you?" I realize the opening I give him and quickly add, "Wait don't answer that." I shake my head laughing and head to the bathroom.

When I come out Jeremy is cleaning up the kitchen and I sit down to finish my coffee. "Thanks for the blanket and pillow last night."

Jeremy faces me. "That wasn't me. When I finally made it up to bed last night you already had the blanket and pillow. Logan must have done it."

It hits me. Logan wouldn't have put a blanket over me or a pillow under my head if he didn't care. Even just a little bit. I get super excited. "You know what this means? He still cares."

"Of course he cares. He loves you, Emma. He would be crazy not to."

Logan walks through the door. "He would be crazy not to what?"

Jeremy hangs up the dish towel and excuses himself upstairs.

Logan grabs a bottle of water out of the fridge and takes a sip. "We need to talk."

Those are never the words you want to hear come out of your boyfriend's mouth. "Can I say something before you break up with me?"

Logan doesn't say anything so I use that as my cue to continue. "Logan, nothing happened. You have to know that. I mean come on, it's your brother. We practically hate each other. What happened to trusting each other? I love you. You are the one I want to be with forever."

I wrap my arms around his waist tightly and lean my head against his chest. "Logan please you have to believe me."

"Emma it isn't that I don't believe you, I just need some time is all." He doesn't hug me back and I can feel him tense up.

"Can I ask you something?" I feel him nod, not wanting to let go in case this is one of the last times I get to hold him like this. "Why did you go for a run when you hate running?"

"I was mad last night Emma. Really mad. Here I was trying to surprise you, and instead I find you in a very tiny bikini in the hot tub with my brother. Not only that, but he was right behind you and you were making all these noises. What am I supposed to think? I needed something to take my mind off everything from last night. Something that I hated more to make me forget." I told myself I won't cry but I can't help the tears running down my cheeks.

Logan softly pulls me away from him and brushes the tears from my eyes. "Emma, please don't cry. Just give me the day to cool down and we can have our talk tonight. I need time to think some things through."

"Are you going to break up with me? Because I want to prepare myself if you are."

"I don't know yet." He gives me one last look before heading upstairs. I collapse onto the floor and feel myself running out of air. I can't breathe. Everything around me is blurry and then turns white. Is this what it felt like to die?

A minute, an hour, or maybe an eternity later, I feel myself being lifted up and slowly everything comes back into focus. I see Jeremy above me. "Emma, are you okay? You were having a panic attack." Jeremy lifts me up. "Let's get you back to your dorm and I'll talk to your coach about sitting out today's practice."

I shake my head trying to find the words. "No. no stop. I have to go to practice. We have that meet tomorrow and I can't miss it."

"Emma, you can barely stand."

"I'll be fine. It will give me something to do or else I will be wallowing and wondering if your brother is going to break up with me tonight. Plus, I'm sure Danielle is wondering where I am."

"I actually texted her from your phone last night and said Logan came into town early and you wouldn't be back. I didn't want her to worry, and I figured you wouldn't be going anywhere till you got Logan to listen. Now let me drive you back to the dorms so you can get your stuff before your practice."

I follow him out to his car because what other option do I have? Logan needs space and I will give it to him. Let's hope I can make it through what I know is going to be a very long day.

Chapter Thirty-four

The day goes by in a blur. I feel like a zombie as I do my laps. I barely even hear Coach Grayson yelling at me. My strokes are sloppy, but I push through and keep swimming.

In the afternoon, he sends the rest of the team to start conditioning and asks to see me. I make my way to his office. "Emma, you're a great swimmer. Even today you still managed to swim almost as fast even with your strokes all over the place. Something has changed though; I didn't see your heart in it today. So please tell me what's wrong so we can fix it before tomorrow."

"I am supposed to have a talk with my boyfriend tonight. He may or may not be breaking up with me." I know I sound like a pathetic high school girl but at this point, I don't care.

"I want you to take the rest of the day off. Go take care of whatever it is you need to and be at the pool tomorrow for warm ups. If I see you there, I expect 110% and no zombie paddling. If I don't see you there, then we will have a talk at a later time about your future in this program. I understand heartbreaks, but I need my swimmers focused at all times when they get into this pool. Do you understand?"

I simply nod. "I need to hear you Emma."

"Yes, I understand."

"Good. Now go change and I will see you tomorrow."

Once in the locker room, I get into the shower stall. I take a deep breath. That went much better than I thought it would. He is so tough on us in the pool, I was expecting him to yell at me.

I turn the water on and let my thoughts drift to tonight. I can't help the tears from falling. Logan hasn't even officially broken up with me yet. I have to be strong when we talk tonight. No crying. I need to get it all out about what happened. I also need to come up with a plan to get him back if he does break up with me.

Logan sends me a text to meet him at Jeremy's house at six. When I get there, I don't see Jeremy's truck so I assume Logan told him about our talk.

I walk to the front door and find it unlocked. Logan is sitting at the kitchen counter. He looks up but gives me no hint of what he is planning on saying. Then again, I have never been good at reading people.

"Hey."

"Hi". I take a seat at the other end. We are both silent for a few minutes, not daring to make eye contact.

"I need to explain." We both speak at the same time.

I look at him confused. "What do you need to explain?"

"Jeremy had a little talk with me this morning after he came back from driving you to the dorms. He told me everything that happened last night and that it was all innocent. He told me he mentioned my ex. He told me how you kept threatening to hit him if he didn't stop with the flirty comments. He even told me he tried to kiss you when you all were goofing off dancing."

I look down at my hands. I know if I keep looking at him, I will start crying.

"I had a few words with him but I owe you an explanation." He pauses before continuing. I still can't manage to look up at him. "There's this girl I was dating in my sophomore year. We'd been going out for almost six months. There was this big end of the year bash we were all invited to at my film professor's house. We went to the party together. When we got there, she said she wanted to go say hi to some friends and would come find me. I figured I would do the same and go mingle. I had brought my camera so I took some pictures. She found me later in the backyard and I drove her home."

I finally look up to see him with his face in his hands, completely devastated. I wonder where he is going with this story.

"The next day I realized I had forgotten my camera bag on the back porch. In the craziness of the party, I only left with my camera around my neck. I drove to my professor's house and knocked on the door. There was no answer so I decided to come back another day. That was when I heard a scream from the backyard. I ran around to the side gate and let myself in. I was not expecting to find my professor in the hot tub behind some girl going at it. I tried to be sneaky and grab my camera bag from the table on the back porch. Unfortunately, the deck was a little squeaky and my professor looked up. So did the girl."

My mouth drops open. "It was your girlfriend, wasn't it?"

"Yes. Ex-girlfriend after that. She tried to explain but I learned it had been happening for the last three months. I came home after that and decided not to go back. Then I met you."

"Can I ask you something?"

He nods.

"Were you in love with her?"

"I thought I was."

"And what was I? Some rebound?"

"No, you're nothing like her. To be honest, you kind of crept up on me. Over the summer, I heard about you from the other kids in our class and what a great swimmer you are. I heard how nice you are to everyone you talk to and not shallow like some of the girls in the class. I knew I had to meet this girl everyone talked about."

What is happening right now? People say those things about me? I barely talk to anyone at school. Sure, most of them I have gone to school with since I was young but I don't hang out with anyone but Ashley.

"Then you literally ran into me in the hallway and I thought it was fate. You seemed very confused though, almost like you had seen me before."

I think back to that day and remember I thought he was Jeremy.

"I went home that day and asked my brother if he knew you. He told me all about you and what an amazing girl you are. I asked him why he wasn't dating you if you were so amazing and he said you were out of his league."

I am shocked that Jeremy even knew who I was back then. Other than the one time I spilled coffee on him, we never had any interaction.

"Then we got assigned that project together and it was like Heaven was bringing us together. The more I got to know you, the harder I fell. I realized I was never in love with my ex."

I know he fell hard for me, but now I want to know what he plans on doing about us.

"Okay I get it that you fell in love with me instantly and I wasn't a rebound. But do you still love me?"

"When I saw Jeremy in that hot tub behind you, all the memories came flooding back. It was like I was reliving a painful time in my life. She was the first girl I really liked and thought I loved. But you're the first girl I ever really loved. It seemed like some bad sitcom or the universe was out to get me. Next, the first girl I marry is going to cheat."

The only thing I hear is "he loved me" as in past tense. I guess that answers my question about whether he still loves me. "The only other question I have is where does that leave us?"

"I owe you an apology for freaking out like I did. I should have heard you out last night. I am honestly more mad at my brother than I am at you. We had it out last night and I told him you were mine. I am sure there will still be plenty of flirty comments because that is who he is. You all have that fire and ice relationship going on but I trust you both. He also knows that if he ever touches you again, I have plenty of blackmail on him I will release. I am sure his team and any future NFL scouts would love that." His lips finally turn up into that grin that I love so much.

"So you aren't breaking up with me?"

He seems to ponder for a second and then smiles. "No, I'm not breaking up with you."

The tears come before I can stop them. He isn't breaking up with me. I feel relief flood through my entire body. I would hate it if things ended because of something that never happened.

He pulls me off my chair so I'm standing right in front of him. "Hey, I thought we said no more crying. Did you not hear me? I said we're not breaking up."

"These are happy tears. You have no idea what you put me through today. I was a zombie all day and hated the thought that you didn't want me anymore."

"Come here." He wipes the tears from my cheeks. "I am sorry I put you through that. What if I promise never to put you through that again if you promise to only wear that little bikini in front of me?"

I laugh at him being the typical guy and nod.

"Good! Now can we stop the tears so I can kiss my girl-friend?"

"Yes!" And he does just that. He kisses me like a soldier seeing his wife after coming back from the war or a baby taking his first breath after being born. It's a kiss of new beginnings and a glimpse of all the "what's to come" in the future. I throw my arms around him, never wanting to let go. He picks me up and carries me over to the couch, never breaking contact.

"Can you all take that PDA somewhere else?" Jeremy walks through the door with a few grocery bags in his hands. He sets them on the table and makes a gagging noise. "I am glad you all made up but I would like to come home and not want to throw up."

I peer over the side of the couch at him and can't help but laugh at his disgusted face.

He smirks pondering his next words and looks at Logan. "I might make an exception if I can get in on this action or better yet we can share her. You can have her during the week and I can have her on the weekends."

Logan gets up from the couch. Just when I think he is going to slap him, he puts out his hand to shake. "Deal".

"Wait what?" I feel my stomach drop. Was this all some huge joke where Logan pretended he wasn't breaking up with me only to actually break up with me and turn me into a laughing stock? They both see my face and burst out laughing. I realize I am completely overreacting and they are the ones joking around.

I take a pillow off the couch and throw it at them, hitting Jeremy square in the chest. I throw another hitting Logan in the arm.

"I hate you both. You're both lucky I have a good throwing arm and I wasn't trying to aim somewhere lower. Now who wants to take me out to dinner? I am thinking I want a big juicy steak!"

I start towards the garage when I hear Jeremy, "I can give you a big juicy steak." I smack him on the back of the head as I pass and hear him laugh. Everything is getting back to normal. I know it may be a little strained for a while, but we'll all be okay.

"Shotgun". Logan gives me a slap on the butt and a wink as he runs by.

Oh yes, everything will be just fine.

After dinner, the guys drop me off at the dorm. Logan walks me to the door and gives me a long kiss. "So any chance you will be wearing that bikini tomorrow at the meet?"

"Don't you wish! I'm pretty sure it would fall off after the first lap." He stares off into the distance and I shove him knowing exactly where his mind just went. "Stop thinking about it you perv. I am leaving now."

"Hey wait one more kiss." He gives me another kiss and brushes a piece of hair behind my ear. He gazes into my eyes, "are we good?"

I pause. I know we are good and we both have trust issues for different reasons. I know his reasoning now but I can't help but wonder why he hasn't said he loves me yet. Maybe he has changed his mind about that part. "Yes, but only because you fed me a nice yummy steak. Now go home and dream only good dreams of me."

"That I can do. I can also pick you up for breakfast tomorrow."

"I promised some of the girls on Monday that I would get breakfast with them before the meet. You're more than welcome to join. I believe we are just going to the cafeteria."

"Sounds like a plan. Until tomorrow." He takes my face between his hands and gazes into my eyes as if he is searching for something. "I love you, you know that, right?"

It's like he knows how to read my mind and what I was just thinking. I nod as relief floods through me. "I love you too, and you have no idea how good it is to hear you say that." He gives me another quick peck. I can't help taking the kiss deeper because I didn't think I would be able to do this again.

He pulls away resting his forehead against mine. "Emma... I need to leave right now or I am going to throw you over my shoulder and make my brother take us both back to his house."

I laugh knowing we can't do that. I give him another simple kiss before pushing him towards Jeremy's truck.

I enter the dorms and see Danielle is still up. "Hey where were you at practice this afternoon? Coach said something about you not feeling well. That wouldn't have to do with a certain boyfriend surprising you last night, would it?"

How does she know? The only other person that knows what happened was Jeremy. I don't think he would go blabbing to anyone. Then I remember he said he texted her from my phone saying Logan had showed up early.

"He did, but I also must have eaten something bad last night. My stomach was all over the place." At least I wasn't lying about that. My stomach really was all over the place all day and

I definitely couldn't keep any food down. I like Danielle and think we can be great friends but I don't know her well enough yet to tell her my secrets.

"Well I am glad you're feeling better. We could use you in the meet tomorrow. I have only seen you in practice but if you swim anything like you do in practice in the meet tomorrow, we will be unstoppable."

"I don't know about that, but thanks for the encouragement. I'm going to go get ready for bed."

I enter the bathroom slightly nervous for tomorrow. I normally don't get nervous during meets but then again, I have never competed at the college level. At least I still have a boyfriend who will be cheering me on from the sidelines.

When I get back in the room the lights are already off.

Chapter Thirty-five

The next morning my alarm buzzes. The swim meet doesn't start till one but our coach wants us there at ten for warm ups. Danielle and I are meeting the rest of the girls at eight thirty for breakfast.

We are about to head out the door when there is a knock. I open it to find Logan with a white rose. "Madam, I am here to escort you and this lovely lady to breakfast." He attempts his best British accent.

He hands me the rose. I attempt a British accent. "Why thank you sir." I look over at Danielle who is looking between us.

"You must be the boyfriend." She plays along in an almost perfect British accent, "It is a pleasure to meet you." She even does a little curtsy at the end.

We arrive at the cafeteria first so we grab food and find a table. When everyone else joins, I introduce them to Logan and he makes small talk. He excuses himself to get more food and asks if anyone needs anything. We all shake our heads.

Sarah who is sitting across from me whispers, "He looks just like his brother. How do you manage to have the two hottest guys falling at your feet?" She stares at Logan like she could eat him for breakfast. It makes me uncomfortable. I felt the same way when Jeremy came to our table the other day. Even though Jeremy isn't mine, I still feel protective of him.

"I wouldn't say they fall at my feet, but I have trained them well." I wink at her. I am still a wreck from the roller coaster of yesterday but it seems better now and I am trying to move forward.

A minute later Logan comes back with Jeremy in tow. He takes his seat next to me and reaches for my hand. "Look who I found milling about."

Jeremy comes up behind me. "It is nice to see you all again. Are you all going to take care of my girl today at the meet?" He gives my shoulders a squeeze.

I feel Logan's hand squeeze mine hard but I bring it to my lips for a quick kiss. I try to tell him with my eyes that he has nothing to worry about. He seems to get the message because I feel him relax.

Sarah nods her head in reply to Jeremy's question. "Of course we will take care of her. Although she'll probably be taking care of us. She is a great swimmer."

"That she is. I've raced her a few times and she beats me every time."

I laugh thinking back to the times when he was so cocky and thought he was a sure win. "Let me know if you ever want to get beat again."

"Yeah yeah. Anyway, I am glad I ran into you. I wanted to let you know I will be at the meet but I'll be a little late. We have practice till two today but I'll head over right after. Just don't mind if I'm a little sweaty." He adds in a wink to the girls on the team. "I wish you all luck." He turns around and leaves.

I knew he added in that last part about being sweaty so all the girls will get ideas in their heads.

Danielle sighs on my other side. "He is so hot."

Logan snorts. "He sure knows it too."

"You could pass as twins though." Sarah says to Logan.

"We've been confused for each other before." He looks at me knowingly. I groan knowing exactly what story he is about to tell.

"There was this one time right after I met Emma. We had a school project and I guess she was trying to surprise me. She saw me lying on a pool chair so she decided to run and jump on me. Turns out it was actually Jeremy."

That was a pretty funny day. I remember how embarrassed I was, and I tried to leave until Logan persuaded me not to. The girls all laugh and ask for more stories of Jeremy.

Before we know it, it is time to head to the pool. Thankfully, our stuff is already in the lockers. When we get there, Logan gives me a quick good luck kiss and heads to the stands.

The meet is a huge success. I come in second in the 400-meter and first in the 800-meter freestyle. After the meet, we go out to celebrate. Coach tells us not to stay out too late because we have to be at the pool for warm ups at 8 a.m. The relays are the second day of the meet.

We go to a local country club for some line dancing. They even have a mechanical bull. Logan tries to persuade me but I don't want to get hurt before the meet in the morning so I tell him to do it instead. He actually does pretty well and stays on for seven seconds before he is thrown off.

We get some water at the bar and I see Jeremy talking to Danielle. "Looks like they're hitting off." I point them out to Logan.

"Looks like you are right." Just then Cotton Eyed Joe comes on and Logan pulls me to the dance floor. We quickly learn the moves. Then comes the part to swing your partner round and round. We switch partners and I am paired with some other guy. We switch again and I am partnered with Jeremy. "Well howdy there darling." He already has a slight Southern accent but he enunciates it even more.

"I see you're hitting it off with Danielle?" Living in Tennessee my whole life, you would think I would have more of a Southern accent but I don't so I try to make it more pronounced. It is so bad but I stick with it. At least it is better than my British accent from earlier.

"Yeah she's pretty cool."

I drop the accent since I clearly fail at them. "Just don't hurt her. She is really nice and I'd like to have a friend when I come here next year."

"Sounds good partner." He tips his hat at me and shuffles off to the next partner. I pair back up with Logan.

"Hey you." The song ends and a slower one comes on. "Perfect timing."

"It is indeed." He kisses me long and slow. I can't help but melt into his arms.

At the end of the night, I say goodbye to Logan at the club and get a ride with Danielle.

On the drive home, I see Danielle dreamy face. "So what is up with you and Jeremy?"

"Oh nothing. He's super sweet and a great dancer."

"That would be the dance lessons his mom made him take when he was little."

"No way!" She is shocked.

"Yep. Logan too. And yes, he has a sweet side that he lets out every once in a while. Just promise me one thing?"

"What's that?" She seems genuinely interested.

"I am only saying this as a friend because I know Jeremy. I went to high school with him after all." I also know how flirty he is with me even though I am dating Logan. I push past the events of earlier this week. "Just be careful. He's a playboy, and he might seem sweet in the beginning but he doesn't commit. I am not saying he won't ever change, but just guard yourself."

"I will. I am not looking for anything serious, just some fun this summer. It could be a summer fling."

"You say that now, but Jeremy knows how to pull you in. I was there once when I was a freshman. You just can't resist his charm until you start dating his brother. Then his charm is easy to ignore."

"Does he have any other brothers?" The more this girl says, the more I think she is an Ashley clone.

I grin at her. "Not that I know of. Just be careful is all I am saying. Have some fun but remember that is all it is."

"Aye aye captain."

The next day the meet goes well and we finish first over all. Coach threw me in the lineup for the relay. I was third in line. Maybe one day I will be the anchor but I am just glad to be a part of the relay team.

That night Logan and I go out for a romantic dinner. He takes me to a fancy Italian place yet we still get the basics. He orders Spaghetti and Meatballs and I get the Chicken Alfredo.

I joke around that we could be like Lady and the Tramp and share his spaghetti noodles. We try it and the noodle breaks before we meet in the middle. We crack up and see people around us staring. I shush him but that makes us laugh even more.

It feels great to be able to actually laugh after the horrible day on Wednesday. I feel so lucky to have a guy like him. I hope we can continue to trust each other and talk before things get out of hand.

Next year, college will be hard but I think we can make it through. I still have my doubts sometimes about how it will work going to separate colleges and I'll have to talk to him at some point about it before we leave.

The next day we head to the game. Sarah and Danielle join us. Despite my reservations about Sarah, she seems really nice and I look forward to swimming with her next year. Danielle reminds me so much of Ashley that it will be nice to have her around next year.

We have seats right on the 50-yard line, thanks to Jeremy. The Seminoles win and Jeremy plays a great game like always.

Jeremy throws a huge rager at his house to celebrate. I end up passing out in the guest bedroom upstairs. Logan being the gentleman he is, takes the other bed in the room.

The next morning, I go downstairs and see I am not the only one that stayed, as people are passed out on the couches and the floor.

I look around at the mess and throw away the cups and plates laying everywhere.

Danielle comes downstairs in a way too big for her t-shirt and short pj pants. She grabs a solo cup and fills it with water.

"Looks like someone had fun last night."

"Yeah it was fun, and yes I am being careful. In more ways than one." She winks and bursts out laughing. I join her. When we finally calm down, Jeremy and Logan join us in the kitchen.

"What is so funny this fine morning?" Jeremy walks over to Danielle and gives her a hug from behind.

"Oh nothing." I give Logan a kiss on the cheek.

"Just girl talk." Danielle gives Jeremy a kiss on the cheek as well, and then links arms with me.

"We'll be upstairs showering if you need us."

Both of their jaws drop open. Jeremy manages to speak. "Together?"

"Wouldn't you like to know." Danielle winks at them. This girl seriously reminds me of Ashley and it makes me realize how much I am going to miss her next year.

Logan still has his jaw down and Jeremy is barely breathing. I look back and forth between the two of them. "You both have a little drool there on your chins. You might want to wipe that off."

We take off running up the stairs and fall on the beds in the guest room.

"That was great. I can't wait to come here next year. I'll finally have someone to team up with." I really hope we can stay friends next year.

"We will definitely have a great time." She leaves for the shower in the master bathroom. I see through the open door Jeremy entering the master bedroom after her, probably seeing if we are actually serious. Boys are so gullible.

Logan follows closely behind and sees me sitting on the bed. "Hey you."

"Hey yourself. What, no showering together?"

"You know I'm not that type of girl." I purr.

"Oh I know you aren't because you are my girl and always will be."

"I like being called yours." I stand, wrapping my arms around his neck.

"Good, you better get used to it because I don't plan on letting you go." He says as he wraps his arms around my waist, pulling me tight to him.

"Good. Now I'm going to take a shower, and no you can't join me. You can wait your turn." I stick my tongue out at him as I push him away and run to the bathroom before he can get to me.

After our showers, we say our goodbyes and head to the airport. This Spring Break was by far one of the most emotional rollercoasters of my life but I guess that is college. You have plenty of ups and downs but the people that stick out the ride till the end, are the ones worth staying with. I can't wait for the next four years!

Chapter Thirty-six

A week before prom, Ash and I shop for our dresses. Ashley goes with a tight black mermaid style dress with a low neckline. I get a baby blue dress with a gathered skirt and a sweetheart neckline.

Logan gets to go this year. Everything that happened over Spring Break is long forgotten and I am so relieved. I hated the whole situation but if anything, it has brought us closer and better at communicating.

Ashley is just as excited as I am because my brother agreed to go with her. She assures me they are only going as friends but I still like to tease her.

The boys pick us up in a limo at my house and we take tons of pictures. Logan gives me a beautiful white and blue orchid that matches my dress and his tie perfectly.

I was speechless when I walked down the stairs to see Logan at the bottom. He had on a black tux with a white shirt underneath and a baby blue tie that made his eyes pop. I had to remind myself to breathe.

We eat a fancy four-course dinner. This year the Prom committee decided not to have a dinner and use that budget for a fancier location on a yacht. I am super thankful because the food last year was not great. Or should I say just boring.

The theme is Under the Stars so the yacht is the perfect venue. We make our way to the docks and board the yacht. They have really outdone themselves this year with twinkling lights hanging everywhere and the back deck is a dance floor open to the night sky.

Inside is a bar where you can order from a selection of mock-tails. Next to the bar is a long table filled with mini desserts such as cream puffs, mini cakes, and brownies. They even added mini stars to the ceiling.

Fifteen minutes later, the yacht leaves the docks and prom has officially begun. We dance and dance just like we did the year before. Only this year, I am with the perfect guy. Don't get me wrong, Jeremy is great, but Logan is the man I love and it makes it that much more romantic.

We dance with a bunch of people from our class and a few girls tell me they love my dress. I talk to some people at school and have known most of them since I was little. I wouldn't say I was popular, but I am surprised at how many people actually know my name let alone who I am. I keep to myself or well I used to before I started dating Logan. He takes after his brother as the super popular jock. It kind of comes with the territory of having to be more social. Doesn't change the fact that I still try to blend into the background as much as possible. If it weren't for Logan and Ashley, I probably would have no social life.

With every slow song, Logan sings in my ear and I can't help falling for him even more, if that is even possible.

I glance over at Ashley and Tyler. Ashley has her head resting on his chest and he has his chin on the top of her head. Both of their eyes are closed and Tyler has a smile on his face. They are so cute together and I wish they would realize how crazy they are for each other. I know they will never admit their feelings for each other. Ashley would kill me if I ever said anything to Tyler, so for now I have left it alone but one day, I may not be able to hold back.

The time comes for them to announce the king and queen. I know Logan is a shoo in for Prom King just like his brother. I don't think I have a chance at all, seeing as I have been a hermit this past year with all my studying and training. I don't normally care about these types of things but a part of me really wants to be standing up there next to Logan as his Queen. It's silly, I know.

Our school does it a little differently. They announce the Royal Court which includes a Prince, Princess, Duke, Duchess, Marquess and Marchioness. Ashley is named Princess. Lastly, they announce the Prom King and Queen. No surprise, Logan's name is called. He may not have been as popular as his brother, but everyone knows who he is and loves him. I always tell him it is the amazing films he makes.

He accepts his crown on stage.

"Emma Collins". I start clapping because I am so happy for the Prom Queen. It was a good thought that maybe I could be Queen. They say it again. "Emma Collins."

Wait, did they just say my name?

I stand there thinking I imagined it. I look up at Logan and he motions for me to come up on the stage. I slowly make my way up the stairs on the side of the stage.

Why did I think I wanted this? I hate being onstage let alone the center of attention. I will leave that to Logan.

I accept my tiara as everyone claps.

Embarrassed, I take his hand as we make our way down to the dance floor for the traditional Royal Dance.

Ashley dances with Ty and the others pick their partners. I take Logan's hand and ask him, "Are you going to make me do the waltz like your brother did last year?"

"Guess you'll have to follow and find out."

The music starts and we begin to dance. "Don't worry, no Jeremy moves or lifts, I promise. I'd rather hold you close." He pulls me into him so there is no space between us. He whispers in my ear, "one day we will be dancing like this but you will be in white and I will be calling you my wife because you will be mine forever. I'll be counting down the minutes till I can whisk you back to our hotel room and show you exactly what it means to be mine."

I literally swoon right there and probably would have fallen if he wasn't holding me. I so wish that night he is describing was tonight. Can you blame me?

He spins me around the dance floor. Unlike when I was dancing with Jeremy the year before, I feel like I belong in Logan's arms.

As the song ends, he dips me — similar to how Jeremy had done not only last year but over Spring Break. This time I look up and see the real Logan staring down at me like he wants to kiss me. And he does. I kiss him back knowing this is the guy I am meant to be with.

The rest of the dance is magical and we spend some time gazing out at the moon lit lake.

On the way home, I cuddle next to Logan. "Thanks for an amazing night."

"Better than last year, right?"

"I don't know that brother of yours..." His face goes blank. I quickly kiss him. "I'm just kidding. This year was perfect and I never expected to be crowned queen. That was a shock since I am not the most social person."

Logan looks over at me. "Are you kidding me? People love you. You may have just been too busy studying or training to notice. People always say great things about you."

"Who did you have to pay to make that happen?" I could think of so many other girls that were way more popular. Then again, they had won the Duchess and the Marquess.

"I may have nominated you but that is it. Everyone else did the voting. They always talk about how smart you are and what an amazing swimmer you are. The guys have plenty to say which I don't always like, but you do have an amazing body and a beautiful face. You are always nice to everyone that you talk to. Plus, it helps when you go to the Prom with the Anderson brothers two years in a row."

I punch him in the shoulder. He may not have as big of an ego as his brother, but he still has his moments.

"Well either way I got to dance with my king under the stars so I was happy."

The rest of the limo ride, I sit quietly thinking about our amazing night. I know that no matter what happens in the future, I'll always remember this night.

"I am going to miss this."

Logan wraps his arm tighter around me knowing what I mean without me having to explain. "Me too."

I stare into the darkness outside the limo and can't help feeling scared. The closer graduation gets, the more I realize I am going to miss everyone. I will have my brother and Jeremy at FSU with me but my family will be here in Tennessee, Ashley will be in North Carolina, and Logan will be all the way in New York.

I can't help but worry where we will all be in a year from now. Will Ashley and I still be best friends? Will Logan and I stay together? Will I make it to the Olympics?

I feel Logan shift next to me and lightly turn my head so he can see my face.

"What are you thinking so hard about?"

"Nothing really." How does he always know when something is wrong? I don't want him to know my doubts.

"You forget I know you pretty well and when you're deep in thought. Now spill."

"I'm just thinking about the future and where we will be in a year from now or even three years from now. You're going to New York and Ashley is going to North Carolina. I feel like I'm losing my two best friends."

"You aren't losing either of us. We have Facetime and a private plane. We will still talk every day and I am not letting you go." He nuzzles my neck with his nose kissing behind my ear. "You and me till the day I die."

"I know but it's college. You will be super busy with film school and getting used to a new city with new people and new things to do. Don't you want to explore and have the college experience without being tied down?"

"Of course, what guy doesn't. But I also have an amazing girlfriend I am not planning on letting go of. I can still experience all college has to offer, just not the girls part. I have everything I want right here in that department." He links our fingers together.

"You make it sound so easy. I am scared you are going to go off to New York and become this huge filmmaker and then fall in love with some actress you cast in one of your films."

"I certainly hope that the first part comes true but as for the second part, the only actress I love is the one sitting right in front of me."

"I am not an actress."

"Well, there was our English project you acted in, and you're the main star of most of my films these days."

"I guess. Aren't you scared at all?"

"Of course, but not about us. We got through my huge over-reaction this past Spring Break. We survived the long-distance last summer. This time it's just a little longer but like I said before we have phones and a private plane at our disposal."

"Just promise me that you'll always talk to me if something is wrong or you have found someone else. I don't want to go through thinking you are going to break up with me again or being strung along."

"Deal, but I don't plan on letting you go. The more I think back to Spring Break the more I feel dumb for reacting the way I did. My past experiences clouded my judgement even though I knew you would never cheat. All I could see was what happened before and not what was right in front of me. For that I'm truly sorry because I caused you so much pain. I never want you to feel that or to feel it myself ever again."

"I know. Now hold me till we get to my house. I want to enjoy the rest of this perfect night."

"Sounds perfect." He pulls me into him as I lay my head against his shoulder thinking back on the night. He gave me reassurance that he isn't going anywhere. I hope we do get our forever.

Chapter Thirty-seven

The second to last day of school, I am called into the office. I have a feeling I know what it is about and I am hoping I will be able to talk my principal out of it.

The secretary points to the door and tells me to go in. The only other times I have been in here was earlier this year with the whole Logan punching Sam incident and then last year when I was asked to show a new girl around.

Principal Evans looks up as I walk in. "Emma, so glad to see you." He folds his hands in front of him. "I assume you know why I called you in?"

"I assume it has to do with the Valedictorian."

"You are correct. We received the final grades and you were at the top of your class. I wanted to personally congratulate you. You have put in a ton of work both with your classes and athletics. I am excited to watch you in the Olympics in a few years."

"I still have to make it sir." I still have two years of hard work ahead of me and that doesn't include actually making the Olympic team. That isn't what worries me though, because he just confirmed what this meeting is about. Being the Valedictorian means I have to give a speech at graduation. I don't do public speaking.

"I have no doubt you will make it. Just go into that gym and look at all the banners with your name on it. You have beaten more records in your four years here than any student in the past fifty years. Plus, you have a full scholarship to FSU and already did a great job at the meet with their team."

Is he stalking me or something? I know this is a small town and a small school, but it's still kind of weird he knows so much. Right? I don't know whether to be creeped out or honored.

He looks at me admiringly. He probably just talks to my dad since he is the Football coach here.

"But I didn't call you in for that. I called you in about the speech you are to give at graduation on Saturday. There are some guidelines I wanted to go over."

"I actually have a question about the speech. Can you have the Salutatorian give the speech instead? I'm not good at public speaking and I'd rather not give it."

"Emma, I have faith in you that you will be able to give it and if I am not mistaken." He checks the papers on his desk. "It looks like you just took a speech class this semester at the community college. That should help."

"I know but sir, I believe someone else would give a much better speech."

"Emma, I would like you to give it. I think you have a lot to say and can really speak to the senior class. If I am being quite honest, it will help give you confidence for future public speaking events.”

I know this is a battle I will lose so I reluctantly agree. “Okay sir, I’ll try my best.”

We go over the guidelines for the speech and order of the graduation.

“Emma, it has been a pleasure having you these past four years and I will see you on Saturday.”

I leave the office. Looks like I have a speech to write.

Saturday comes too quickly and I wake up in a cold sweat. I rehearsed my speech multiple times in front of Logan and Ashley. They even helped me write it but I am not any less nervous.

I hear a knock at my door and tell whoever it is to come in. My parents run in with confetti and balloons. My mom has a plate of french toast and fruit on the side. Stuck in the middle of the french toast is a candle. I laugh at my crazy parents as they set the tray down.

“You get to clean up that confetti.” My mom laughs and says, “deal”.

“Now make a wish and blow out your candle.” My dad points at the plate of french toast.

“You know it’s not my birthday right?”

My dad chuckles. "Yes. We know full well when your birthday is, but we think you can still make a wish on your graduation day. This is the day you become an adult and move on to greatness."

My dad always has a great speech ready to go. Probably has to do with being a football coach and giving a motivational speech before each game.

I look down at the candle and up at my parents. I think about my life. I have an amazing boyfriend. I am going to an amazing school in the Fall. I may not know what to major in, but everything in my life is great. I even have a big chance at making the Olympic team. I think hard and decide on my wish as I close my eyes. I blow out the candle.

"That must have been some wish." My mom sits down on the bed next to me. "Are you ready for graduation?"

"I am a little nervous about my speech, but I can't wait to graduate."

"You're going to do great." She kisses me on the top of the head. "Now get changed and I will have this ready for you on the kitchen table." She takes the tray but not before I grab a piece of fruit.

I change into my baby blue knee length dress. The top is a halter and according to Ashley, shows off my toned shoulders.

In the kitchen, Ty jumps up from the table to give me a hug. "When did you get in?"

"Late last night with Jeremy. I couldn't miss my little sister graduating and her giving a speech. That is something worth seeing."

"Yeah the speech..."

"Just imagine everyone in their underwear."

I smack him on the shoulder. "Thanks Ty. That helps a lot."

We get to the high school and I spot the Andersons. We make our way over to them.

Logan gives me a hug and kiss. "You ready?" I nod trying not to think about it.

Jeremy walks up. "Congrats Miss Valedictorian".

"Thanks Jer." I give him a hug and then accept hugs from their parents. Just then Ashley runs up to me.

"We're graduating!" She yells. "Let's go get our seats."

I laugh. Logan, Ash and I wave at our families before heading to our seats. Logan is seated on the ground but Ashley and I are up on the stage with the other top ten students.

Ashley graduated number six in our class and I am so proud of her. She is going to The University of North Carolina at Chapel Hill and double majoring in Communications and History.

The graduation ceremony begins and Principal Evans speaks first. He introduces our guest speaker and then announces the top ten students. Per our discussion, that is my cue.

My hands holding my speech begin to shake. I find Logan in the crowd and he smiles, giving me a thumbs up. Everything in me calms. He has come to be my rock and I hate to rely on him so much. That is why it scares me so much with us going to different colleges.

"Welcome friends, family and graduates. I am honored to be up here today, and I will admit to being a little nervous about this speech. We started out as scared freshmen, but these past four years have turned us into ambitious, driven seniors. I look around here today at the many people that helped us get here."

I go on to thank all our friends, family and teachers for teaching us lessons and helping us set goals. I tell funny stories that have everyone laughing and crying. I talk about how all of our relationships and life lessons we learned made us into the people we are today. They pushed us out of our comfort zones to do things we never thought possible.

"As we leave here today, we have a wide open road in front of us. These past four years have made that road a little clearer and pushed us closer to our dreams. Just remember the relationships we made here and the lessons we learned will help us make those dreams a reality. I will leave you with this quote, "Don't let the fear of striking out keep you from playing the game.""

Everyone applauds and Logan is the first to stand, followed by my family and the Andersons.

I am so relieved that my speech is behind me. I go back to my seat and Principal Evans takes the podium to begin the presentation of diplomas.

Those of us onstage, the top ten, stand first.

Principal Evans makes a few remarks before he begins, "Emma Collins." I take a deep breath and walk towards Principal Evans to accept my diploma. He shakes my hand and whispers, "Wonderful speech. I knew you could do it." I smile and move the tassel to the other side of my hat before circling back to my seat.

"Ashley Gallagher." I clap and holler loudly as Ash accepts her diploma.

When the top ten are done, they move onto the rest of the class. "Logan Anderson." I jump up from my seat and clap. Logan accepts his diploma and gives me a quick kiss as he walks by before making his way down the stairs to his seat. I hear whistling from the audience and I am guessing it is either my brother, Jeremy, or both.

I am shocked he did that in front of everyone but then again, he is always surprising me.

The rest of the class is called and Principal Evans says the words we are all dying to hear, "I now present to you the graduating class of Marshall Creek High School." We all stand and toss up our hats.

I run down to Logan who catches me when I jump to give him a hug. "You did amazing and I am so proud of you." He kisses me way more passionately than is probably appropriate for where we are but I don't care. I am thankful he didn't give me a kiss like that on stage.

We pull away as all our families walk up already with their cameras out. They congratulate us and tell me how much they loved my speech. Jeremy gives me a hug. "Nice baseball reference there at the end of your speech."

"Thanks but it is actually from the movie, *A Cinderella Story*. Have you seen it?" He shakes his head. "Looks like you'll have to watch it. It's a romantic comedy!" I tease.

Jeremy secretly loves romantic comedies but only Logan and I know. He says he can't have people thinking he isn't the big bad football player. That's how I know he will go watch it when he gets home.

My parents take tons of pictures of Logan, Ash and I. Then we do every combination of pictures — family pictures, just Ash and I, Ash and my brother, just Logan and I, and even Logan and Jeremy holding me.

It feels great to finally graduate from high school, but it also makes me nervous. I don't know much about what the future holds but I am currently surrounded by the people I care most about in the world, and that is all I can ask for.

Chapter Thirty-eight

The summer passes way too quickly. I still have a strict swim training schedule, putting in six to seven hours a day. I am typically done around three in the afternoon.

All my free time is spent with Ashley and Logan. Logan is headed off to New York, Ashley to North Carolina and me to Florida. I hate going to separate schools but we plan on visiting each other whenever possible. Logan says he is going to try to come to plenty of his brother's games.

At the end of the summer, we have a cookout at the local park with some friends from school as a last hurrah before going off to college.

I stand in the gazebo and admire the mountains in the distance. I'll miss this view when I go to Florida. Last I checked, there were no mountains there.

Logan puts his arms around my shoulders, resting his head on mine. I love that he is that much taller than me so I can feel like I am completely engulfed in him when he hugs me. "What are you thinking about?"

"Everything — college, swimming, the future, us..."

"Uh ohh. This better not be the part where you break up with me."

He can't see my face but if he could, he would know how much his statement will never be true. I have no plans of ever breaking up with him or giving him a reason to break up with me.

"No, never. I was just thinking how hard it is going to be not seeing you every day and how much I am going to miss you."

"Hey, look at me." He gently turns my chin towards him. "We are going to be okay. I love you so much. More than you know, and I am not letting you go ever. We will talk on the phone every day. I will try to make it to whatever football games I can."

"I know, I just wish I had you around with me."

"You have my brother. He already said he would look out for you."

"Oh thanks, just hand me off to your brother." I shove him and he falls to the side before catching himself.

"Just no hot tubs in tiny bikinis." I give him a funny look. We are at the point now where we can look back at what happened last Spring Break and laugh at it. "For real though, if anything ever happened to me, I wouldn't trust anyone more than him to help you move on."

I am speechless. Nothing better happen to him.

Logan laughs. "I'm not going anywhere — well except New York, but before you know it Thanksgiving will be here and then Christmas."

"Yeah and I know swimming is going to be taking up most of my time when I am not in class or studying. I still don't know what to major in."

"I know you love science. Have you ever thought about being a doctor of some sort?"

"I don't know. I've never really liked viruses or sick people."

"No, I mean something to do with Sports Physical Therapy. With swimming, you have already had to learn about the different muscles and how to prevent them from cramping up or tearing after hours of training."

"I never thought about that. It would definitely help in swimming the more I learn plus I won't be able to swim in the Olympics my whole life. Why not do something helping future generations of Olympians. I have a meeting with my advisor the first week of school so I'll see what she thinks. You are amazing!"

"Of course I am." He grins but before I can push him again, he grabs onto me and the side of the gazebo. He grins even wider. "Have you figured out about your credits yet?"

"That is what my meeting with the advisor is for. I think I'll have enough to graduate in two years depending on what I major in. If I do sports physical therapy, that is probably another two to three years on top of that for a masters. I am assuming you need a masters for that."

"I don't know how you managed to get so many college credits." He sighs. "I am going to miss you even if it is only to watch you swim or bite your fingernails as you study."

I put my head on his shoulder. "Like you said though, this semester will fly by and soon we will be right back here for Thanksgiving and Christmas."

Ashley joins us and puts her head on my shoulder. "I am going to miss this. With everything wide open like you said in your speech, anything can happen." She pulls out her phone and takes a selfie of the three of us. "Picture perfect moment."

She is right. Anything can happen and we need to capture every moment.

Ashley is the first to leave. I go over to her house to help her pack. She is sorting through her clothes when I get there. I stand in her doorway, watching her contemplate which dresses to take and which to give away. I see her throw a blue and purple sundress in the giveaway pile. "Hey I like that dress."

She picks it up out of the pile and throws it at me. "Take it. Looks better on you anyway."

I sit down on the floor next to her. "How's the packing going? By the looks of it, you still have a way to go. Don't you leave tomorrow?"

"Don't remind me. I have to somehow narrow my closet down to these three suitcases. That is all that will fit in the car with the rest of my stuff."

"You realize you're only going to school about six hours away. That is close enough to come home on the weekend for anything you forget."

"Aren't you forgetting I have nothing to come back here for? My parents are always traveling for work and you'll be away at school."

"You could always hang out with Amber. Isn't she going to the University of Tennessee? That is an hour or two from here."

"Oh yes. Amber and I are best friends forever, especially after I caught her with Daniel too." I can hear the sarcasm in her voice.

Turns out Daniel had been cheating on Ashley with Amber and Mallory. When Ashley confronted him, she had only mentioned Mallory and he wasn't about to come forward about Amber. It was later that Ashley found out about Amber and she made it well known that it had been going on for a while, before Ashley and him had broken up.

"Do you want this? I never wore it." She holds up a bright pink strapless blouse.

I scrunch up my nose. "I think I'm good." She tosses it in the giveaway pile.

"Well, I'm just about done. I need to put these four piles in these two suitcases and those two piles of shoes in the third suitcase. Want to help?"

I nod and we get to work on making everything fit. When we finally close the last suitcase, we take everything out to the cars. The car is already filled with everything else like towels, sheets, pillows and then the extra stuff like her own mini fridge and a dry erase calendar. I end up with a box full of clothes she no longer wants.

Before she heads out, we go to Jack's for some burgers.

"What am I going to do when I don't know what to wear?"

She pulls out her phone and presses a few buttons. My phone starts to ring and I look to see Ashley is Facetiming me. I hold the phone up to her. "Why are you calling me?"

"Just answer." I hit accept and see her face. "You see there is this great thing called Facetime where you can actually see the other person."

I just shake my head before ending the call and looking at her for real across the table. "I am warning you now, you may be getting a lot of calls."

"Fine by me." She smiles over at me.

"Are you scared at all for college?"

"I'm scared that I won't fit in anywhere. You have swimming and Jeremy and your brother. Logan has his films. What do I have?"

"Ash you have you! You fit in everywhere you go. Talking to people and making new friends has always come easy to you. I never knew how you did it these past four years. You're good at everything you do. You can play an intramural sport or join any club, or even be president of the mathletes." She stares at me like I just told her I killed someone.

We burst out laughing at the same time. When we finally calm down after getting a few amused looks I say to her, "Maybe not that last one because math is the worst unless you're Logan. I just meant you can do anything. No one will know you and you can have so much fun trying new things and meeting new people. I am actually kind of jealous. I will already be so busy with swimming that I won't be able to try new things, plus I will have Jeremy and Tyler constantly watching me."

Ashley seems to think about it for a while. "I guess you're right. It'll just be different. What about you? Are you scared?"

"I am scared that everything is going to change and I am going to be left behind. Jeremy and my brother have their lives there already. I'm scared Logan is going to love life in New York and forget about little old me. You're going to go take over the University of North Carolina and forget our small little town here."

"First off, you are crazy if you think Logan is going to fall for anyone else besides you. Second, we have been friends since we were born and I haven't gone anywhere yet, have I?" I shake my head at her.

"Why are you always right?"

"I think I just know my best friend." She grabs my hand. "Now are we ready for one last sleepover before I leave tomorrow?"

"Will there be pillow fights and prank calls?"

"Of course. It wouldn't be a sleepover without it."

We pay our bill and link arms as we make our way to my car. We took mine since hers was packed.

I am going to miss her so much. I know she will always be there for me if I need her just as I am for her, but it'll be different not having her actually with me.

I start classes a week after Ashley. I have to show up a few days before that to move into my dorm.

On my last night in town, my parents take me out to dinner. I invite Logan too. I am going to miss my parents but they remind me that they will always be here if I get homesick or just need to do laundry.

After dinner, Logan takes me out for ice cream. We eat as we walk hand in hand around the town. It is a breezy night and we eventually find ourselves at our park. It used to be my park but after Logan kissed me here the first time, it quickly turned into our park.

We sit in the gazebo and I wrap my jacket around me a little tighter. Logan pulls me into his side. We stare out at the sky and enjoy the silence. I wish I could stay like this forever.

When it comes time for goodbyes the next morning, Logan reassures me that he isn't going anywhere. The Homecoming game is several weeks after school starts and he is going to try to come for it.

I give him a hug. A long hug that I never want to get out of. I feel safe and loved in his arms. Logan cups my face in his hands staring into my eyes. He does that thing where he looks deep into my soul. "One day we won't have to do the goodbyes but until then, I love you Emma Collins. Don't you forget it."

"I could never." As I feel the first tear fall, I lean forward and kiss Logan. He deepens the kiss. It has so many emotions in it from love to sadness to goodbye for now.

When we pull apart, he rests his forehead against mine, wiping the tear that has fallen to my cheek. "I love you too, Logan."

"Now go before I whisk you away and lock you up so you don't have to leave."

"Okay." I give him one more kiss before getting in my car. The last thing I see before I turn the corner is Logan blowing me a kiss.

As I pull onto the highway, I can't help but feel like things are about to change. I don't know whether it will be a good or bad change, but for once I am excited to see what the future holds.

I am going to my dream school, swimming and training for the Olympics, and even possibly majoring in something I could have a lot of fun with. I will miss my best friend and my boyfriend but I know neither of them are going anywhere.

College will be a new adventure and I can't wait to see what it has to offer.

Chapter Thirty-nine

Turns out Danielle is my roommate. She requested me and I couldn't be happier. She still reminds me so much of Ashley, that it makes me miss her even more. It is nice having Danielle as a roommate because with us both being on the swim team, we have the same early hours. I never have to worry about waking her up in the morning.

It is already the end of October. My first semester in college has been so busy that I haven't had a chance to make it up to New York to visit Logan. He did come down for the FSU Homecoming game against Georgia. We beat the Bulldogs.

With the semester flying by we won't be able to see each other again until Thanksgiving or so he thinks. We planned to see each other for Halloween, but I told him something came up with my classes and I wouldn't make it. Really, I am planning on surprising him.

My coach had to leave early for the weekend so he gave us Friday practice off. I only have one class at 8 a.m. and plan on leaving right after.

I ask Jeremy if he can set up the jet for me so I can spend as much time in New York and not deal with the airport.

When I finally land in LaGuardia, I call an Uber to take me to New York University — Hayden Hall. While I wait for the car to arrive, I think of all the ways I can surprise Logan.

I didn't have much time to plan it out on the plane because I was trying to finish my paper. I wasn't lying when I said that something for class came up. One of my professors assigned us a five-page paper that is due next week. Thankfully, it is a topic I could write in my sleep so I was able to finish it on the plane.

I glance down at my phone and see my Uber is two minutes away. His name is Elijah and he is driving a red Prius.

When he arrives, he helps me put my carry-on in the trunk. In the car, I text Logan to see what he is up to.

Emma: *Hey you. What are you doing with the rest of your Halloween Eve?*

It's a few minutes before he texts back.

Logan: *Just heading out to grab a bite to eat at the Spaniard place right around the corner from my dorm. It's this little pub that has delicious burgers. Next time you come, I'll have to take you here.*

I can just imagine how good the food is. New York has some of the best food and I'm sure Logan finds all the best places.

Emma: *Sounds delicious. I wish I was there to eat with you right now.*

I smile to myself knowing I will be in several minutes. I ask my Uber driver if he can drop me off at the pub right around the corner from the dorms. I give him the name and he says he knows the place and that it is no problem.

Logan texts me back before I put my phone in my pocket.

Logan: *Me too but Thanksgiving will be here before you know it. I have stuff to do anyway and you would be a distraction.*

A distraction? I hope he isn't mad that I really am here. Before I can even think about it more, another text comes through.

Logan: *A wonderful distraction and I so wish you were here but I am counting down the days till I have you in my arms again. I'll text you in a little bit. My partner just got here.*

He must be working on a project but that is okay. I can occupy myself while he finishes and then he can show me the sights.

We pull up to the Pub and Elijah helps me with my luggage. I only have my carry-on and my backpack so I can easily manage it.

In the Pub, I spot Logan in the back corner. I hide behind a fake tree to watch him and plan my next move. If he is working on a project, I don't want to disturb him just yet. I can sit at another table and just let him work for a little and then I will make myself known. I want him to get his work done so we can actually have time together.

I peer around the tree and notice a girl walk over to him and sit down rather close. I see Logan pull out a small bag of what looks like white powder. He hands it to the girl who very discreetly hands him a wad of cash. He then puts the cash in his pocket. She stands up and walks by me.

I can't believe what I am seeing. *Is Logan dealing drugs?*

I don't even allow my conscience to talk me into staying and listening to whatever he has to say. I go to leave but the wheel on my luggage catches on the tree. I pull and the tree falls over, exposing me to Logan.

Just my luck!

He looks up and stares right at me. His face immediately breaks into a wide grin. I need to get out of here as fast as possible.

I don't have time to wait for an Uber. I do what they do in the movies and raise my hand. It actually works when a cab pulls up. I throw my suitcase in the backseat and hop in.

Right as I am about to close the door, Logan grabs it. "Emma, what are you doing here?"

"I was trying to surprise you until I saw you dealing drugs. I can't be with someone that is doing that, not if I want to make it to the Olympics."

He tries to get in the car but I push on his chest.

"Please Emma, let me explain. It isn't what you think. Please just scoot over and I will tell you everything."

"No, get out. It's over." I give him a good shove and pull the door closed. I tell the taxi driver to take me to LaGuardia. Maybe the jet hasn't left yet and I can get it to take me home.

We pull up to the private jet section and I call Jeremy. He answers on the first ring and I say, "Does the jet have anywhere else to be today?"

"I don't think so. I believe my dad is using it tomorrow morning and then it is coming back to New York to pick you up on Sunday. Why what's up? I thought you would be with my brother by now?"

"Plans changed and I need to come home."

"Okay. I know you won't tell me anything until you have processed whatever happened. Just go up to the gate and tell them you're there for the Anderson Jet. I'll take care of the rest."

"Thanks Jer."

"Call me if you have any problems." He pauses. "Emma, whatever my brother did, was probably nothing. He loves you and wouldn't do anything to hurt you."

"Yeah well this just might be that thing. I have to go. Talk soon."

I hang up before he can say anything else. I know after what happened last Spring Break Jeremy has been making sure nothing comes between Logan and I. Don't get me wrong, he is still his annoying, huge ego, flirty self but he will never put us in that situation again.

Between him and my brother always watching me at school, I am glad to be dating Logan because I would never be able to date anyone. They won't let me out of their sight enough to go on a date let alone approve of any guy. Well... I guess now... No, I don't even want to think about dating.

I tell the gate I am here for the Anderson Jet. They look at their schedule and tell me nothing is set to leave till later today. I tell them there is a change of plans and I need to leave. The attendant gets a call. He nods a bunch and right before he hangs up, I hear, "will do, Mr. Anderson."

I figure it must have been Jeremy calling to tell them I was good to go because the attendant lets me through and leads me to where the jet is refueling.

They tell me to make myself comfortable on the jet and we will be headed to North Carolina as soon as the jet is fueled. I thank them and then pause. Wait, did he say North Carolina?

Before I can ask the attendant, my phone buzzes in my pocket with a text message.

I glance at it to see it's from Jeremy.

Jeremy: *I told them you were headed to North Carolina. I thought you might want to spend the weekend with Ashley. Girl time and all.*

Why did I not think of that? Jeremy is always looking out for me. Maybe I should start dating him. I shake my head as soon as the thought pops in my head. It is way too soon to be thinking about dating, let alone dating Jeremy. He is way too annoying.

I shoot Ashley a text.

Emma: *How would you feel about some company this weekend?*

She replies immediately.

Ashley: *Uh ohh... I thought you were supposed to be in New York with that boy of yours?*

Emma: *Well plans change. I'll explain everything when I get there?*

Ashley: *You're always welcome here. Let me know your eta and I'll be there.*

She always seems to know how to cheer me up.

Emma: *Okay!*

The crew confirms the flight plan with me and I agree to whatever airport is closest to the University of North Carolina.

The pilot lets me know as soon as they are done fueling that we will be on our way.

When the flight attendant comes over with a glass of champagne, I ask what time they think we will land and then text Ashley the details.

Ashley: *See you soon. I'll be the one waiting with flowers.*

Sometimes all you need is your best friend.

The plane lands and sure enough Ashley is waiting. I walk down the stairs of the jet.

"Where are my flowers?" I ask, jokingly.

"Well you see the store was out but my freezer is filled with ice cream and my DVD player is cued up with chick flicks."

The crew member hands me my luggage.

"Good because I am going to need it. Although, maybe not a chick flick."

The ride to Ashley's dorm is only twenty-five minutes away. She was correct when she said the freezer was stocked with ice cream. She has everything from triple chocolate fudge to cookie dough.

"Do you normally have this much ice cream in your freezer?"

"No, but I happened to be at the store when Jeremy called to ask if he could send the plane here. I didn't ask why but I knew something must have happened since you're supposed to be in New York. I figured I should probably have ice cream ready."

"Jeremy called you?"

"Yeah he did."

Jeremy is getting major brownie points today.

Stop thinking about Jeremy. You just ended it with Logan.

My brain is all over the place. It is time for ice cream and to stop thinking about either of the annoyingly charming Anderson boys.

We settle onto her bed with big bowls of ice cream and turn on the first movie.

Sisterhood of the Traveling Pants is a favorite of ours and while it may have romance in it, I like to focus on the friendship.

Halfway through I turn to Ashley. "Logan was dealing drugs."

Ashley sets her empty bowl on her bedside table. "I'm sorry what?"

"I was going to surprise him and he said he was at a pub right by his dorm. I walked in and saw him in the back corner. Then some girl sat down. He handed her a bag of white powder and she handed him some cash. What else am I supposed to think?"

"So you just left?"

"Yeah and he saw me. Chased me down the street and tried to get in my cab. He told me to listen to him as I didn't know the whole story."

"Why didn't you listen?"

"I probably should have but I was just so mad that he would be dealing drugs. He knows I can't be around that if I want to go to the Olympics. They take that all very seriously and I don't want to be caught up in whatever he was doing."

"Emma... I really think you should talk to him."

I pull my knees to my chest. "I'll let him sit for a little bit. I just don't know how he can explain dealing drugs. I mean it isn't like he needs the money or anything."

She wraps her arms around me and pulls me to her. "Emma, I'm sure it wasn't real. Let me get more ice cream."

Ashley jumps off her bed and goes over to her small kitchenette. I see her pull out her phone and text someone. She glances at me suspiciously and then back at her phone.

Why is she looking at me? She better not be texting either of the Anderson boys. "Ash, who are you texting?"

She sets her phone back on the counter and pulls out the ice cream. "No one. Just a friend in one of my classes asking if I wanted to go out tomorrow night. One of the bars is throwing a Halloween Bash."

Oh, that explains it. She probably thinks I don't want to go but that sounds like the perfect distraction. "Sounds fun. We should go."

"You sure?"

"Yes. It'll help get my mind off of everything."

"Okay. I will text her back then. What do you want to dress up as?"

I think for a second. All I can think about are the signs I kept seeing in New York for the new Cat in the Hat Musical. "Thing 1 and Thing 2! I actually have that little red dress we bought together. Do you still have yours?"

"Yes, but Emma you realize it is in the fifties and only getting colder."

I think again because the dresses are pretty short and we will definitely freeze. "Well I have knee high black boots, tights and the dress is long sleeve. We can print out Thing 1 and Thing 2 and tape them onto the dress."

"Looks like my fashion sense is rubbing off on you. I will turn on my computer." She puts the ice cream away before it melts.

We print out our signs and laminate them with the awesome machine her roommate has. I guess she is very OCD about things spilling and laminates everything so nothing will get ruined. Ashely told me she even laminates her papers for class because she had a few times where coffee spilled on them or they got rained on and her papers were ruined. I guess it makes sense but it is still a little crazy. Either way I am thankful for it now.

By the time we are done it is super late and we are ready to pass out. Her roommate is gone for the weekend and said I could use her bed for the weekend.

The next day I sleep in till nine. It feels nice to not have to get up early. We head out to get some brunch and then pick up some blue feathers to put in our hair as part of our costumes.

Around six, Ashley leaves to get takeout. About an hour and half later, she finally gets back.

"What took you so long?" I ask her.

"Halloween gets everyone excited and people are everywhere." She sets the bag on her desk and pulls out a container. It smells delicious. She went to this new healthy Chinese place, if you can call it that. Instead of regular noodles, they use zucchini or sweet potato noodles. It is all low carb and low sodium. It may not taste exactly like the regular stuff, but it still tastes delicious.

Chapter Fourty

We enter the bar and there are people in costume everywhere. I guess that makes sense since it's Halloween. I try not to think about what Logan and I would be doing right now.

At the bar, we order two Manhattans. "They didn't card me." I say surprised.

"What did you expect? It's a college bar so let's have fun. Here's to us having a great night and listening." She holds her cup out.

"Listening to what?" I ask what she means by her comment.

"Just the music." She holds her cup up higher. "Just cheers me." I clink my glass with hers and take a sip.

We finish the first round and head to the dance floor.

"This is Halloween" comes on. We attempt to dance to it but end up laughing hysterically because this is not a song you can dance to. Try it next time you hear it.

A few more songs play and then they go with a slower one.

We take a break and start heading to get more drinks when I hear someone behind me. He sounds familiar but it is so loud that I don't really know. "Can I have this dance?"

"No sorry I have a boyfriend." I yell over my shoulder. The last thing I want is to dance with some creep. I look for Ashley but she has disappeared. Great, this is just what I need.

He grabs my waist and whispers into my ear. I am ready to punch this guy out when I instantly feel electricity run through me. "Glad to hear I'm still your boyfriend." I turn around and see a guy dressed as the Cat in the Hat.

"Logan?" I peer under the hat to get a glimpse.

"Hey Emma." He takes off his hat. "I had to find you. Ashley told me where you all would be tonight. I want to explain about what you saw."

"I need a drink." I finally spot Ashley at the bar. He grabs my hand before I can leave.

"Please Emma. One dance so I can explain, and if you still don't believe me then I'll go back to New York."

I feel him squeeze my hand and I can feel the electricity coursing through me, once again. I know I at least owed him the chance to explain.

"Fine."

I wrap my arms around his shoulders making sure to leave plenty of space between us. If I get too close, I know I will melt in his arms and believe anything he says.

"You have till the end of this song."

"Okay. What you think you saw was not actually what you saw. I am working on a film project and that is one of the scenes we were shooting. I was trying to show the actress in the film, that girl you saw, what I wanted. The actor in it was sitting at the table right next to us."

I peer into his deep blue eyes trying to see if he is telling the truth. Normally I can see everything in his eyes but I can barely see his face with the flashing lights.

"Right, and how am I supposed to believe that you aren't just saying that?"

"Emma, would I lie to you? You know me. I would never try to jeopardize your future or our future. I want to spend forever with you, but if you can't trust me then maybe this isn't going to work."

"Yeah maybe it isn't." I remove my arms from his shoulders.

He releases his grip on my waist. "Goodbye, Emma." With one last look, he walks away.

I stand there and watch him walk away. It feels like he yanked my heart out and took it with him which doesn't make sense. I should be glad because he is lying and dealing drugs.

Or is he? Do I believe him? Was it really a project? Did I just over react?

Ashley makes her way towards me with a drink in her hand. I grab it and chug the whole thing. "Is Logan not staying?"

"No he isn't...Wait how did you know that was Logan?"

She can't seem to look me in the eye. "I may have helped him come here."

Now I briefly remember Logan saying that. "Of course. Well, he told me it was for a film project."

She looks hopeful. "So you believe him?" I shake my head. "Why not? That sounds more like Logan. The whole dealing drugs thing doesn't sound like him."

"I just know what I saw and it looked too real." I remember back to the way Logan was very secretive about handing the drugs over. He looked around like he was going to be caught. He took the money like it wasn't the first time he had done it.

"He is going to school for film not acting." It looked too real for him to be acting.

"Don't many directors come from actors? Isn't it some requirement that those going to film school need to have an acting class to learn the other side?"

"How do you know all this?" I am surprised she knows so much about film school.

She shuffles her feet embarrassed. "A guy I know is in film school."

"A guy huh?"

She finally looks up at me. "Yes, a guy. We've been on one date so don't get too excited. Anyway, do you really think Logan would do something like that?"

"Honestly, no. It just looked so real. I just need time to cool down from it. Let's get another drink."

I head to the bar and realize Ashley is still standing in the same place. She shakes her head like she knows more than she is telling me. I leave the topic alone for now. I don't want to talk about it anymore. She eventually follows me to the bar.

Later that night, Ashley helps me into bed. I don't really remember much after Logan left. I drank way too much hoping it would make me forget. It did, for a while.

I wake up in the morning with a pounding headache. Everything comes rushing back. That is the thing about getting drunk. It may seem great during but after is so not worth it.

I see a bottle of water with two Advils next to it. There is a note, "Went out to run errands. Be back soon. Ash." I swallow the Advil and chug the bottle of water. It feels great going down my very dry throat.

I hear the click of the door and Ashley walks through. "Oh good you're awake. I brought you some breakfast."

"Yes, breakfast would be great and coffee."

"That I have right here." She pulls a coffee cup from behind her back.

"You're an angel." I take a giant sip. When the caffeine starts to sink in, I sigh and say. "Ash, I think I made a mistake."

"Aww come here." She pulls me in for a hug and rubs my back.

A tear rolls down my cheek. "I should have just listened to him last night. I knew he was telling me the truth, but I was just being stubborn and insecure."

"Hey everyone can get like that in relationships."

"Everything was just going too perfect. We never fight except that one time over Spring Break. I just feel like something is wrong and we should fight more. Relationships shouldn't be this easy."

"Em, you two are perfect for each other and that is why it's so easy. You both light up when the other walks in the room. You get this glow whenever you talk about each other. You finish each other's sentences. You are his muse for all his films while he is your number one fan at all your swim meets. Do I need to go on--?"

"No, you can stop now. I get it. I messed up. How do I make it better?"

"I may know something you don't. I figured you might have realized you made a mistake so I went to his hotel this morning to stop him from leaving before he talked to you again."

"What did he say?"

"He had already left so I called him and texted but he didn't answer."

"How is this helping, Ash?"

"Let me finish. I called Jeremy and asked if he could get his flight information. You have the private plane so he is on a commercial flight. I told him the whole story and he said he would see what he could do. He called me right back and told me which flight he was on. He has a noon flight and it is already ten. So eat this..." She hands me the carton of food and I start scarfing it down. "Then we will get you showered and to the airport to stop him."

On the way to the airport, I buy the cheapest ticket I can find. I only need something to get me through security.

By the time we get to the airport it's already 11:15 a.m. I quickly go through security. Thankfully the line isn't long.

I run down the terminal looking for his gate number. I see him standing in line to board at his gate at the other end of the terminal. He is towards the front. I start to run as I shout his name. "Logan!"

He must not hear me because he doesn't turn around. There are two people ahead of him when I get to the gate.

I shout his name one more time. "Logan!" He turns around. Instead of walking over to me, like I thought he would, he moves forward in line. I run over to him.

"Please Logan. I made a mistake. I should have listened to you. I believe you. I don't know how I never did." He continues to ignore me. "Logan, please look at me."

Slowly, he steps out of line. "I thought we trusted each other, but you obviously didn't trust me. How can I believe that next time you will talk to me before running off?"

"I could say the same thing about you. Spring Break hot tub ring any bells?"

"I already apologized for that and we agreed to always listen before we come to any conclusions no matter how the situation looks. You didn't even give me a chance to explain in New York and then last night when I did, you still didn't believe me."

"I did." I really did but I was so blinded by what I was seeing to realize that it wasn't actually real.

"I don't want to be hurt like I was last night when I thought it was over. We need to talk before running off, Emma. I don't want to lose you."

"I know a little something about being hurt when I thought it was over too. So will you please just forgive me for running off? I don't want to lose you either."

Logan hesitates for a minute. "Yes, now come here so I can kiss you like I wanted to when I saw you on Friday."

I don't hesitate to close the gap and throw my arms around his neck. I kiss him like there is no tomorrow.

Everyone around us cheers but I don't care that people are watching. I barely even hear them.

When we finally pull away, Logan is smirking. "You know this feels like a movie. The whole running through the airport to stop me before I get on a plane."

"I thought you would appreciate it. Although it was all Ashley and your brother."

"I wondered why my brother was randomly asking me what I was doing today and then what my flight information was." We hear them call last boarding for his flight.

"I wish you didn't have to go."

"Hold that thought."

He talks with the flight attendant for a few minutes before coming back with a new boarding pass. "Looks like I'm not leaving till later today. You can leave whenever you want on the jet. We can just call them and change your time. I know it doesn't have to be anywhere till Wednesday to pick up my dad. Now let's go grab some food because I am starving. I also need some quality time with my girl before I don't see her for three weeks."

He puts his arm around my shoulder and pulls me in tight. It feels so good to be next to him again.

We've both made mistakes by not trusting the other and I believe that moving forward, we won't do it again. After all, no mistake is too big for us to handle as long as we trust each other.

Chapter Fourty-one

Thanksgiving is finally here and I can't wait to see my family. With classes and swimming, I haven't been home since summer. I am meeting Jeremy and my brother and we are driving home together.

I'm waiting for them as I pull out my phone. I have a text from Logan.

Logan: *Hey you! I can't wait to see you. Be prepared for some serious kisses and hugs. Love you <3.*

"Awww how cute." Jeremy reads over my shoulder. "Remind me to not be around when you have your little reunion."

I swat him on the shoulder. "For that you can carry my bag. I have an amazing boyfriend to get home to."

Jeremy takes my bag. "That is my brother you are talking about. You can leave out the details, but I'm glad you worked everything out on Halloween." He lifts the bag. "Now what do you have in this bag, a bunch of books." I shrug. "You're the only girl I know that packs more books than clothes."

He throws my bag inside the car as my brother walks up. "Shotgun". My brother doesn't put up a fight so I climb into the passenger seat as he gets in the back.

"It is all good. I am going to sleep."

I reach for the radio and Jeremy grabs my hand before I can change the song. "You're not allowed to pick what we listen to. Your taste in music is terrible."

"Hey, it's not that bad." I cross my arms over my chest.

"But it is." Tyler agrees from the back seat.

Jer glances at me. "You keep telling yourself that." He puts on country music and I gaze out the window, counting down the minutes till we get home. It's not that I don't like country music. I do, although I would never admit that to Jeremy because I like to annoy him with other music.

We pull up to my house around 10 p.m. and I am surprised to see Logan walk outside. I jump out of the car and run up to him. He catches me, spinning me around.

"What are you doing here?"

"I couldn't wait till tomorrow. I knew my brother was dropping you off so I was bonding with your dad."

"Bonding with my dad?" I look at him suspiciously.

"Yeah, we talked about all sorts of stuff, but enough talking." He bends down to kiss me. He deepens the kiss and I wrap my arms around his neck.

"As great as this is watching you two reunite, I'd like to get home at some point." Jeremy says sarcastically as he sets down my bags.

Logan picks them up. "Let me help you get these inside and we can get away from Mr. Prying Eyes."

"You have five minutes before I leave." Jeremy points at his brother.

"Good luck with that." Tyler comes up behind him laughing before going inside the house.

"Where is your car?" I ask Logan.

"My mom dropped me off on the way into town. I figured I would get a ride home with Jeremy."

Inside, my parents give me big hugs. I tell them I am headed to bed but will see them in the morning. Logan helps me carry my bags to my room. He gives me another kiss. "How was the trip up here?"

"It was fun, other than him not letting me pick the music. We talked a lot on the drive and I never realized how smart he was. He gave me fitness tips that should help with swimming. My brother basically slept the entire way."

"I'm glad you bonded with him. I should probably go so my brother doesn't leave me. I'll see you tomorrow." He gives me another quick kiss before leaving.

I wake up the next morning and smell the turkey wafting into my room. My mom must have put it in the oven already. I see it is 9 a.m. I get out of bed and take a shower before going downstairs to help my mom.

The Andersons are coming over soon and I can't wait to see Logan. I know I am a little obsessed.

Thanksgiving is delicious. I enjoy spending time with my family and the Andersons who already feel like part of our family. Maybe one day they really will be. Logan and I have talked about the future but we are still young and have plenty of time.

Ashley wasn't able to make it back for the holidays so we don't get to do our annual Black Friday shopping trip. It just wouldn't be the same without her. All is well though because Jeremy is making us leave at five in the morning to head back to FSU because he has practice later in the day.

Logan is coming with us to go to the game on Saturday and then he will fly back to New York on Sunday.

Sunday comes way too fast and I say my goodbyes to Logan. It isn't as hard this time because I know I will see him in three weeks for Christmas break. He kisses me goodbye. "I love you and I'll see you in a few weeks. Don't miss me too much."

"I love you too. I can't make any promises about not missing you."

He walks through the gate of the private plane area and waves back at me. I am already counting down the days before I get to see him again.

Chapter Fourty-two

Exams are over. I feel good about them. I have declared an Athletic Training major but with it being a limited access program I still have to be accepted. I am supposed to hear back anytime now.

Ever since Logan put the idea in my head, I know it is what I want to do. It will help with my swimming and one day I can use the knowledge I learn to help others.

In the meantime, I am meeting the boys at the airport before our flight. Jeremy is coming right from practice to the airport. We beat him and board the jet. My brother sits down and immediately starts texting someone. I just laugh. I think he is seeing this new girl but I don't really know much.

I am offered a drink, sipping it as I lean back in my chair. I could get used to this whole private jet thing.

I fell in love with Logan before I realized who his dad was. I thought his dad just worked at Andertainment but he is actually the owner. I should have put two and two together with the name Andertainment as in Anderson Entertainment but I just never cared. I still don't, but the perks are nice. Like dating the son of a guy with a private jet.

My phone rings interrupting me from my thoughts. "Hello?"

"Is this Miss Emma Collins?" My hands start to sweat as I realize this might be the Athletic Training program calling. They only call if you are accepted, right? Or maybe they have more questions.

"Yes, this is Emma. May I ask who is calling?"

"This is the FSU College of Human Sciences Admissions. We want to congratulate you on being accepted into the Athletic Training program."

"Are you serio... I mean that is great to hear."

I got in?

"We are very serious Miss Collins. Your grades this past semester and the credits that transferred from your high school are outstanding. We are honored to have you in the program and hope to see great things from you."

"Wow! Thank you so much. I'm very excited to start the program."

"An advisor will be calling you in the next few days to go over your classes for the Spring semester, and you will receive an email with a list of the required courses for the program as well as some other useful information. Congratulations again, and we look forward to having you in the program." Before I can say thanks, she hangs up.

I jump out of my seat and put my hands in the air. I dance around in a circle. I turn to see Jeremy standing in the door of the plane watching.

"What are you so happy about? Don't tell me my brother asked you over the phone."

"Asked me what?" I ask confused. Jeremy immediately starts busying himself with his bag. I glance at my brother and I can tell he is pretending not to be listening.

"Oh umm... nothing. Just your Christmas present he had a question about."

"Well speaking of your brother, I need to call to tell him my good news."

"Which is...?"

"I have to tell him first but you'll hear when I tell him." He picks up on the second ring.

"Hey you! I thought you would be up in the air by now."

"Jeremy just got here so we'll be taking off shortly. I only have a few minutes but I wanted to tell you I got accepted into the Athletic Training Program."

"What? That's amazing! I knew you would. They would be crazy to deny you."

"It is all thanks to you. I never would have declared a major if you hadn't encouraged me to do something I love."

There is some rustling on the phone. "Are you there?"

"Yes sorry, just finishing up some editing for my final project. I only have two finals left and I'll be home with you."

"I can't wait. Oh, by the way, Jeremy said something about you having something to ask me..." There is silence on the other end. "Something about my Christmas present."

"Oh uhh yeah. I was going to ask... to ask if you prefer gold or silver?"

"Silver, but why?"

"Oh nothing. Listen babe, I have to finish up this project but text me when you land. I love you."

"Love you too." We hang up and I look over at Jeremy. "That was weird. He seemed really distracted." He's always very attentive on our phone calls and makes sure to give me his undivided attention. It makes me feel special.

"I am sure he is busy finishing up exams. On the other hand, congratulations on your acceptance. I have heard those programs in the Health Science school are extremely selective."

"Thanks! I am excited. I just wish Logan was more excited. He was after all the one that helped me decide what to major in."

"Like I said, he's probably distracted with his exams. You will see him in a few days and everything will be great."

"I hope so." I put my head back against the seat preparing for takeoff. I have this feeling in my gut that things are about to change and I can't help wondering if it will be good or bad. I really hope for the former.

A few days later, I pick Logan up from the airport. The second he walks off the plane, I know everything is perfectly fine. He must have just been stressed with finals. We spend Christmas

Eve catching up. Even with our daily phone calls and constant texts at school, we never get to actually talk for long.

I spend Christmas Eve with the Andersons. His mom does a great job cooking and has been getting much better. Apparently, she has been taking cooking lessons once a week.

For Christmas, Mr. Anderson surprised her with a trip to Europe. They will be visiting multiple countries and meeting with renowned chefs for private cooking lessons. Mr. Anderson is wanting to expand Andertainment over there and this is part of that. He promised that he would not work that much but he is simply getting a feel for the restaurants over there.

Christmas Day is with my family. Logan comes over for Christmas dinner.

As the meal is cooking, we sit outside on the porch to exchange gifts. I open Logan's first gift and inside is an elegant long sleeve evening gown in midnight blue. I lift it out of the box and there is a crystal beading on top that cascades down to the waist where the silky skirt sways as I move it. Wrapped inside the dress is a small jewelry box. My pulse picks up because it is the same size as a ring box.

I look up at Logan and he can see the question in my eyes.

He kisses me quickly. "This is not what you are thinking, but I hope one day soon to be asking you that question and sliding a ring on your finger."

He takes the jewelry box from me and opens it. Inside are the most gorgeous diamond heart earrings.

"They are beautiful and I can't wait to wear them, but you didn't have to do this. You always spoil me."

"I thought you could wear them to the New Year's Ball, if you want?" I nod.

I hand him my much smaller box in comparison. He opens the box and inside is a framed picture of Logan and I. It is from the New Year's Ball right after we started dating. Someone had taken a picture of us dancing and we were gazing into each other's eyes. That was the night we first told each other how we really felt and the picture shows it all.

"I love it. Who took this?"

"I think the photographer. I was talking to your mom and she showed me the picture. I knew it was perfect and thought it might remind you of me on those cold nights all alone up in New York."

"Yes it will. It will go on my bedside table so I wake up to your face. Then I'll move it to my desk, although that might be distracting. So maybe I will just put it in my backpack to bring with me wherever I go."

I laugh because he is ridiculous. He gazes deeply into my eyes. "I love you so much Emma." He looks like he has more to say but doesn't. Instead, he kisses me.

As he pulls away, he rests his forehead against mine.

"I love you too." I whisper. "Now let's go inside and get warm by the fire." Logan gets up and takes my hand as we head into the house.

Chapter Fourty-three

Logan calls me as I am getting ready for the Andersons' Annual New Year's Ball. He is sending a car for me around 7:30 p.m. He said he has to help his parents with some last-minute things or else he would come get me himself.

Ashley was here earlier but had to run home because she forgot something. She was very vague about what she forgot but knowing her it could be anything. She said she would meet us at the party.

I finish getting ready, making sure not to mess up my hair or makeup that Ashley did. She curled my hair and did some sort of half up half down braid. She left my makeup simple, adding just enough to make my eyes pop and give me a glow although she mentioned something about how I will have a natural glow after tonight. I didn't comment because I was guessing she was talking about the new year.

I persuaded my parents to go this year and my brother is even joining us. It didn't take much convincing for any of them.

The car arrives and I go outside to get in but I realize my parents and brother aren't behind me. I pop my head back inside. "Hey I thought you all were coming?"

"We'll be right behind you. I made your dad go change. He came down in his Zebra print suit." She laughs and pushes me out the door. "Now go."

"I'm sure the car will wait for you."

"It's fine. We'll see you at the party."

I get in the car thinking my mom is acting weird but then think about my dad. There is no way he is going to be allowed to go to the party in his Zebra suit. I don't even know why he has it. I guess it was from a college party and he somehow still has it. I am surprised my mom hasn't thrown it away.

A few minutes later the car stops and I hear the driver get out. The drive was way too short for us to already be at the Anderson's house. I glance outside and see the park. My door opens and the driver helps me out.

"I think we're supposed to be going to the Anderson house."

"This way ma'am." He takes me to the path leading to the gazebo and I stop suddenly. The path is lined with rose petals and there are candles dangling from the trees. I follow the path to the gazebo and see Logan with a bouquet of white roses. He hands me the roses and leans down to kiss my cheek.

"You look gorgeous my love." He takes my hand and twirls me as my dress sways.

I love this dress!

"Logan what are we doing here?" I look around to see if anyone else is here but as far as I can tell it's just us.

"Emma, ever since I met you in our junior year, I haven't been the same. When I came back home, I had lost focus on what

I really wanted. For as long as I remember, I wanted to be a filmmaker but the program in Europe just took the joy out of it. This past semester at NYU, we focused on finding the right subject. Something you are passionate about and something you want to spend a lot of time on. When we did that film project in English class, it brought back that joy and the reason was because I was filming something I loved."

I nod for him to continue.

"You, Emma, were that subject I was passionate about. You brought the joy back into filmmaking and I realized I don't want to spend any more time away from my favorite subject. We've been through so much in a short time but I love you, Emma, so much and want to know if you will spend the rest of your life with me?"

I gasp as he gets down on one knee and pulls out a ring box. "Emma Rose Collins, will you marry me?"

The tears fall. "Yyee...Yes." I shake my head up and down. "I'll marry you!"

Logan jumps up, slides the ring on my finger, and kisses me. He picks me up and spins me around. I giggle and feel like the luckiest girl. He rests his forehead against mine. "I haven't even told you the best part."

"There is something better than this?" I laugh at him, pulling back so I can gaze into his eyes.

"Come Spring semester, I'm transferring to the FSU film program. I don't want to be away from you any longer. I'll follow you wherever you go, whether we have to travel for the

Olympics or you get into a Physical training program on the other side of the world."

I kiss him again, so happy he's the man I get to spend the rest of my life with. I don't know how this became my life and I got so lucky, but I wouldn't change it for anything.

On the way to the New Year's Eve Ball, I admire my ring. In the midst of him proposing, I hadn't gotten a good look at the ring.

It is a princess cut with diamonds around the band. The center stone is decently big, at around one carat. It is gorgeous!

"Do you like it?"

"I love it almost as much as I love you." I kiss him on the lips.

"Good. I bought it back in mid-October and was scared I wasn't going to be able to give it to you when we had that misunderstanding. I'm glad we cleared it all up."

I lean my head on his shoulder still looking down at my ring. "Me too."

We pull up to his house and step out of the car. As we walk through the ballroom doors Logan shouts, "she said yes". Everyone immediately circles around congratulating us.

I see my parents. "You knew about this?"

"Yes. You picked a wonderful man." My mom kisses me on the head.

"He asked me over Thanksgiving break for our permission." My dad adds.

I glance at Logan. "So that was the bonding with my dad?"

"Yep. You didn't think I wouldn't ask him first did you?" He kisses me on the cheek as his parents and Jeremy walk up.

"Welcome to the family." Mr. Anderson gives me a hug.

Mrs. Anderson takes both my hands. "We couldn't ask for a better daughter-in-law."

"I am lucky to have met the wonderful son you raised."

Jeremy comes over and puts his arm around my shoulders. "It's not too late to switch brothers."

"I think I'm good." I grab Logan's hand and squeeze.

I point at Ashley and Ty and we excuse ourselves to say hi. Ashley gives me a big hug. "Look at you catching Mr. big bucks." I glare at her. "Kidding. You two make a great couple. I knew you would last forever the first time I saw you together. I am so happy for you."

"He is pretty amazing." I look at him talking to my brother. "And this ring is insane." I lift it up so she can see. Ashley shrugs. "You helped him pick it out didn't you?"

"I may have given him some hints, but he picked it out himself before Halloween. Why do you think I kept trying to get you to listen to what he had to say?"

She winks and turns to Logan. "You two may be engaged but I still have the right to kick your butt if you hurt my best friend." Logan nods.

Ty walks over to me. "Congrats little sis. I am so happy for you. Glad you chose to marry the brother of the FSU quarterback. Free games for life." He pinches me lightly in the shoulder.

I put my hands on my hips. "Haha."

We hear a glass clinking. Mr. Anderson gestures for us to join him on the stage. I stand next to Logan with my family next to us and his family on the platform above us. "Welcome everyone to another year. This year has been extra exciting for us as our youngest son just got engaged to an amazing girl." He smiles at us. "If everyone would raise their glasses as we toast to Logan and Emma." I raise my glass and clink it with Logan's before taking a sip. "As we move forward into the next year, let us remember what is most important. Here's to many more years to come."

Logan kisses me and whispers in my ear, "Let's go outside." I follow him outside where we sit on our favorite bench by the fire and wrap up in a blanket. As I rest my head on his shoulder, the stars twinkle above us and I swear I see a shooting star.

We wait for the New Year and I can't help thinking about the past year. It was a tough year but we made it. I truly have the perfect guy, an awesome family, a bright career path, and I am Olympic bound.

We sit there for what feels like hours but also not enough time. We hear the countdown as everyone makes their way outside for the annual fireworks show.

"Are you happy?" Logan asks me.

"So happy!" He kisses me while everyone shouts, "Happy New Year."

I watch the fireworks excited for what is to come. After all, I get to plan the wedding of my dreams to the man of my dreams. What more could I want?

Chapter Fourty-four
Almost 2 Years Later

"Jingle bells, Batman smells, Robin laid an egg," sings Logan loudly.

"That is not how the song goes." I tease Logan as I turn down the radio.

"That is the better version of it."

"If you say so." He knows how much I love Christmas and he always likes to sing the extra lyrics of every Christmas song. I don't care but my mom is strictly against it when we go caroling every year.

"I need to get it out now before caroling."

"Deal. Think your parents will be upset that we won't make the New Year's Ball this year?"

"No. They know we want to have a special trip before the new semester starts. They just don't know the other reason."

I smile knowingly at him. I reach out to grab his hand and give it a squeeze. "They'll know soon enough." I rest my head back against my seat. "Can you believe we've been married for one year?"

"One year and nine days to be exact."

"I thought you would have the hours and minutes too?"

Logan glances at the clock on the car. "One year, nine days, one hour, four minutes, and..." he looks at his watch, "twenty-two seconds, twenty three, twenty four..."

I can't help but laugh at him as he continues to count the seconds. His phone dings with a text message and that is the only reason he stops. I am pretty sure he would have kept counting for the next ten minutes or so till we got home.

"My mom is asking how far out we are. I'll tell her we're passing the park."

I nod and continue driving as Logan gets back to work. "Just enough time for my video to finish rendering."

As we pass the park, I can't help but think back to that day just over two years ago. It was a cold winter day just like this. Only this year seems to have more ice which is why it has taken us so much longer to get home than normal.

Our wedding was better than I ever dreamed. We got married in the gazebo overlooking the mountains. The sun was peeking through the clouds and the mountain peaks as it got close to sunset. There were candles hanging and rose petals scattered about just like when Logan proposed.

We had a tent set up on the far side of the park that was enclosed with heaters so we could stay warm, not that we needed them much with all the dancing.

Ashley was my maid of honor and Danielle, my roommate and fellow swim team member, was my bridesmaid. Jeremy was Logan's best man and Tyler was his groomsman.

The most perfect part was when it started to snow right as we had our first kiss as a married couple.

As promised, we did have a short honeymoon at the same resort of our Senior Ski Trip. It was everything I could have hoped for.

Our longer, actual honeymoon was spent in Greece five months later when it was a little warmer. We enjoyed a biking and boat tour that took us all over the Greek islands. The whole trip was breathtaking and one we will have to do again.

Logan places his laptop on the backseat still open so it can finish rendering. He wedges it between the Christmas gifts so it doesn't slide forward then he turns towards me. "So I received an email."

"Was it a good email or a bad email?"

"It was a good email. The University of South California saw one of my projects and offered me a scholarship to finish film school there and then move into their Masters program." Before I can say anything, he holds up a finger. "At first I said no, but then I started looking into the program and other programs like the Physical Therapy program which is one of the best in the country, I might add."

"I thought you liked it at Boston College?" I glance at Logan.

"I do, but I think this would be an amazing opportunity for both of us. "

I sigh because I don't want to transfer. I love my Master's program and the swim center I am training at is amazing. "We would be so far away from our family and friends. Plus, my coach is here and if I want to go to the Olympics again, I need him."

"Em, I'm sure there are other coaches out there or maybe he will even follow us out there. He came up here but if he doesn't then he probably knows someone. I put out feelers for coaches in the area just in case."

"Logan, it sounds great but the Olympics were this Summer and I am settled here with my program and training. I don't want to go. If you really want to go then go without me."

"Remember that time I transferred from NYU to FSU for you? Then I transferred again when you got accepted into Boston College for your Masters this past Fall. I'm asking you to do the same."

I pull up to a red light trying not to get mad. "You decided to transfer. I was more than happy to have you close when we were engaged and I have been super happy to have you nearby while we are married." I start to raise my voice. "Don't you dare use that against me."

"I am not using it against you, but why can't you ever make a sacrifice for me? I transferred both times so you could stay on the East Coast."

The light turns green and I hit the gas pedal. "I make sacrifices for you all the time. Can we please stop talking about this until we get to my house? I will think about transferring schools. Now let's just get home. It has been a long day, there is tons of ice on the roads, and we're almost there."

"Fine, but we will talk about this."

I can't help raising my voice, fed up with him for not being able to drop it. This isn't the first time the conversation has been brought up about going to the West Coast. He wanted to go there before I started my masters at Boston College. He has hinted at it a few times since then. I would think he would be sick of transferring at this point.

"LOGAN, yes we will talk about it. Please drop it." I pull up to a stop sign just outside Logan's parents' neighborhood.

"You know I love you when you get all angry at me. It is so cute. The last thing I will say is we will figure out the right next step for school but this is an amazing chance. You should see the list of things they offer. I just wanted to tell you about it. I don't like fighting but as long as I have you by my side, it'll be perfect. I love you, Emma."

I can't help but smile at his words. Even when I am angry at him, he still knows how to make me calm down. "I love you too." He entwines his fingers with mine and kisses my hand.

The road is clear and I hit the gas once again. "I will look at it and maybe..." I see the lights as the car spins and I feel the impact only seconds later. I feel the car spin again and I hear my screams pierce the air. I feel pressure on my right leg before excruciating pain shoots up it.

Glass shatters and I feel warmth trickle down my cheek. I touch my forehead and when I pull back my hand, there is red. I look over at Logan and see red everywhere.

"Logan!" I yell.

I lunge toward him to feel for a pulse but my seatbelt is in the way. I try to undo it but it is stuck.

I can't breathe. This can't be happening.

Why now? Is this the end?

I feel my lungs start to give out as I look over at Logan once more.

"Logan, don't leave me." I whisper as everything goes black.

A Note from Kaitlyn

Is your heart pumping? What is going to happen next, you might ask? I am sorry I left you on a cliffhanger but, all will be revealed in book two. She will get her happily ever after then. I promise!

Thank you so much for reading about Emma and going on this journey with me. Funny story, this book and book two were originally the same but, I had so much more to write. I wanted to do right by my characters and give my readers a chance to fall in love with them as much as I did.

Emma is a small part of all of us, whether that be: chasing your dream, finding love, being insecure at times, relying on your friends, and expanding your wings.

If you'd like to know what happens next, head to my Facebook group for updates, spoilers and hints.

Thanks again for picking up 'I Will Always Love You"! If you have a chance, please leave a review.

Until next time,
Kaitlyn Calicott

Acknowledgments

A special thanks to:

My husband, Lloyd, for always believing in me and letting me spend hours writing this book. Also, for keeping the kids occupied while I edited, formatted, worked on marketing and everything else that goes into a new book. Thanks also for helping create an amazing cover!

My sister, Kelsey, for reading this book for what I am sure feels like a million times and giving me tons of feedback, even though this is not your favorite genre.

Lynne, for helping me create the blurb.

My dad for looking at all the pictures I sent of the cover.

My mom for reading through my book and sending me edits.

Ivy Smoak, Ryan Hauge, and Jillian Dodd for answering my millions of questions about self-publishing.

My editor, Jessie, for fixing my errors, adding all the commas, and making my book the best it can be.

About the Author

Kaitlyn Calicott writes romances with a guaranteed happily ever after; sometimes, it just takes a while to get there. When she isn't writing, she loves reading and getting lost in the world of books with a glass of wine. She also loves spending time with her husband and two boys, cuddling on the couch watching movies, playing with their chickens, boating, and baking delicious treats. For upcoming releases, spoilers, and so much more, check out her Facebook Group or website at Kaitlyncalicott.com.